SISTERS

sisters

LISA WINGATE

Tyndale House Publishers, Inc.
Carol Stream, Illinois

Visit Tyndale online at www.tyndale.com.

Visit Lisa Wingate's website at www.lisawingate.com.

TYNDALE and Tyndale's quill logo are registered trademarks of Tyndale House Publishers, Inc.

Sisters

The Sea Glass Sisters copyright © 2013 by Lisa Wingate. All rights reserved.

The Tidewater Sisters copyright © 2014 by Wingate Media, LLC. All rights reserved.

The Sandcastle Sister copyright © 2015 by Wingate Media, LLC. All rights reserved.

Author photo taken by Amber Zimmerman, copyright © 2013. All rights reserved.

Cover photograph of girl copyright © Norbert Schaefer/Corbis. All rights reserved.

Designed by Stephen Vosloo and Dean H. Renninger

Edited by Sarah Mason

Published in association with Folio Literary Management, LLC, 630 9th Avenue, Suite 1101, New York, NY 10036.

ISBN 978-1-4964-1341-3 (International Trade Paper Edition)

Printed in the United States of America

21	20	19	18	17	16	15
7	6	5	4	3	2	1

Contents

The
Sea Glass
Sisters

CHAPTER 1

The more time that passes before it happens, the better. Usually that isn't the case on any given day of any given week. Life is all about running breakneck, half-exhausted, from one thing to another—the kids, the job, the bills, the PTA, the school concession stand, the cheerleaders' fund-raiser garage sale, the marriage . . .

Sometimes I wonder if she's sleeping under there— the *old* Elizabeth Gallagher, the woman who seemed to have it all together. Or was she always just a fantasy? A figment of the hype she created eighteen years ago, when an unexpected pregnancy led to a hurried marriage between high school sweethearts? She was so determined to show all the naysayers that she could make a go of it, defy the statistics. Create the perfect family. A life to be proud of.

Pride is a steamroller. It'll clear the path for a while, but sooner or later it'll shift into reverse, and then . . . look out. Maybe everyone else saw it coming, and that's why they're backing away lately.

3

And now *this*.

I gaze out the bay window of the house that was supposed to be our dream home. Even the oak trees have grown up now, resolving our original objection to building on two acres of centennial family farmland deeded to us as a wedding gift. The trees, once they grew, were supposed to make life in this house picture-perfect.

Fall leaves blow across what we lovingly call *the family compound*, the bits of seasonal color dancing into the yards of aunts, uncles, and cousins. Unfortunately, a layer of pretty colors can't fix what's wrong here. Nor can it remove the For Sale sign across the street—the one that makes me feel like a drugstore mannequin in a 1950s government staging area, about to unwittingly take part in a nuclear test. I'm just waiting for the bomb to drop. I know it's coming.

It couldn't possibly hit the mark on a worse day.

I'd like to get the kids off to school before it happens. See if I can cajole a hug—one that doesn't feel like it's just me hanging on. But chances are, if they can slip by and get to Jessica's car, they'll be gone like bank robbers on the lam. They'll probably be rushing, in danger of getting a tardy, Micah complaining that his big sister has made them late by lining her deep-blue eyes and fluffing her golden curls. She reminds me so much of myself in high school, it almost hurts. Exchange the blonde hair for brown, and our cheerleading photos would've been almost interchangeable side by side.

As they swerve out of the driveway, she'll give her brother a dirty look, just like I would have. She's frustrated with him for horning in on her senior year by choosing to take extra courses and graduate while he should still be a junior. She doesn't want him in her car, and he's only there because we force her to drive him. She saved her money for the car, but we pay for the gas and the insurance.

The kids most likely won't even notice the sign across the road. The one that will bring a blinding explosion and a mushroom cloud of family fallout as soon as Uncle Butch sees it. There's no way he'll sit still for his sister selling that property.

I let my head sink to the table, let my eyes close next to the bowl of steel-cut oatmeal that is both breakfast and supper after working a night shift. Something mild that won't make me throw up once it hits my stomach, which has been churning since 3 a.m., halfway through my work hours.

There's a little girl missing this morning, and if I'd only been quicker, if I hadn't screwed up, vapor-locked for the first time ever, my mind whirling in a pool of exhaustion and family issues when the call came into the 911 dispatch center, that girl might be home right now. Safe in her mother's arms.

Instead I'm petrified that the worst has happened, and it's my fault. If a child isn't found within the first three hours, the chances are immeasurably less.

I hear the call again as sleep mist floats over my

mind. I re-create the moment in my thoughts, try to alter events, to fix the damage.

The caller is sobbing, panicked, alone in the Cappie's Quick Mart parking lot, except for a kindly trucker who has seen her screaming hysterically and stopped to investigate the problem.

"Sh-sh-she was h—!" The word *here* disappears into a moaning howl, animal-like. "Jus-s-st you . . . Sh-sh-she . . . she was . . . sleeping . . . in the seat. In back, with . . . with the babyyyy. I only went . . . just one mm-minute . . . Mm-maybe two . . . in . . ."

I try to calm her down, to discern what has happened, exactly. She's been hysterical for several minutes, difficult to work with, though I've managed to get her name, the name of the store, and that this is a possible abduction, then send the information through Computer-Aided Dispatch. Response units are on the way, but the Cappie's Quick Mart is out on Old Collier Road, not close to anything. It'll take a while.

The caller is slurring her words. I'm beginning to suspect that she's drunk or on something. But she could just be emotional. I do the thing that 911 operators are trained to do. I use her name, Trista. She sounds incredibly young, and so much like my Jessica. I wonder if she is the missing girl's sister or babysitter or friend or mother. I'm still trying to establish what has taken place.

There's adrenaline rushing through me, but my mind hasn't kicked in the way it should. It's like a disk drive spinning and spinning but not coming up with the correct response. I reach for the scripts on the shelf above the desk—the ones we use with new operators doing on-the-job training.

So many of these instances turn out to be nothing, I think. I've said it to trainees before. Often the child either has been picked up by another family member or has wandered off to play or is in trouble and is hiding to avoid punishment.

Please let this be nothing. The words in my head seem to drift into empty space. Even that seems wrong. I used to know those words were going somewhere. That someone was hearing them.

I read off the script instead of winging it. I know it's slower, but it feels safer tonight. There's something wrong with me, and the truth is, I've known it for a while. I've been afraid something like this would happen.

This is my nightmare, playing out.

I ask her if there's anyone else I can speak to. Anyone who was with her when the child disappeared. There is only the trucker, and he knows nothing, other than that he's found a crazed woman in a parking lot at three in the morning. In the background, traffic whizzes by. The trucker tells me that the people in the convenience store didn't see anything either—just a woman going hysterical in the parking lot a couple minutes after she left the store.

I ask him to give the phone back to Trista, then

please go check on the car and keep an eye on the baby, if there is one. Do we have two missing children here or one?

"Okay, Trista, I need you to take a breath, calm down, and talk to me. You're not alone. We are going to do everything we can to bring this girl home safely." My stomach turns over. I taste the 1 a.m. ham sandwich and the shot of energy drink. "Is she your sister or your daughter?"

"Mm-my girl . . . my little girl . . . ," she sobs.

The alarm meter ratchets upward inside me. I'm pretty sure I'm talking to a teenage mother with two babies on her hands. "What is her name?"

"Em . . . Emily."

"And how old is Emily?"

"F-f-four . . . f-five. She just turned f-five." Trista seems more lucid now, her speech clearer. "We w-were gonna have her birthday par-party this weeken-n-nd. . . ."

I note that she used the word *were*. I taste the bile again. It's a bad sign when a parent uses past tense in reference to a missing child.

She breaks down sobbing, and it's a couple minutes before I can get her to listen to me. I feel the burden of time ticking by, even as I'm sending information through dispatch. I need a description of this girl.

"Trista . . . *Trista!* I'm harsh now, like a teacher demanding a student's attention. "What is Emily's hair and eye color?"

"B-blonde . . . b-blue."

"I need to know what Emily was wearing the last time you saw her. Exactly. Everything."

Instead, she repeats location details. She's at Cappie's Quick Mart. She came out to buy cigarettes.

At three in the morning? I wonder and glance at the screen.

The caller's voice is far away for a moment. I hear her screaming the girl's name. It echoes against the traffic and a blaring horn. I cringe.

"Trista!" My voice fills the dispatch center, echoes down the hall. "Don't put down the phone. Don't hang up. Keep talking to me."

Carol comes running from the break room. She's heard me yelling.

I cap the mike, quickly whisper, "Missing juvenile, female, five years old." My heart is pumping wildly. I point to the dispatch screen.

Then I open the receiver again. "Trista! *Trista!* What was Emily wearing? I need you to tell me what she was wearing."

"She's go-o-one! She's go-o-one!"

"What was Emily wearing?"

"A . . . tee . . . a tee . . . a T-shirt," Trista hiccups out finally. "One of W-Wade's wor-work shirts. He . . . he . . . I-it was his . . . his . . . last . . . c-clean . . . M-maybe she thought sh-she was in troub . . . troubl-l-le . . ."

I note several things at once, send them through dispatch in random bits. There's a male involved, possibly a domestic dispute, no known location on the male at this time.

"What color was the T-shirt?" If it was a man's shirt, it was oversize for a five-year-old, probably worn as a nightgown.

"Re-red . . . or blue. I don . . . don't know. He has . . . he has . . . I d-don't . . . My *babyyyyy*. Where's my babyyyy?"

"I need you to stay focused, Trista." So much time is passing. How much longer until officers reach her? I glance at the screen. They're still several miles away. "What else was Emily wearing? Pants? Shoes? Coat?"

"No!" Trista sobs, frustrated with my questions now. "Only the shirt! Only the shirt."

A chill passes through me. It's cold at night in central Michigan in mid-October. I picture the little girl wandering along some roadside, shivering, barefoot, her blonde hair tangled around her face, her eyes filled with fear.

And then I hope that's all it is. I hope she's wandering somewhere. Alone. Far from the traffic that's whizzing by in the background.

Beside me, Carol has picked up a headset to listen in on the call. She leans over my shoulder toward the screen as I try to work more information out of Trista, who has collapsed into unintelligible sobs again.

Carol looks my way, squints, shakes her head. Her eyes meet mine, gray eyebrows lowered and drawn together. "The Cappie's Quick Mart out on Old

Collier Road isn't open late. There's no highway traffic out there, either. She has to be at the new Super Cappie's—the one they just opened near the bypass."

I close my eyes, just for the flash of an instant, feeling sick, then hot, then dazed. Then I'm hit by the white-hot lightning of panic.

I've lived in this county all my life. I should've realized there wouldn't be traffic noise by the Cappie's on Old Collier Road. I should've realized she had to be somewhere else. . . .

The phone rings, and at first I'm still in the dispatch center, trying to answer the incoming call through my headset. But it won't work. It's just ringing and ringing and ringing.

It's about to roll over to voice mail when I jerk awake, lift my head off my own kitchen table, and scramble for my cell. The house is quiet, the full light of midmorning pressing through the window now.

A half-dozen thoughts strike me at once. The kids have slipped off, not bothering to wake me as they passed by on their way to the garage. Across the street, the real estate sign has caught the sun like a beacon. My car sits alone in the driveway, meaning that Robert has gone to the cabin in the north woods for the weekend instead of coming home after his business trip. Again.

The phone call is Carol from work.

I want to crawl to the nearest closet, curl into a ball, and cry. But instead, I answer the cell.

"They found something in the ditch a couple miles from the new Cappie's," Carol informs me flatly. "An auto supply store T-shirt. Red."

CHAPTER 2

I walk into the master bedroom, strip off the muddy clothes, and let them fall to the carpet, not even thinking about the fact that it's afternoon and the kids might come home from school anytime.

After a week of spending my off time tromping through the woods with volunteer search parties, poking in trash piles and moats of last year's dead leaves, I just want to fall into bed and sleep. I'm in family-conflict-avoidance mode, and I know it. Right now, the girl drama of a new school year and the wrangling over the For Sale sign across the street are like static, turned up impossibly loud. All I want to do is find little Emily, be the one who turns up the evidence that leads to her discovery. Alive.

I must, in some way, atone for my screwup. I have to make things right again.

My family doesn't understand. They don't get why I've spent endless hours joining the volunteers looking for Emily. Oh, they're aware of the search, of course. There are posters everywhere, constant coverage on TV.

Pleas from Emily's mother and frantic grandparents. But my family doesn't know I was the one who took the call.

I'm not even sure why I haven't said anything. Maybe I just can't bear to speak it out loud, to have them see what a mess I am, how afraid I am that, while officers were racing toward Old Collier Road, Emily's abductor was slipping off into the night, somewhere near the new Cappie's Quick Mart near the bypass. Maybe I'm afraid that if I reveal the facts, admit to the guilt, the response will be a face buried in a cell phone. A disinterested *Well, you can't control everything, Elizabeth.* And then a quick redirecting of the conversation, to rehash the ongoing family drama about the land sale. Even the kids are involved in it now—taking up sides with my mother and Uncle Butch.

In Robert's case, the reply would more likely be a manufactured *Sorry you had a tough week. Listen, I'm going up to work on the cabin. I just need to get away for a while.*

I wonder if that's really where he is, and at the same time, I don't want to know. It's just one more thing cycling through my mind, the worries flashing by like the fins on a pinwheel.

Jessica skipped the SAT test she was supposed to take last weekend. Just skipped it. *You never told me you signed me up,* she argued. *Great. Now I'll probably have to miss a volleyball tournament to do a retake.*

Micah has a new girl chasing him. One who

transferred here from another district because there were problems. At least that's the warning I got from a mother whose son was involved with the girl last summer.

Outside, as I look down the street, Uncle Butch and Mom are in a heated discussion in front of the little house she built for herself after Dad died and she sold the farmhouse to my brother and his wife.

Uncle Butch is in Mom's face, his arms flailing, his six-foot-four-inch bulk dwarfing her five-foot frame. But she's not backing down. My mother's hair may be auburn, but she's got the fire of a full-blown redhead.

Right now, she's lifting her hands palm-up in frustration. I know what she's saying. She has called my aunt Sandy in the Outer Banks of North Carolina repeatedly, and Aunt Sandy isn't backing down either. She's determined to sell her twenty acres of the farm in order to save the seaside store that has eaten up most of her cash reserves after the hurricane damage last year.

So far, Uncle Butch has threatened everything from a legal filibuster involving easements on the farmland to the equivalent of a family shunning. It won't do any good. Aunt Sandy is the baby of the family, and only slightly over five feet tall herself, but she is a force of nature. The rebel. She won't cave, no matter how much everyone espouses the logic of finally letting go of the beachfront retirement dream that has kept Aunt Sandy and Uncle George away from the family compound for the past eighteen years.

I haven't ever seen her little store by the sea, even though it's just a day's drive away. If I did anything to encourage this post-empty-nest life my aunt and uncle have carved out for themselves, I'd never hear the end of it, especially now that they're getting older. My mother can't fathom why *anyone* would want to live more than a stone's throw from their children and grandchildren.

But lately I understand it. Sometimes when I'm coming home after a long third shift on the boards, I want to run away to the beach myself.

I watch the fight across the street until it finishes. Uncle Butch stalks off to his vehicle and drives away, spewing gravel and burning rubber all the way up the street, a skill he undoubtedly perfected as a high schooler with Elvis hair, cruising in his '57 Chevy. The maneuver loses some of its effect when it's done in an old, potbellied Suburban and you're only going a half mile up the street.

The next thing I know, I'm laughing, and I wonder if I've really lost it this time. Maybe this is the final tipping off some invisible cliff.

You're just tired, I tell myself. *You need to catch a few hours' sleep, then go to work. Stay on the routine. Keep up the hope.* Dispatchers aren't supposed to get involved with the cases that come through the 911 phone lines, but the truth is, the calls stay with you. You go into the profession because you want to help people. You can't just turn that on and off.

A blonde curl peeks from the shadows of my

purse—the photograph on a flyer seeking any news of Emily. They called off the search for her today. There's simply nowhere else to look.

I remind myself again to have hope. *If you give up, it's like saying that little girl isn't coming home.*

But the tears press anyway, and I pull the shades, slide into bed, and close my eyes. I'm just . . . so . . . tired. . . .

The doorbell rings downstairs as I finally start to drift. Who in the world? No one in the family would bother ringing the bell. They'd come in through the garage.

I ignore it, hoping it's just a package delivery, something Robert ordered online for the cabin. With so much vacation built up after seventeen years with the auto company, he has plenty of time to work on the place.

The doorbell rings again. Twice. Close together. Insistent.

I get up, put on a robe, and head downstairs. Before I reach the front door, I recognize the halo of auburn hair on the other side of the leaded glass. Mom. Why she's ringing the bell, I can't imagine.

I open the door, and she thrusts a white pet carrier my way. She has her cat, Honey, dangling under one arm and a sack of kitty chow under the other. "You'll have to keep Honey for me." As usual, it's an order, not a question. She jabs the pet carrier outward again. "Here. Take this."

I relieve her of the carrier and the cat chow as she breezes past me into the house. "Mom, what are you talking about?"

She strokes Honey's head so hard that the cat's eyes bug out with every pass. "I'm going to Sandy's and talking some sense into her. It's the only way. I am *not* having this family, or this farm, torn apart so my sister can sink the last of her money into that stupid shop of hers. Mother and Daddy didn't give us this land so we could sell it and run off to some hut on the beach."

"Mom, in the first place, it's a store, not a hut. In the second place, she's a grown woman. And in the third place, she's been there for almost twenty years now. She knows what she wants."

"She doesn't know anything. She's sixty-five years old, for heaven's sake. How much longer does she think she and George will be able to stay there anyway?" Mom paces down the entryway, Honey's rear end swinging against her hip. The cat's feet flail, searching for a toehold. I know the feeling.

"Mom, you can't *make* Aunt Sandy and Uncle George pull up stakes and come back. Maybe they never will. Maybe when they finally can't run the shell shop anymore, they'll just . . . retire there on the Outer Banks." It sounds nice. Retiring on an island.

Mom pulls a sheet of instructions from her pocket and leaves it on the dining table as she passes. Honey braces a claw on my mother's hip, tries to retract herself from the elbow hold. Mom hasn't even noticed so far.

"I'll tell you what'll happen. She'll sell that property and throw the money into that shop, and then when another storm comes along, or she or George experience a health crisis and they can't live in such a remote place anymore, they won't have anywhere to come home to. And we'll be stuck with strangers building houses *right* in the *middle* of all of our places. Butch doesn't have the money to buy the land from her, and neither do I."

Honey has finally gone into full-out escape mode. My mother releases her, and she jumps to the floor and skitters away, skidding on the tile as she disappears around the corner.

Mom barely gives the cat a second glance. She has bigger fish to fry. "I'm going there to talk some sense into her, face-to-face. That's all there is to it."

That's the second time she's said it. And this time, it genuinely worries me. "Mom, you've never once been out to Aunt Sandy's place in all these years, and now, suddenly, you're going? And then what? You'll kidnap Aunt Sandy and Uncle George and force them to come back to Michigan?"

Her green eyes flare, then narrow beneath wind-blown shocks of hair. She's not used to being talked to like this. No one talks back to the principal. It's hard for her to get used to civilian life. Even harder, since, after nearly thirty years of dedicated service, she was caught in the squeeze play of an unpleasant consolidation between two schools.

Retirement isn't suiting my mother. That school

was her heart and soul. "George isn't even there with her right now. He's in Kalamazoo, taking care of his mother. He has *been* there off and on for months. The poor man is commuting back and forth between Michigan and Hatteras Island, trying to see to his mother's care and help Sandy keep that shop afloat. It's ridiculous. Their family is here. Their children and grandchildren are here. Someone has to force Sandy to see reason."

"Mother, you cannot fly to North Carolina on your own."

"I'm not flying. I'm driving."

"You definitely can't drive to North Carolina." I'm guessing that trip would take twelve to fourteen hours. Just a couple months ago, Mom ran her car into a ditch during a three-hour drive to my great-aunt's house. I think she fell asleep at the wheel, but she won't admit it.

"Oh yes, I can. There's some worry about a storm on the East Coast mucking up the airports. I don't want to fly and end up trapped out there."

"So your solution is to *drive*?" Like Uncle Butch burning rubber in his old Suburban, this would be funny if it weren't so serious.

"Yes, that's my solution. And if you're so worried about it, you can come with me. We'll only be gone a few days."

Her gaze catches mine, and suddenly I realize this is why she's really here. This is what she's had in mind all along.

CHAPTER 3

He's there in the woods. I hear him moving in the shadows. A sense of warning slides under my sweatshirt—cold, visceral, trailing along my skin like the edge of a blade. Not deep enough to cut, just touching in a way that makes me shiver.

I pull up the stick I've been using to probe leaves, then whirl around, catch a breath, but I can't see anyone.

Is he there? Is it just my imagination? Where have all the other searchers gone? We are supposed to work in pairs. Always in pairs. There's a danger that he might come back, seeking to snatch the evidence left behind and relocate it. If there is any evidence . . .

"Who's there?" I whisper.

"Elizabeth . . ." He knows my name. His voice sends another shiver through me.

What if he knows where I live? Where are Jessica and Micah? Could he come to my house, take them away like he took little Emily? Has he been to my house already? Stood over the beds of my children while they were sleeping?

"Who are you?" My voice echoes through the woods, bouncing off shadows and trees, rising into the canopy of birch and pine, startling birds into flight. "You give her back, do you hear me? You give Emily back!" Suddenly I am bold. I expect him to do as I have commanded.

I scan the forest, checking for the blonde girl from the photo on the flyer. I can almost see her, running through the trees. I think I do, but then she's gone.

"Elizabeth!" He calls my name again, louder than before, insistent. His voice seems to come from the sky, from everywhere. "Elizabeth!"

He grabs me then, seizes my arm, shakes me. The back of my head strikes something solid yet soft. His shoulder, I think. He has me now.

How will the news reach my family? How will they find out? Who will help Jessica pick out her dress for the prom? Who will make sure that Micah doesn't get left out of all the festivities, since he's decided to graduate this year?

I picture them rattling around the house, alone, while Robert spends his time in the north woods. Will he come home and pick up the slack after I'm gone?

I fight, jerk an elbow back, flail my arms, try to grab something—his hair, his nose, his eyes. I go for the most vulnerable targets, the things I've learned in self-defense classes offered by the department.

"Elizabeth, for heaven's sake! Wake up!" The voice rings high, echoes. It's a woman's now. My mother's.

My head bobbles side to side, bumps into something hard this time, and I wake just as the car is wobbling from the shoulder back onto an old two-lane road.

Around the ribbon of blacktop, pine, maple, and sweet gum trees stretch skyward like the pickets of a privacy fence, concealing all but glimpses of what lies beyond—a house, a barn, a cotton field, white-crested and ready for harvest, and the sky darkening toward the first evening hues.

Beside me, Mom is wide-eyed, both hands back on the wheel. She sends a concerned look my way, but mostly she's irritated. "What in the world is wrong with you? You're lucky we didn't end up in a wreck."

I stretch the stiffness from my neck and sit up, surprised that I've let myself fall so deeply asleep. I'd intended to stay awake, to watch for any signs of Mom dozing at the wheel or zoning out and doing something dangerous. If she shouldn't be making car trips anymore, I need to know. But even that seems strange—my questioning my mother's competence in anything. She's always been the one in charge. Of the school, of the family. Of the world, really.

I don't want to take over the world, or even the running of the family compound. Or the running of *her*. It's all I can do right now to hold my own house together and keep from committing mayhem in the daily struggle of parent versus teen.

There's a town ahead, and I spot a Dairy Queen billboard. "Let's stop for an ice cream." I'm surprised when another sign informs me that we have driven through a whole state since I fell asleep. "We're in Virginia? How long was I out?"

"Three hours at least, maybe four." Mom rolls *the look* my way, frowning. "I've been trying to tell you that you don't get enough sleep. I had to go up to the school and sign Micah's permission form the other day. You stretch yourself too thin. It's no wonder you forget things."

"They would've waited for it." I really don't need the bad-mother guilt trip. Does this woman have any idea how many times I forged her signature because she was tied up with football game crowd control, school board meetings, the courses for her doctoral degree, the task of working out class schedules for five hundred kids? It was just a good thing that my siblings and I went to a different school and that our administration never bothered checking the signatures.

In my eighteen years as a parent, I've attended fifty times more PTA meetings, sports practices, and school plays than my mother ever did for us. It's funny how family histories seem to differ, depending on whom you ask.

"The school administration needs things *when* it needs things. It's hard enough coordinating hundreds of students without tracking down every little thing for every individual kid," Mom lectures. So far, this trip across four states is like being stuck in a cave with a bear waking from hibernation. She's ramping up for the confrontation with Aunt Sandy and using me for sparring practice.

I've really had enough of it. "You know what, Mom? I rearranged everything on the spur of the moment to come on this trip with you. I took four days off work and stuck Carol with a weekend shift. I made arrangements for the kids. I called Robert home from the cabin. I really don't deserve this. And to tell you the truth, I don't need one more person complaining about me, okay?" The last words are out of my mouth before I realize that I have fully snapped and started digging a little too close to the pool of angst I've been trying to ignore. I've revealed more than I meant to.

A curious eye slants my way. "*Who's* complaining about you?"

"You just were. That's all I meant." Deflect. Distract. Sidetrack.

"You said you don't need anyone *else* complaining about you. Clearly there's a larger problem here."

Suddenly I wish I'd stayed asleep. "No. Nothing. It was just a figure of speech." We pass the Dairy Queen, and I watch it go by. I really need an ice cream cone right now. Chocolate. Anything chocolate. Maybe chocolate ice cream dipped in chocolate. I need comfort food, the kind of thing I would not normally allow myself to eat.

"Is it Robert?" For months now, she's been nibbling

around the situation with Robert and me, trying to sniff out the reasons he's gone so much.

It's never occurred to her that if there is something going on, I don't want to know. At least not yet. Two kids graduating in one year and the end of family life as we know it is enough to handle. I refuse to let some big upheaval blow my kids out of the water during their senior year of high school. I wonder if this is the reason Micah has decided to hurry up and graduate. Maybe he's afraid that something bad is coming and thinks he'd better get out of the house while he can.

"Oh, look! There's a Piggly Wiggly!" Mom cheers, and I'm glad we've veered off course. Literally so— Mom turns in to the parking lot. "Remember when we lived in Biloxi? You used to get all excited about going to the Piggly Wiggly."

"I don't remember." The family compound is the only life I've ever known. My father's stint in the military ended when I was three years old. "I was just little."

"I always thought that was the strangest name for a grocery store. . . ." Her face turns solemn as she leans forward to get a better view of the Piggly Wiggly sign. For a moment, there's a mist in her eyes. "You were such a cute little thing . . ." The sentence goes unfinished as if she knows that I've reached a point in life where a sense of yearning for the past strikes me too. There's something magical about that time when your babies are small, when you're the center of their world, the person they love the most.

"We always used to sing a little song, remember?" Mom offers. "'To market, to market, to buy a fat pig. To market, to market, jiggety-jig . . . ,'" she sings. Having taught preschool for several years before she had children, my mother always had a song or a nursery rhyme to suit any occasion.

It plays in my mind, a long-lost track I didn't know was there. I join in on the second stanza. "'To market, to market, to buy a fat hog. To market, to market, jiggety-jog.'"

We laugh together at the end, and I have a flash of a memory. Heat boiling off asphalt around my white Mary Jane sandals, Mom and me sitting on a bench in front of a store, eating ice cream. There's a scent in the air, and I smell it again today. It's not a Michigan scent.

"I guess I do remember after all." An image wavers in my mind, heat-washed and misty—my mother as a young homemaker, before my little sister came along and then my brother. Before Mom decided the June Cleaver life wasn't for her, that she wanted a career.

But before all that, there was just a young mom and a first child and a quiet summer day with ice cream cones. There will always be those memories that tie us together, those invisible strings. The careless stitches of mother and daughter.

Suddenly I'm glad I've come along on this trip. The Piggly Wiggly seems healing in some way, though I can't explain it.

"Oh, let's go back and get an ice cream." The car

wheels around in the parking lot, and we head back to the Dairy Queen. "Dinner can wait. We don't have a schedule to keep."

The last words trouble me a bit, because I know my mother. She never makes a trip without a schedule in place. She never arrives late or unannounced.

It hadn't even occurred to me that she might be making this trip without having ironed out the plans ahead of time, but those words, *We don't have a schedule to keep,* clue me in.

This is a stealth attack. Aunt Sandy doesn't know we're coming.

CHAPTER 4

Evening is setting in as we drive over the wide, four-lane bridge from the North Carolina mainland onto the Outer Banks. The highway is strangely quiet heading onto the islands, but it's busy going the other direction, crowded with vehicles stuffed full of possessions and trailers piled high with sofas, mattresses, ATVs, shelves, and store fixtures with tarps tied over the top. Even though the last miles after looping Norfolk are fairly rural, we've already passed numerous homes and businesses boarded up with hurricane shutters. I'm starting to feel the insanity of what we're doing, and living in Michigan, I know nothing about hurricane evacuations.

The crazy meter is ringing off the charts in my head. It does this often when my family is involved.

"Mom, grab my phone for me." I take one hand off the wheel and try to reach my purse on the passenger-side floorboard near her feet. "I want to check the weather."

"Not while you're driving."

"Give me my phone."

"For heaven's sake, Elizabeth. Have you looked around? What if you get distracted and drive us off into the drink?" She indicates the waters of Currituck Sound below us. They are perfectly placid this evening, slightly pink-tinged as the day works toward its end. It'll be dark before we can travel all the way down the Outer Banks to Hatteras Island.

"I just want to make sure you're not about to get us stuck in a hurricane." The horror stories I've seen on TV come to mind. I'm way out of my element here, and Mom only knows whatever she learned during those three years living in Biloxi. Which, presumably, is practically nothing.

Her arms cross, and her foot slides the purse far out of my reach. Our Piggly Wiggly peace evaporated about the time the Dairy Queen faded from sight in the rear-view mirror, and we've been butting heads ever since.

She snorts. "I checked the weather before we left. What do you think I am, some kind of addle-brained idiot?" The claw of deeper issues scratches up a morsel. Once again, we're feeling our way through this difficult dance of changing roles. And stepping on each other's toes. "We've got almost forty-eight hours before it is supposed to even be in the vicinity, and it's only supposed to pass by here, not make landfall. Those people are just taking precautions." She waves blithely toward the vehicles going the other way, heading for higher ground that's not surrounded by water.

"This is stupid," I mutter under my breath. Overhead, a formation of pelicans wings its way toward the mainland. The birds know. They are smarter than we are. The word *birdbrain* comes to mind.

I keep driving because we're here now. What other choice is there, really? We might as well see Aunt Sandy.

But in the morning, I am insisting. If I have to hogtie my mother and throw her in the car, we are leaving. Preferably with Aunt Sandy safely in the backseat. I've heard the stories of Hurricane Irene hitting the Outer Banks. Of Aunt Sandy's shop flooding, the roof of her house being blown partially off, and the bridge to Hatteras Island washing out, cutting the island off from all highway traffic for weeks.

Aunt Sandy shared the details with us when she was home last Christmas. She made the hurricane sound like one ginormous adventure, filled with heroic acts of neighborliness and personal sacrifice. She always makes her life sound idyllic, partly to counteract all the family disapproval, no doubt. The relatives consistently provide a united front against this runaway island existence of hers.

It's a form of bullying, I guess, but it's what we do. We keep our own close to home. Period.

I give up on the phone. I'll check as soon as we get to Aunt Sandy's place, and if there's anything dire, we'll just get back in the car and drive the other way. After the long nap this afternoon, I feel pretty good. I could drive for several hours tonight if I had to.

But as we pass through the intersection that allows us a choice of turning north toward Duck and Corolla or south toward Kill Devil Hills, Nags Head, Rodanthe, Avon, and eventually the tip of Hatteras Island, where Aunt Sandy lives, I hope we really do have a day or two to spare. The windows are down, and the scents of salt breeze and sand slip into me. I need this.

Maybe now the nightmares about Emily will stop. I haven't turned the whole situation over and over in my mind for a couple hours or tried to mentally rewrite the way things happened. Here, with the live oaks bending over the road, the Spanish moss dangling in lacy chains, and the palm trees swaying, Emily seems like a story on the evening news. Something terrible but far away.

I ignore homeowners shuttering windows and crews covering storefronts with plywood as we pass. It's hard to believe anything could be wrong in a place like this.

We drive by the giant sand dunes of Kill Devil Hills, and I can't help slowing down. I've read about this place in books.

Mom leans toward the window. "Oh, how beautiful! Maybe tomorrow on our way off the islands, we can stop and visit the Wright Brothers Memorial, see where Wilbur and Orville took their famous first flight."

I don't know whether to agree or look at her like she's crazy. This trip isn't a vacation. At the same time, I'd like to pull over, throw my arms out, and run wildly up that giant dune, see what the view looks like from the top. I'll bet you can watch the water on both sides of the island from up there. What kind of freedom would that be?

I can taste it, almost, that burst of something unplanned and completely different. Something I wouldn't normally do. My heart quickens for the first time in a long time. Maybe that's what I need, I decide. Maybe that's the secret to surviving this change in life, this ending of all the things I've put my heart and soul into, of motherhood as it has been. Maybe I need to plan a vacation—go bungee jumping or zip-lining or skydiving. Something wild.

"Well, that's a faraway look if I've ever seen one." Mom's observation breaks into my thoughts, and I realize some time has passed. "What's that about?"

"Nothing." The whole thing is a can of worms I'm not ready to open yet. With my mother or anyone. It's like I've been stuffing emotions into a bottle for a couple years now, and if I open the cork, everything will rush out at once.

"Oh, there it is!" She's distracted by a glimpse of the ocean. The waves, white-tipped and frothy, brush against the shore with a different kind of power than I'm used to seeing in Lake Michigan. They seem determined to pick up this place and move it bit by bit.

A lit sign echoes my thoughts: *Life on a sandbar. It's beachy!*

We continue down the Outer Banks, pointing out

beautiful multistory vacation homes, interesting shops, and glimpses of the water that quicken my pulse each time. No wonder Aunt Sandy has run away to this place. It's incredible. I wish I'd come sooner, brought the kids all those years she invited us to visit.

The sun sinks lower as we drive, and the last blush is gone by the time we finally reach Hatteras Island. Overhead, a spray of stars seems close enough to reach for. My mother has relaxed in her seat, gazing at the sky. She tells me about a time she and my father went on a picnic to Lake Michigan. The day he asked her to marry him, and she said yes. They lay beneath the stars for hours, making plans, talking about their future. A young couple in love.

Mom has dipped her toe into the waters of the past now. As we drive through Buxton and Frisco, she tells me about her wedding. The day, the dress, the conflicts with her own mother that seem petty now. "Sandy was only fifteen then, and your grandma was convinced that she was too young to be a bridesmaid. I think that was the first time my mother and I ever went head-to-head about anything. But I was almost twenty, I'd been out on my own working, and I was paying for a lot of the wedding. I wanted my sister in it."

"Did you get your way?" The GPS on the dashboard shows us drawing ever closer to Sandy's house, and I almost regret it. I'm enjoying the conversation. It's amazing that the GPS knows its way to places like this, so far off the beaten path. We've been driving down the Outer Banks for roughly two hours. From near the top, almost all the way to the bottom, where the ferry landing leads down to Ocracoke, the last of the developed islands. I know these places because Aunt Sandy has told me stories about them. They already live in my mind.

"Yes, I did. My sister and I had slept in the same bed since she left the crib in my parents' room, and I couldn't imagine not sharing that day with her."

"That's really nice." I picture my mother and my aunt, a little over four years apart in age, curled up in the same bed, sharing innocent games of Let's Pretend. It makes the present situation seem that much sadder. Should geography and real estate signs outweigh the bonds formed by the shared milestones of childhood?

The pressure of that question grows as we continue down the island and finally wind through a small neighborhood toward my aunt's place. Around us now, the houses are a combination of historic clapboard homes built closer to the ground and more modern ones constructed on stilts where historic homes have undoubtedly surrendered to the wind and the floods.

"Mom, maybe you shouldn't do this. Maybe you should forget what Uncle Butch says and just let it go."

The profile of her chin is stiff. "I won't have this family torn apart." I recognize the stubborn look. I've seen it many times in my daughter, who is her grandmother's spitting image—in personality and mannerisms, if not in appearance.

What if this is the thing that tears the family apart? I wonder. We're pulling into the driveway now, so there's no time to ask. The house is a gray, cedar-shingled structure on stilts with a carport underneath. Hurricane shutters cover the windows, but over the front door, a cheery sign, just visible in the glow of the headlights, proclaims, *Sandy Feet Welcome Here.*

The house is dark. It's obvious that no one is home.

"Maybe she has evacuated already," I suggest, grasping at a hope that perhaps this ill-fated journey will end in a missed connection. Somewhere on the road I learned that Aunt Sandy has quit answering calls from my mother and Uncle Butch, hence this wild trip.

"She's down at that shop of hers. You can bet on it." A frustrated huff punctuates the words. "Let's go."

We drive back to Highway 12, then wind our way past more shuttered houses, through Hatteras Village, and a short distance toward the ferry landing, where my aunt's shop comes into view as we round a corner. It's just like the pictures on the postcards she sends us at Christmas. An antique clapboard house in the I-style that's traditional in the Outer Banks, painted yellow and converted to a shop. The wide front porch looks like a perfect place to sit and watch the traffic headed to the Ocracoke ferry. In back, the water of Pamlico Sound twinkles beneath the full moon, and some sort of outdoor lamps cast a colored glow onto the grass. The lights are on in the shop, the upper dormers reflecting against a carved sign that labels the place.

SANDY'S SEASHELL SHOP
An Ocean of Possibilities

It looks like the showdown of the O'Bannion sisters will happen after all.

Mom doesn't even wait for me to put the car in park. She flips the lock and is out the passenger door, climbing the steps before I can turn off the engine, but she stops on the second stair from the top.

Exiting the vehicle, I hear music. Mom has tipped an ear toward it too. She glances over her shoulder at me as if she needs backup. I don't want to be backup. I'm realizing how completely I hate this mess. And I wonder how much of this is happening because my mother wants it and how much is because Uncle Butch is a bully and my family is set in its ways?

The shop door is open, but no one is around when we walk in. Furniture and store fixtures have been stacked in the main room, with soft things like chairs and sofas raised onto metal shelves and wooden tables. Clearly someone has been preparing for the possibility of floodwater. But even in its present condition, the shop is adorable. There's a coffee bar along the left wall, an antique display case bearing a vintage cash register, an actual indoor sandbox in the middle of the store, and a bay window on the front wall with beautiful stained-glass suncatchers hanging inside. Hummingbirds. Dozens of them.

The well-worn plank floors of the main room and

the beadboard wainscoting are clearly original to the house. Above the wainscoting an array of shell art and signs offers beach-related bits of wisdom, ready for tourists to take home. A rack of hats and sarongs makes me want to stroll a few miles down the shore and see what the tide might wash up. The music seeping from outside adds to the mood. It's an island tune, heavy on the steel drums and wooden flutes.

"She must be out there." Mom turns toward the light spilling through the back doors that lead to what appears to be a deck. The accordion paper shades are lowered partway over the glass, so all we can see is the first foot or two of weathered wood. "She has her stained-glass workshop in the old garage building in back. She told me."

My moment of beach nirvana evaporates as we cross through the shop and open the French doors. The deck comes into view, and of all things, it looks like there's a party going on. At the patio tables, a dozen or so people are laughing and talking and feasting on piles of food dumped unceremoniously atop splayed-out newspapers.

Mom stops in the doorway, clearly surprised to have walked in on a gathering of some sort. She's not at all prepared for this. From where I'm standing, it looks like we've shown up at a convention of old hippies. The people on the deck are an eclectic collection of long hair, grungy T-shirts, sagging tattoos, and leathery skin. They range in age from perhaps forty to seventy or so.

Aunt Sandy spots us, and her eyes fly wide. She stops with a crab claw halfway to her mouth, a cracker still dangling in the other hand. She blinks, blinks again. I have a feeling she's hoping we'll disappear. But of course, we don't.

Here come the relatives, like it or not.

Finally she sets down the crab cracker, which I figure is a good sign, and stands up. Her round cheeks rise beneath her spiky blonde hair, and a measure of relief trickles through me. At least we're not going to have all-out war right here and now.

To the contrary, she waves us outside, like she's not a bit surprised to find us on her doorstep. "Well, don't just stand there!" she bubbles cheerfully. "Come on out here! Grab a plate! We're having a hurricane party!"

CHAPTER 5

I open my eyes, stare at the evenly spaced metal bars above my head, wonder where I am.

For once I've slept the whole night, rather than spending the hours dozing and waking, dozing and waking in a sweat. I haven't tromped the woods in my dream, stirring the leaf litter and hoping to find a little blonde girl running through the trees.

The realization should come with relief, but instead it comes with guilt. If I give up on looking for Emily, even in my dreams, isn't it the same as accepting the worst?

I don't accept it. I won't. Little girls shouldn't be stolen from their mothers in the middle of the night. They should be safe at home in their beds, tucked in after a storybook and good-night prayers.

I figure out two things as I look up at the bars. The first is that I'm in the extra bedroom at Aunt Sandy's house—the one with two sets of bunk beds, where her grandchildren stay when they come to visit. Mom has already vacated the bed across the room, but the quilt is turned back and rumpled still. She must have gotten up in a hurry. Probably to go argue with Aunt Sandy some more, before my aunt can escape for her morning walk along the shore. There's a path out the back of the house, and it eventually leads to the ocean side of the island.

Yesterday morning, Aunt Sandy slipped away before Mom could catch her. They've been locked in mortal combat for over twenty-four hours now. Today we have to leave, and sooner rather than later. We've pushed the timeline as far as we dare.

The second thing I realize—with startling clarity, as I listen to see if I can catch the rhythm of the waves far off in the distance: I am angry with God. So incredibly, bitterly, hotly angry. I'm boiling over with it.

Why? I want to scream. *Why? Why? Why?* Why is evil allowed to come in the night and snatch up an innocent little girl? The world shouldn't be this way. And if it is this way, maybe I don't want to live in it anymore. . . .

I know that is a selfish thought. I brush it away as soon as it comes.

I wonder if the advice Carol has been giving me at work is more spot-on than I've realized. She thinks I need to see somebody—a doctor or a shrink. *It's nothing to be ashamed of,* she says. *This job is stressful, Elizabeth. You deal with people's worst situations, year after year, and it adds up. On top of that, major life transitions are hard. They can knock you completely off-balance. And then sometimes it's all as simple as hormones and body chemistry. You should go get checked out. Life's too short to be walking around with one foot in the ditch.*

I sit up, catch a breath, remind myself that my problems are small. I know where my children are, for one thing. They're both safe. There's never been a time when I couldn't kiss them good night, at least over the phone. And even though these years of tearing away are difficult, there's a part of me that knows it's normal enough. Kids are supposed to grow up and cut the apron strings. I just never dreamed those sharp scissors would leave so many wounds. Who *am* I, now that I'm not Mom-in-charge anymore?

I put on sweats and tennis shoes, grab a jacket in case my mother and Aunt Sandy are outside, engaging in an early morning battle. Yesterday, the only peaceful moments were those when Aunt Sandy brought out her sea glass, shells, and freshwater pearls and showed my mother how she makes one-of-a-kind jewelry pieces. *Jewelry from the sea,* she calls it. She almost lured my mother into the idea of being a long-distance designer of artisan pieces before Mom realized that she was unwittingly being pulled into the Seashell Shop dream. After that, she pushed away the salt-frosted glass and said, "For heaven's sake, I don't have time for this kind of thing. I came here to talk about the property, Sandy."

Then the war was on again. It lasted all day and kept us from leaving last night.

Maybe they've gone down to the water together this morning, but I hope not. We need to get on the road, and from the sounds of the conversation after the moments of sea glass sisterhood, it will be just the two of us leaving. Mom and I. The taproot holding my aunt to this place reaches straight through the salty soil and all the way to the floor of the ocean. And with Uncle George gone, there's no way she's leaving their house and the store without someone watching after them. She has a generator, bottled water, batteries, nonperishable food, Uncle George's old ham radio, and all the other hurricane necessities, including numerous cans of gasoline.

Besides, she doesn't expect the storm to be that bad. The last thing we heard on the television was that it was expected to pass by Cape Hatteras, not coming onshore until farther north. The greater fear seems to be that it will strike hard around New York City and up the Jersey coast.

I don't know if it was a show of bravado or not, but at the hurricane party the night before last, the old hippies were tipping their glasses to the storm, thumbing their noses at the weather bureau, and eating enough discount seafood to choke a whale. What else is there to do but feast when the power may be out for a while and the food will spoil anyway?

These people are either the heartiest souls I have ever met or the most foolhardy. I can't decide which, but they are very nice. While helping to pack shop goods yesterday—and listening to Mom and Aunt Sandy argue—I met several women Aunt Sandy refers to as the Sisterhood of the Seashell Shop. Teresa, Elsa, Callie, Crystal . . . I can't remember all the names, but most of them own shops up and down Hatteras Island.

They are as close to my aunt as sisters, and as I watched them, I noted something. This is lacking in my own life. Over the years, I've gotten so busy with work and my kids' activities that I've let friendships slide off the map. Other than Carol at work, there's literally no one to talk to who *gets it* . . . no one I'm close enough to that I'd admit the ragged truth, anyway.

I find my mother in the kitchen, trying to make heads or tails of some sort of professional coffeemaker that has undoubtedly been brought home from the Seashell Shop.

Mom looks like you might expect a former high school principal to look without her morning coffee.

And Aunt Sandy is nowhere to be found. That, of course, is the first thing Mom complains about, after letting me know what she thinks of the fancy coffeemaker.

I decipher the brewing machine because I am, after all, trained to save lives, and this is a life-or-death situation. We need coffee. Now. Or heads will roll.

We perch on barstools on either side of the small island as the pungent nectar of morning perks nearby. Some fresh strawberries are waiting in a bowl. I don't know if they are for us or not, but I help myself.

I wait for the brewing to finish and for Mom to take in the requisite amount of coffee before I bring up the obvious. "We need to get on the road this morning."

Mom is drumming her fingernails on her cup. *Ching, ching, chang. Chang-chang. Ching-ching-ching.* That's not a good sign. "She won't listen. She's being ridiculous. It's insanity." Mom squints toward the back window. I gather that *Mrs. Insanity* has indeed gotten up early and escaped for her walk. "And I'm not the only one who thinks so either. That woman who owns the ice cream stand down the road, that *Teresa person*, she agrees with me. Not only was she sending her own elderly mother to the mainland to stay with relatives, she agrees that Sandra Kay is in no shape to be riding out a storm here, and especially not by herself." She's calling my aunt by first and middle name this morning, adding a parental tone to the battle. She is Big Sister Sharon now, and big sister knows best.

"Well, she's done it before. They've been here for years, Mom. Surely she knows what she's getting into." I'd noticed my mother canvassing the crowd at the hurricane party, soliciting opinions, support, or information—or all three. She pulled Teresa aside again yesterday, when Teresa stopped by the Shell Shop to check on us. We were out back, packing up supplies in the glassmaking shop. Aunt Sandy was sweating like crazy, despite the fact that the day was seasonally cool.

On the one hand, I realize that what my mother has been doing, she's been doing with the best intentions.

Mom is not a mean person. She's worried about her sister. On the other hand, I hate it when she does this to me. And I'm not unaware that in these months since her retirement, she has been nosing around in my life.

"Mom, I think you're just going to have to let this . . ."

Her glare could fry an egg at thirty paces. "They *all* agree with me, Elizabeth. *Every* one of them I talk to. But especially Teresa. She knows the most because she's the one going to the doctor appointments with Sandy."

An uncomfortable wrinkle in the universe travels my way. "What doctor appointments?"

My mother lifts the index finger that says, *I'm right, and you'd better listen.* "Oh, you don't know the half of it. And neither does George because Sandy's been keeping secrets from him since not too long after they went through the last hurricane. She doesn't want him having to worry about it, considering all the trouble he's having with his mother and her dementia and the nursing home back in Michigan."

"But what's going on with Aunt Sandy?"

"Diabetes that's out of control. She won't take her medicine. And near blackouts behind the wheel of her car. Eating things she's not supposed to. She refuses to monitor her diet. And if anyone tries to tell her what she should do, she makes excuses. She says there's been too much going on since the last hurricane, and she doesn't have time for the adjustment to the medicine. It makes her sick and takes away all her energy, so after just *one week* of trying it, she went off the stuff. She says she's been making it okay all these years—she'll be fine until things settle down and she has *time to be sick*. Can you believe that? Can you believe the ridiculous stubbornness?"

Oh yes, I can. I'm looking at the mirror image. Different hair. Same personality. These women run the world, or else.

I take a sip of coffee, savor the taste on my tongue, try to come up with a solution that doesn't include throwing a gunnysack over my aunt's head and tossing her into the trunk of the car.

"Well, maybe when we get back home, we can—" I don't even get *talk to Uncle George* out of my mouth.

"I'm staying."

The hammer drops, and I hear it ringing against my ear. My brain sloshes back and forth in my skull, and it's a minute before I can form a coherent thought.

"What do you mean, you're staying?"

"I'm not leaving. That's it. She can't be here by herself. And she won't let any of her friends stay over with her because they have houses of their own to look after. And she refuses to weather this thing at their houses because she wants to keep a watch on this place."

"Mom, you can't stay here."

"Oh yes, I can. And I am. What's my sister going to do? Throw me out in the ocean? Once you leave, she'll be stuck with me, whether she likes it or not. If she's that worried about my safety, well then, she'll have to get in her vehicle and drive to the mainland, now won't she?" My mother gives me a lemon-lipped smirk, pleased with herself. All those doctoral classes are paying off. She has outmaneuvered everyone. She thinks.

"I'm *not* going to drive off and leave you here with a hurricane coming." No way. Nohow. Not happening.

"Oh, it's not even supposed to be that bad. You saw the weather report last night. Just a little brush."

"Yes, and I see the eighty-seven gas cans piled on the deck out there too. It's a hurricane, Mother. You can't tell from one minute to the next what these things will do. Even assuming that it doesn't cause some kind of catastrophic damage around here, there could be travel problems on the East Coast for days, maybe weeks. Who knows?"

She focuses out the window, as in, *La la la, I can't hear you.* "I'm capable of making my own decisions, Elizabeth. They may have put some young know-nothing in charge of the school that should've been mine, but I'm still a fully competent adult."

This is a fine way to prove it. My cell phone rings in my pocket, and if it weren't for the fact that the kids might need me and the investigation into Emily's kidnapping is still ongoing, I wouldn't pull the phone out to look at it. As it is, Mom gives me a disgusted look as I check.

It's Carol.

Something cold and solid sinks slowly from my

throat to the pit of my stomach. "I need to take this." I can barely get the words out.

Mom lodges a complaint about young people and bad cell phone manners as I head outside to the second-story deck and pull the door closed behind me.

I answer, and Carol sounds emotional on the other end. I know before she says the words. It's bad news.

"Elizabeth, they've found a body out by Palmer Lake. They haven't got a positive ID yet, but I didn't want you to hear it somewhere else if you were following the local news over the Internet. Jason says it's her." Carol's son, Jason, is one of the officers on the case. He's looked at that picture on the flyer a thousand times. If he says it's her, it is.

"Is he sure?" I ask anyway. I can't think of what else to say. I feel myself breaking inside. Shattering into a million pieces.

How can this be? How can this be happening?

"Yeah. But they haven't done an ID yet," she repeats as if that extends a ray of hope. As if it would be better for some other little girl's lifeless body to be found in the woods. "You okay?"

I don't really need to answer. She knows me well enough to guess. "No."

Once again, I cycle through those moments. Those moments after the call came in, the time wasted because my mind was lost in a fog of my own problems. Could it have made the difference? Would the outcome have changed if Carol had taken the call?

"They don't know any details yet," she warns. "Elizabeth, don't go jumping to any conclusions. That won't help anything, okay?"

I don't answer. I can't.

"Okay?" Carol repeats, louder this time.

"I have to go." Somehow I manage to thank her for letting me know. Then I'm walking across the deck. And then I'm running, down the stairs, across the lawn of wispy salt grass and weeds, down the path through the scrubby bayberry bushes, toward the dunes and over them onto the thin strip of sand that hasn't been overtaken by the storm-swelled tide.

I run and run, shoes sinking into the sand, the weight of it pulling and tugging, slowing me down, not letting me get away fast enough. The waves claw the shore, and tears blur my eyes. Far out to sea, the first hints of a change in the weather blacken into a formless darkness.

I pant and I scream, but other than quiet, shuttered houses, no one hears me. As far as I can see down the beach, there's not a sign of another living soul. Nothing to stop me from running, except myself. My own weakness.

Eventually I can't go any farther. I can't put any more distance between myself and that phone call. My lungs burn and my legs go numb, and all I can do is collapse into a dune and watch the waves violently strike land, and feel myself going out to sea with them, piece by piece.

CHAPTER 6

I'm chilled to the bone by the time Aunt Sandy finally finds me. Overhead, the sky has narrowed, the clouds closing in. The waves have taken out the beach, the water already brown and churning with a mix of sea foam and debris. There's only a few feet now between the shoreline and the dunes. Aunt Sandy is driving on it in the little ragtop Jeep she uses to run around the island.

The vehicle slides to a halt, and she hurries toward me in a stocky shuffle as I rise from the dunes. I have no idea how long I've been here, watching the storm slowly work its way toward us. That is the beauty of the ocean, even when it's angry. It steals all perception of time. Right now, I need to lose myself more than anything.

But as I catch my aunt's frantic look, I realize how selfish I've been, and guilt strikes me like a cold splash in the face. Undoubtedly they've been looking for me all this time. I've kept them from last-minute hurricane preparations. By default, I have probably sacrificed any possibility of talking them both into leaving. If Aunt Sandy is really having as many health problems as my mother indicated, she doesn't need to stay here.

"Where have you been?" She grabs me and rubs her hands up and down my arms. The sweatshirt is wet, stiff, and practically icy. The spray is so cold now.

I like the numbness it has created.

"I'm sorry." I think I've gotten myself together. I intend to say that I had a call this morning with bad news. Instead, I manage, "The call . . . the call . . ." and then the flood wall bursts. Sobs come rushing forth, and I cry, bent over her shoulder for who knows how long. Against me, she seems strong, her feet spread a distance in the sand, bracing to hold back each strike of wind. I huddle on her leeward side like a clump of sea oats, seeking to ride out the storm.

She does me the favor of not asking for more information, here and now. The surf is so loud, it isn't a place for talking. Finally she guides me to the Jeep, buckles me into the passenger seat like a child, continues up the dunes until we find a place to cross through, then motors between beach houses and down the highway. In the distance, the cylindrical black-and-white stripes of the old Hatteras lighthouse stretch skyward, seeming to promise that it is possible for something well built to survive the storm.

I wonder if I have what it takes. I don't feel as solid as that lighthouse.

Instead of taking me home, Aunt Sandy steers

toward the Seashell Shop. She lets us in and calls my mother's cell phone from the landline. The service is patchy right now, so the call ends abruptly.

"We need to get you out of here, and you need to take your mother with you," she says, suddenly all business. The storm comes first, and I'm glad of it. I don't want to talk about the news from work. I don't want to think about it. "There's probably still time for you to get off the Banks and over to the mainland, at least if the traffic cooperates. But you need to go *now*. Just let me check everything and get the shutters in place on the door. And then we'll hurry home."

She walks around the room, muttering to herself, reviewing a mental checklist that makes me realize how many times she must have been through this procedure before. "All the furniture up . . . glass cutters and saws at the house . . . inventory on the high shelves . . ."

How does somebody do this—face storm after storm as if it's to be expected? Why hasn't she just given up?

She stands in the center of the shop, her hands braced on her hips, her face partially hidden by a base-ball cap she has grabbed and pulled over her short blonde hair. "You might want to get one off the rack," she says, motioning to the hat. "It's about to be a bad time for hair around here. And depending how far inland you two make it—which, like I said, is all about the traffic—it may be a while before there's a hot shower."

"I'm not going." The words come out in a rush as

if I've just discovered them myself, but I've known for hours that I couldn't bear to return home. Not right now. Suddenly, riding out a hurricane seems like the lesser of two evils. I can't watch the discovery of Emily's small body as it's broadcast on TV. The confirmation that it's her. The pictures of her sobbing mother clutching her baby brother. The interviews with the grandparents, who have stood rock solid through this entire process, their faces stricken with grief. I can't bear to hear the behind-the-scenes details coming out bit by bit. I can't go back to work. I can't take another call. What if I screw up again, cost someone else the time that's needed to save a life?

"Oh *no* . . . ," Aunt Sandy begins, but when her survey of the store turns her my way, she catches my face, studies me a moment. I feel like she's reading everything inside me. "All right," she says then. "Okay . . . but let's just hope this one passes on by without being anything like Irene was."

I nod, and then she hands me the phone and adds, "You'd better call your family while you can. Tell them not to worry if they don't hear much from us for a few days. You never know about communications after one of these things." *For a few days* slides past me, plucking a disquieting note. "And take those suncatchers out of the bay window, would you? I forgot those were there. Wrap them in bubble wrap and tuck them in one of those boxes with the egg-crate slots. Put it up high somewhere. Two dozen suncatchers are worth some money, and if, heaven forbid, we get any damage out of this storm, we're gonna need it."

The ominous tone should scare me—I think she means it to—but instead it produces one last burst of determination. I find myself slipping into my mother's role. Maybe Aunt Sandy will listen to me. She knows I'm not trying to take over her life. "I understand how much this place means to you. But listen, I was talking to Mom this morning, and she's legitimately worried about your health."

She turns away with a quick shake of her head. "Don't start on me. Just help me do these last few things and get the doors shuttered, okay? I've heard everything your mother has to say. I've already promised her that I'll get checked out and see what I can do about finding a medication that doesn't put me flat on my back, *when there's time*." A backhand hatchets through the air in a maneuver so like my mother's, it's scary. No wonder they drive each other crazy.

I hope it's not genetic, this ridiculous determination to ignore all the people around me and answer a concern with a laissez-faire flip of the hand. *If I ever catch myself doing that, I hope I smack myself upside the head in the process.* "Okay, okay . . . but how about if we just go inland and get a hotel for a few days? All of us. I'll drive. I'll help you shutter up before we leave. It really doesn't seem like a good idea for you or Mom to be here during this storm, just in case it's . . ."

A look comes my way, and it aborts the rest of the

sentence. There's no point. Mind made up. Those blue eyes say it all. "Elizabeth, storms are part of living on an island. Every decision you make in life has benefits and consequences. Sometimes you just have to go on faith, and even that comes at a price. It means you have to give up the idea that you're the one in charge of the universe. This old house and I have been through all the storms before, and we're going to get through this one. Whatever I need, whether that's provisions or friends to help in the aftermath or the kindness of strangers, like the volunteers who helped after the last storm, God's going to bring it my way."

I don't have an answer for that. Aunt Sandy is the expert in this area. She's the Bible study teacher. But I think, *What if the provision this time is a sister who's telling you to get yourself to the doctor?*

I don't say it, though. She won't hear me anyway, and I'm so ragged right now, I don't have any more energy for arguing. Instead, I take the phone outside so I can call Robert and tell him I've decided to stay for a hurricane.

I catch him in the office, and I know he's busy or he wouldn't be working on a Sunday. Aunt Sandy's cordless-phone battery is low, so I should make it quick, but there's a part of me that yearns for some form of normalcy, for a touchstone. I want to run through the list of kid issues: Micah's calculus-teacher problem, Jessica's cheerleader tiffs, signing up for another SAT test.

I want to talk. Just talk about all the normal concerns. Pretend there are no such things as storms and sad ends to troubling missing-persons cases.

"What's up?" he asks. I've let the line hang too long.

"Well, there's been a little hitch in my plans. . . ." I start into the saga of my aunt's health concerns, my mother's insistence on staying, and the fact that I'm afraid to leave them here alone. I downplay the hurricane reports, basically intimating that there's no chance it will actually hit full force here. "Just a lot of rain and thunder, and maybe flooding in low-lying areas, but Sandy's house is up high and fortified, so it shouldn't be any problem."

Robert is distracted but sympathetic. "Sounds like the O'Bannion commotion continues," he says in a tone that indicates he doesn't want the details or have time for them right now. Generally he tries to sidestep the family wrangles. "I have to travel early next week. Four days. A test track out in Arizona."

"I'm sure we'll be home by then." I run some quick mental calculations. Next week is seven days away. With any luck, we'll be through the storm and have convinced my aunt to make a doctor's appointment by then.

"Be careful on the way back home." This is Robert's way of ending the conversation nicely, but also letting me know he has other things to attend to.

I feel issue-creep coming on, and before I can stop myself, I'm unloading a laundry list of questions. Really, I'm just not ready to let go of the lifeline yet. I want Robert to ask for a few more details about Aunt Sandy and the storm, help me make sure I'm doing the right thing by staying here. I want him to act like they miss me at home. "Did Jess get signed up for the SAT test again? You know, I was thinking that really both kids should go even though Micah's last score was pretty good. Oh, and I think I forgot to tell you— Jess found a leak below her bathroom sink. I stuck a bowl under it, but we better get a plumber in before it springs loose and floods the second story . . ."

"Got it under control," Robert bites out.

"I wasn't trying to nag. I was just wondering. You know, I'm nine hundred miles from home, and I'm stuck in the middle of this stupid fight between my mom and my aunt. I'm not there to take care of things at home. I just want a couple minutes of your time to find out what's going on there." My voice trembles at the end, but I harden myself against it. There's no room for a breakdown right now, but there's a part of me that wants him to pick up on the emotion and ask what's wrong. I want to tell him everything—the 911 call, Emily's mother, the wasted minutes . . . everything.

That little girl on the news, I want to say. *I took the call. I made assumptions. I botched it.*

"If you're going to leave me in charge, Elizabeth, then let me handle it," he snaps, and I'm stung.

I stand there gritting my teeth, my lips tightening against the swell of emotion—anger, irritation, disappointment, sadness. Loneliness. When did we get to this point, always brushing by each other in a rush or taking our frustrations out on each other?

He hates his job. I hate what our lives have become. We're both stretched so thin that neither one of us has a soft place to fall. I wonder again if he's seeking solace somewhere else. He wouldn't . . . would he? Robert is one of the most honest people I know, which is why some of the things going on at work drive him crazy. There's a lot of cutting corners in the auto industry during these times of economic pressure.

"I'm sorry." He sighs into the phone. "It's just been a bad day here, and I wasn't planning on being out of town next week. I'll miss the homecoming game."

"Homecoming," I mutter. "I'd forgotten about homecoming. . . ."

"Are you okay?" This time he seems like he's really asking. I realize I've been wiping my eyes and sniffling.

"Yes . . . yeah . . . fine." He doesn't need any extra pressure today. I know how he is when things aren't going well at work. "I'd better sign off. I'm trying to help Aunt Sandy get the shop closed up before the storm. She's hoping the water won't come in this time."

"Listen, keep in touch." His note of concern gives me comfort. Then I tell him what Aunt Sandy said—communications could be spotty.

We finish the conversation, and I call into work, explain that I may be off a couple more days than I'd planned. Fortunately, no one else is on vacation right now, so it's not a problem.

All the bases are covered by the time I go inside to help Aunt Sandy finish up. I do as I've been asked. It feels good to have something to occupy my hands, a manageable task. I can save these little glass hummingbirds. They are beautiful things, my aunt's creations—hummingbirds and flower vines, captured in colored glass and leaded metal.

"There's one extra." I hold it up after I've filled the box of twenty-four. The straggler dangles from its green ribbon, suspended in flight.

Aunt Sandy smiles at me as she crosses the room. "Must be that one's for you. We'll take it home with us, and you can tuck it in your suitcase. Then when you hang him in your window, he'll be a reminder of an ocean of possibilities." She spreads her arms like she's Vanna White offering up a prize package, then looks at the pile of goods in the center of the room and adds, "Although my ocean's a little bit of a mess right now, sorry. I wish you could see this place on a regular day."

"Me too." I'm one half inch from saying, *I'll come visit again, maybe bring the kids after graduation,* but I stop myself. We're supposed to be persuading her to give this place up, after all.

So I follow her from the shop instead.

I help her work the hurricane shutter onto the front door and tap the sliding latches into the brackets with a small hammer. By the time it's done, we're both sweating and Aunt Sandy has called her husband an ugly name or two. Uncle George designed and built this special door covering after the last hurricane flooded and decimated the shop. He calls it the floodgate. It is weather-stripped to death around the lower edges, in hopes of preventing water from seeping into the building if it comes up that high. The guys from the surf shop helped Aunt Sandy install the ones on the back door after the hurricane party. It never occurred to her that she and I might test the limits of our strength to put the front floodgate in place today.

When we're done, she pauses, braces both hands against the doorframe, and scares me half to death by dropping her head forward and wheezing huge breaths.

"Are you okay?" I touch her shoulder before I realize that she's not having a heart attack. She's praying.

I close my eyes and bow my head, and a couple things strike me in the darkness of my own mind. I realize how much my aunt loves this place. How much it means to her. Much more than twenty acres of farmland she never uses and probably doesn't intend to. I'm also struck by the fact that, in the hours since I learned about little Emily, it hasn't occurred to me to pray. There's been nothing in my mind but grief and crazy rage. My last prayers went unanswered, after all. Emily didn't run through the trees to a rescuer. She wasn't delivered safely home.

I try to force myself to offer up words for her family, to plead that, in her last moments, she wasn't terrified and alone and cold. But all I find myself doing is reliving what those last hours may have been like—a stranger speeding away with her in the car while I sent the first responders in the wrong direction.

"Let's go." Aunt Sandy is all business again. We return to the Jeep, and instead of going home, we make the rounds, as she calls it. We visit the other shopkeepers. We check on the homes of friends who have evacuated. We canvass neighborhoods and ensure that the elderly women from the Sunday school class have gone to relatives' homes or that they at least have a caretaker staying with them.

We work our way through traffic, on the shoulder about half the time, to Fairhope, a little fishing village around a marina, where the boats are now bound and double-bound to the docks. I wonder how they will fare in the storm.

Inside Bink's Market, the Fairhope locals are discussing the incoming storm. We listen as we nibble on crab-and-sausage balls and crab rangoons, which the owner, Bink, assures us are famous. Meanwhile, three men at a table swap stories about the last hurricane and the one before that and the famous Ash Wednesday nor'easter that tore a hole through the island, bisecting it.

I wonder again where these people get their fortitude. The weather hasn't ruined their appetites. As customers rush in and out, buying the last of the water, the bread, and the canned food, the fishermen play cards at a table in the corner and enjoy some of Bink's shrimp po'boy sandwiches. We buy some to take home.

"George and I love the food at this place," my aunt remarks as Geneva Bink wraps up our sandwiches.

I check out the size of the homemade bun and think of Aunt Sandy's diabetes. Clearly she's in denial if it's as bad as Mom said.

Before leaving Fairhope, we pull into the driveway of a giant Victorian house. With its three-story turret, wide front porch, and wraparound veranda, it makes me think of the graceful, quiet life of days gone by. Dressed in faded paint and crumbling gingerbread trims, it looks like a bride who has fallen asleep beneath the live oaks and forgotten to wake up, her wedding gown weatherworn now.

"*Pppffff!*" A disgusted sound escapes Aunt Sandy as she looks at the house. "Well, at least she's had someone put up the hurricane shutters for her, but I'll bet she's here. She sure doesn't need to be. Ninety-one years old and still determined to ride out the hurricane. Ridiculous."

I survey the place as we walk up the steps and knock on the door. "Ninety-one and she lives here? Alone?"

The reply is a frown of genuine concern. "One of my longtime customers. I don't think she has any family. Haven't ever heard her mention anyone for as long as I've known her."

I try to imagine a ninety-one-year-old woman going through a hurricane, all by herself in this enormous house. "That's terrible." Having lived on the family compound as long as I can remember, I can't

fathom not being surrounded by relatives, not having someone to take care of me if I needed it. It occurs to me that I've never been as grateful for that as I
should've been.

"Well, Iola Anne Poole is a woman of the Banks,
through and through." Aunt Sandy says it like that
explains everything. "This place gets in your blood."

The little woman who opens the door looks like
a native. Her skin is a deep olive color, wrinkled and
leathery in the way of things that have lived long by
the sea. But her silvery-blue eyes are bright. She's tiny,
stooped over, and thin, yet she seems strangely capable
as she assures my aunt that she has made all the proper
preparations for the storm. "Oh, you know, this old
house and I have been through quite a few."

"I understand that, Iola Anne." My aunt touches
the little woman's shoulder tenderly. "But I just wanted
to check and see if you won't consider coming and
staying over with me, or if there is anything you need.
I could run to the store for you or . . ."

"No, no, no. Now don't bother about me. I don't
want to trouble anyone." A pat of my aunt's hand and
a shrug seem to assure that this slip of a woman has
everything under control, though the general condition of the house says otherwise.

She catches me checking out the porch, asks who
I am, and quick introductions are made. I shake her
hand, which is cold, the skin as thin as parchment over
bone, yet her grip is surprisingly strong.

My fingers stay trapped between hers for a moment as she turns back to my aunt. "I'll be just fine." A scrappy black cat with a damaged ear slips past her feet and skitters out the door, skirting us warily. "You'd better hurry back, Mr. Muggins!" she calls after him, letting go of my hand. "You'll end up with Dorothy and Toto in Oz."

The three of us laugh, and Aunt Sandy promises to check on her after the storm. Iola Anne Poole assures her it's not necessary. "You know how it is. The storms come and it's water and wind as far as the eye can see for a bit. But winds calm and the waters drain. We find our feet again, and the ground under us sprouts a new crop of seed. That is always the way of it. I don't suppose this storm will be any different."

At my aunt's insistence, Iola promises to at least call after the storm and let us know everything is okay in the big white house. We offer to fold the shutters over the door for her, and after calling Mr. Muggins in from the overgrown flower bed, she allows us to do it. She waves from behind the leaded glass as the hinges groan and we close her into darkness before hurrying back to the driveway. We've almost pushed our luck too far, I can tell. The weather's coming in now.

The wind buffets the Jeep as we travel back down the island. By the time we reach home and drive the Jeep onto one of the flatbed trailers Uncle George cleverly uses to keep the vehicles and various machinery above the reach of low-level floodwater, I can feel the storm arriving in earnest. So can my mother. She's a nervous wreck.

I don't blame her. I feel pretty much the same way myself.

CHAPTER 7

The storm has been raging for hours now. It's worse than was predicted. It's hitting Hatteras pretty hard as it lumbers by, the eye staying out at sea. We've pulled the mattresses and one of the sofas into Aunt Sandy's dining room to camp out away from the exterior walls. From time to time, I'm sure the roof will go any minute.

Outside, the hurricane shutters rattle, and the house sways in gust after gust of wind. The rain flows in ribbons, stronger as each band of the storm bears down, but even the ebb is incredibly intense. I've never heard rain like this. The sound on the roof of Aunt Sandy's little saltbox house is deafening.

The storm wants to push its way inside. It's like a demon. Determined. Relentless. Seeking out the faintest cracks to breach our fortress and find its way past the walls. During the ebbs, we hurry through the house, replacing the towels and bedsheets we've stuffed in the wet spots around the windows and door stoops. Weather stripping is no match for the fury of this beast.

I have to give my mother and Aunt Sandy credit. They are an efficient team. Two commanding generals who have temporarily joined forces to fight a greater enemy. There is no arguing about whether or not we should have stayed.

During an ebb, we hear a rhythmic *clang, clang, clang* below the house.

Aunt Sandy pinches the bridge of her nose, closing her eyes. I notice for the first time how flushed she looks. "Water's coming up. The boat's floating off its trailer down there."

The noise suddenly makes sense. There's a little aluminum johnboat outside. Before the rain started, we unhooked the straps binding it to the trailer and tied it to the piers of the house instead. Now I understand why.

She seems matter-of-fact about it, but I know this is not good. For the water to float that boat, it must be a couple feet high already. The weather radio has been belching out flood reports for a while, and our hiding place has become an island.

"No way out but through the storm now." Aunt Sandy sits down beside me on the sofa and pats my knee. She meets my gaze purposefully, as if she knows there's a deeper meaning that can be taken there and wants me to grasp it. "I'll bet about now you're wishing you had beaten it toward home while you still could."

"Nope," I lie.

I expect her to ask about why she found me having a breakdown on the dunes earlier, but she doesn't. Instead, she curls an arm over me and pulls my head onto her shoulder.

"No way out but through the storm," she whispers again. "We're not alone." She combs her fingers through my hair, and I close my eyes, relaxing against her. "We're never alone."

I know what she's referring to. She's a woman of great faith. I don't confirm what she's said or refute it. I just drift away with the boat downstairs ringing like a church bell, her words the last ones on my mind.

There's peace for a little while, and then I'm in the woods again. I'm forcing my way through briars, ignoring the sting as they claw at my skin, slice through my clothing. I hear something in the distance. Music. People singing. A choir.

Pushing back vines, I move toward the sound, stumble through the trees until I see light ahead. There must be a clearing. The singing is so loud now, it eclipses everything.

And then I'm in the hollow, standing outside a funeral tent. There's a tiny white casket. A gasp steals from me, and I throw my hand over my mouth. All the mourners turn my way accusingly.

Emily's mother motions toward the grave, her eyes still fixed on me. And then I'm standing at the edge of the hole, looking down on the casket, and it isn't Emily in there, but Jessica. My daughter, lying on white satin, only four or five years old, her face soft and chubby-cheeked and pale. Lifeless.

The mourners begin throwing in handfuls of dirt. A scream tears from me, and I try to shield Jessica from the spray, but they hold me back.

Men begin adding soil by the shovelful. I scream again, and then Aunt Sandy is shaking me awake.

I come to consciousness lying on the sofa, trying to fight my way out of a quilt.

It's a moment before I realize that the storm sounds different.

"The eye went past, out at sea. The wind's hooking around the other way now, which means it's going to pull the water up on the sound side even more. The weather radio is full of overwash reports on both sides of the island," Aunt Sandy explains. She looks like she's been dozing herself. On one of the mattresses, my mother is sitting up, watching me. I realize I've awakened everybody.

Aunt Sandy turns up the battery-powered lantern, then taps my legs so that I swing around and let her sit.

"Sweetheart," she says when she looks at my face, "what's the matter?"

My eyes sting and brim with tears, and suddenly I'm like this old house. I can't keep the storm out any longer. It forces its way through the cracks.

Mom gets up and comes to sit beside us on the sofa, and I pour out the whole story. Emily, the fact that I was the one who took the 911 call, how I botched it.

How I feel like I must be coming apart at the seams lately. There is something so wrong with me. I don't even know who I am anymore.

As the storm increases in intensity again, I fold over myself, lower my head into my hands, and Mom and Aunt Sandy close ranks on either side of me.

"Elizabeth, you can't take this on yourself," Mom insists. "In the first place, it isn't your fault that woman took her little girl out in the middle of the night and left her alone in a car. In the second place, you don't even know what has happened yet, or *when* it happened. That woman might just as easily be lying about how long she was away from the car and how soon she called 911 when she couldn't find her little girl. You don't know if there's one thing you could've done to change how this ended." It's exactly what you'd expect a mother to say, what I would say if anyone were trying to lay this on Jessica or Micah. Defend first, ask questions later.

Aunt Sandy rubs my back. "Honey, I can't tell you why this has happened. It's a terrible thing. One of those happenings you can question and discuss until your mind goes numb. But I do know that you're still here, and if you're still here, no matter how much it hurts, there's a reason for that. You may not feel it right now. And it's okay to grieve. But it's not okay to quit living. You've still got kids to raise and the family to take care of and work to do. I know it seems like your babies get to a point in life where they don't need you anymore, but they do. There are just a few hard years here where everything's changing, where the kids are testing their wings, and then it gets better. I promise."

"It does," my mother assures softly. "You just wait, Elizabeth. In a few years, that girl who's driving you crazy right now will be a woman you are incredibly proud of. She'll be your best friend, and when you look at her, you won't be able to believe that you raised someone who has so much going for her."

They lock themselves around me in a three-way hug, and we rock back and forth, joined together, a sisterhood against the storm.

CHAPTER 8

The sun is out and the water has begun to drain away by the time Aunt Sandy backs the Jeep down from the flatbed trailer that has kept it above the brackish soup of overwash, runoff, and debris. On the piers under the house, the flood has left a line almost three feet high, which we know is not a good sign for the shop. This house is on higher ground.

We've spent just under forty-eight hours waiting for the storm to pass and the floodwaters to drain. With the power out in Aunt Sandy's neighborhood, we've been listening to weather-radio stories and getting word-of-mouth reports on the conditions farther north via the Hurricane Watch Net on Uncle George's scanner and ham radio. There's flooding and damage all the way up the Banks. Where the storm came ashore along the Jersey coast, the damage is catastrophic. Homes and businesses have been lost. And lives.

In Aunt Sandy's house, other than the leakage we mopped and sopped around the windows, everything remains high and dry. The generator is running on the deck, providing enough power to keep the essentials going, but crews are expected to restore the electricity soon. Even the food in the refrigerator will survive, it seems. To preserve the gas in the cans outside, we maintained our campout lifestyle and left the refrigerator closed throughout the storm.

Now it's time to move from survival mode to assessment and recovery. I know this process. It reads like a script in a 911 reference manual. Life preservation first, then damage control.

Aunt Sandy directs my mother to stay behind with the house and enlists me to go along on the reconnaissance mission to the shop.

Mom seems amenable enough. Working our way around storm wreckage and piles of sand transported by the raging water is more of an adventure than she really wants. She doesn't seem to regret the fact that we stayed through the storm, even though North Carolina Highway 12, the one road in and out of Hatteras Island, has been lifted and buckled at Rodanthe and Mirlo Beach, and the bridge at Pea Island Inlet is out of commission. Emergency ferry runs will be starting soon to reconnect Hatteras with the mainland, but it'll be a while before transportation on and off the island becomes routine again. For now, we are just here, like everyone else who rode out the storm.

"You watch her," Mom mutters under her breath, leaning close to me as Aunt Sandy and the Jeep splash across six inches of water in the flooded yard. "She doesn't need to be doing this. Whatever has happened in that shop has happened. There's not a thing she can do about it now."

"I will."

"Don't let her start hauling things out of the place and whatnot," Mom insists. "She almost took a tumble in the hallway this morning. I know she was dizzy. I saw her feeling her way along the wall."

I've seen things too, but I don't share them with my mother. I do plan to try to talk to Aunt Sandy today. Maybe she will listen to me. I'll probably sneak a call to Uncle George if I can, assuming the landline phone is working at the Seashell Shop. Cell service is out due to a damaged fiber cable up island. Aunt Sandy won't be happy with me for butting in, but her husband needs to know what he's coming home to.

"Don't worry," I say and kiss my mother on the cheek. There's a new feeling between the three of us after the night of the storm.

On the way down the island, skirting logs, displaced patio furniture, and leaning telephone poles that have been cordoned off by emergency workers, Aunt Sandy talks about the most routine things as I stare at beach houses sitting in water, storm-damaged cars encased in sand wash, bits of relocated pavement, pieces of decks, and shreds of houses.

Aunt Sandy wants me to know that an empty nest isn't the end of the world. It's normal, what I'm going through. Even the distance between Robert and me.

"It's the leap from one phase of life into another," she assures me. "Like when you went from being a young couple to being parents. Remember how hard that was? Remember those moments when you realized that you'd never again just hop in the car and go somewhere? That your life would always be tied to this new responsibility now? But it was the beginning of something too. It was the beginning of this great big adventure of raising a family. And that becomes your center point for a lot of years. It's normal to feel lost when you suddenly realize that's going away now. It's normal to grieve something you've loved."

I nod, still taking in the distractions. I consider what these people have been through, and I feel ridiculous. We shouldn't even be talking about my problems right now.

The salt air blows into the Jeep and tries to steal my aunt's baseball cap. She grabs the bill and pulls it lower, the sun reflecting off rhinestones that spell out the words *Beach Time*. "The trick," she says, "is to find a new dream for the next part of your life. Then empty nest becomes a beginning, not an ending."

"I know." I try to shift her off the subject. "I just want to get through this year, through the graduations and everything, and then I'll think about it."

A stern look comes my way. "That's not soon enough. Do you think those kids want a mother boohooing at every one of their little milestones this year? They want you to celebrate with them, Elizabeth.

They've got enough of their own worries. They don't need to be worrying about you. They need to know that you'll be okay when they're gone. That you and Robert are looking forward to new frontiers too."

I try to think of it this way. I try to think of Robert and me doing things together again, just the two of us. Maybe going up to the north woods and spending time in the cabin?

Then I wonder if he's even interested. I can't tell Aunt Sandy that, of course.

"Like when George and I came here." She takes a breath, and I can tell she has a story she wants to share. She tells me about their first trip to the Outer Banks—a vacation Uncle George won through a sales contest at his job. She admits that they argued all the way from Michigan that first day. She wished they hadn't even taken the trip. "But you know, the vacation gave us a new dream, a dream we could share together. We saw that old house by the highway in Hatteras Village, and I think we both knew. Putting a shop in there was our future. It seemed crazy, but it was what we needed. We never looked back, and we've never been sorry. This part of our life has been one of the best parts. The shop, the grandkids coming to visit, our house with the path to the shore. A whole new experience, instead of sitting around mourning what's gone. I'm just . . ."

Movement on the side of the road catches my eye, and I shut out the rest of her sentence. There's a woman running from a beach house, sloshing through the water in the front yard with something in her arms. I lean down and look in the side mirror after we pass. Something's wrong. . . .

"Wait! Stop!" I reach across and clutch Aunt Sandy's arm, strain against my seat belt to get a view over my shoulder. "Turn around! Somebody's got a problem back there."

Aunt Sandy cuts the wheel, circling a sand-covered pile of flotsam at the edge of the road. Our view is blocked momentarily, and then we see the woman. She's in the ditch now, running. There's a baby in her arms. Limp. My heart lurches upward, my mind rushes, and for a moment I wonder if this is a dream— if I'm really back at Aunt Sandy's house, asleep.

But it's real. It must be.

We squeal into the ditch, and the Jeep rams into a sandbank as it slides to a stop, tossing me against the seat belt hard enough that I'm addled for a moment before I spring the buckle, jump out, and run to the woman.

She's carrying a toddler, a little girl. The baby's wispy blonde hair is plastered to her head, muddy and wet. For an instant, my thoughts stall. I wonder again if I'm dreaming of Emily, but this child is younger.

"She fell!" the woman screams, her face flushed and covered with dirt and tears. "She fell off the deck into the water. I only turned my back for a minute. Oh, dear God, save my baby. She's not breathing. She's not breathing! Help my baby!"

There's a split-second fear that I will freeze, but I don't. A calm slips over me. A clarity of thought. A step-by-step logic that comes from training. "How long?"

I take the girl and lay her on the storm-washed sand alongside the road, shaking her to see if I can stimulate a response, but there is none.

A four-wheel-drive truck pulls over and two men run our way, but I'm barely aware of them. The script is in my head, but not only the script. There's also the emergency training I've been through as part of the department.

Until you're in the situation, you always wonder if you could do this in real life. Now it feels like second nature. "Find a landline and have someone call 911!" I say. Then I check her airway, give a quick breath into her mouth, feel for the rise and fall of her chest, try again to rouse her as the men in the truck race to the fire department, not far away.

I start chest compressions, count to thirty, give two breaths. She doesn't respond.

Come on, come on, come on, I think.

Beside me, Aunt Sandy is on her knees, praying.

The baby's mother keens and wails, calling out, "Sarah, Sarah, Sarah. Wake up, baby. Wake up for Mommy. Wake up!"

I repeat the process. Still no response after the second cycle. This child isn't going to die right here beside the road. She's not. This little girl will live a full life. She'll build sand castles along the shore, celebrate birthdays, hunt for Easter eggs, and wear her favorite dress on the first day of school.

Please, God . . . please. This can't happen. . . .

I begin a third cycle, then a fourth. There's a siren in the distance. Help, I hope.

Finally . . . finally . . . there's a thready pulse. A hint of life. And then a tiny cough. It is the most beautiful sound.

"Praise God!" Aunt Sandy lifts her hands heavenward.

I roll Sarah onto her side, support her head as she gags up a combination of water and stomach contents. When it's finally over, she fights back as I try to scoop out her mouth, and then her wide blue eyes blink at us. She's confused at first, disoriented. Her lip trembles and she starts to cry. I gently sit her up and let her mom cradle her so tightly that there's not a whisper of space between them.

"Thank you," the mother breathes, tears streaming down her cheeks. "Thank you. Thank you so much."

I hear clapping, and all of a sudden I realize there are people around. A first responder runs in with a medical kit. At least a half-dozen bystanders are forming a circle around us. I don't even know where they've come from.

I'm shaking as I stand up, and I just want to get to the Jeep and sit down. Catch my breath. I can't believe this thing that has just happened. We watch until the first responders finish assessing the child and the crowd begins to disperse, then we leave with everyone else.

It all starts to seem unreal as we continue to the Seashell Shop. I sit looking at my hands, thinking, *Did I do that? Did it happen?*

"If you hadn't been here, that little girl would probably be dead right now," Aunt Sandy points out as we skirt a piece of toppled billboard near the Seashell Shop parking lot. The area around the store is a swamp, water still pooled over the parking spaces and probably a foot or two deep in the backyard, all the way up to the deck. The flood-line mark on the building pronounces the verdict without our even needing to go inside. When the eye of the hurricane passed by and the wind reversed direction, the overwash here was bad enough to cover the porch and reach partway up the long bay windows in the front.

Neither of us speaks as we wade through six inches of water, then climb the steps to the front porch of the old yellow house. Above the front door, the cheery ambers, blues, and yellows of a sign seem out of place now. The gold letters read:

SANDY'S SEASHELL SHOP
An Ocean of Possibilities

"Well, I hope this thing worked." She indicates Uncle George's homemade floodgate on the door while fishing a hammer and screwdriver from the antique iron mailbox. "Looks like this storm may have made it in through the windows, though." She glances toward the nearest one, which is clearly below the dirt line left by the water.

Even so, she seems upbeat. This is the thing I love about my aunt. She never gives up, even when the prognosis looks grim. Somehow I know that, no matter what we find inside, the water will not defeat her. And perhaps, after what we've experienced on our way to the shop, she realizes what I realize—that no matter what happens now, this day is already golden.

The fact remains, though, that the storm has been much worse than anyone anticipated. The hurricane hung over the island forever, dumping water. Yes, it's only property damage, and property can be replaced, but I know that Aunt Sandy wouldn't be selling the land in Michigan if she and Uncle George weren't already tapped out from the last storm recovery.

I help her clear driftwood away from the front door. We pile it near the porch steps. The collection looks almost like art, if you don't think about what it is and how it got there.

The scent of the air slipping from the building answers the looming question even before we loosen the last of the latches and move the shutter away from the door. It smells like our clothes washer when one of the kids throws in a load and forgets about it for a couple days. In a flash, I wonder if anyone is taking care of the laundry at home. How are they faring without me?

Am I really as unneeded as I sometimes feel these days? Probably not. I know that's the truth of it.

I think about what Aunt Sandy said to me in the Jeep, about making the leap to a new phase and it all being part of the plan. Parenthood is the only career in which the better you do your job, the sooner you're fired.

I'll have to share that with Carol when I'm back at work. The thought makes me smile for about half a second, before I catch a glimpse through the glass door into Sandy's Seashell Shop.

My aunt grabs a breath and lets it out through pursed lips. Her shoulders square before she turns the knob. "No point avoiding reality. It is what it is." As she pushes it open, the door catches on a soggy floor mat we forgot to pick up. It's the first thing she grabs when she's able to squeeze partway inside. The drips create a waterfall as she hands off the mat and tells me to throw it over the porch railing. "Gotta start somewhere. That's the only thing you can do with a mess. Start cleaning it up, a little at a time."

Inside, the shop not only smells like mildew already, but it is a mess. The water reached over two feet high in here, swamping the old plank floors and the antique wooden beadboard around the lower parts of the walls. The moisture has seeped upward into the drywall above the wainscoting, drawing uneven mountainscapes in dirty shades of brown and gray.

"We just got all that fixed." Tears sparkle in Aunt

Sandy's eyes, and she blinks rapidly, trying to deny them. "One season. *One*. That's all we got out of the repairs we spent so much money on before a storm hit again. It doesn't seem fair, does it?"

"No, it doesn't."

She pulls another breath, then puckers up and kisses the air on its way out. "Then again, this day is already a blessing." As she echoes my earlier thought, a smile spreads from one side of her face to the other, dimpling her round cheeks and spilling the tears over. "You saved a life today."

"*We* saved a life today." Through all the gloom and the smell of newly forming mildew and the merchandise that has tumbled to the ground and been covered by the slime, an incredible light falls over me.

"Divine providence." Aunt Sandy gives the events a name and an author.

She picks up a muck-covered glass box that has inexplicably been left sitting in the middle of the floor. We stand there and smile at each other as she fingers the lighthouse ornaments atop the box, and the moment could not be more perfect. It's odd when I think back on the events of the past week and a half—the unpredictable, uneven chain that began with the frantic call about little Emily's disappearance and eventually led us here today. The fruitless searches, the nightmares, the trip to the Outer Banks, the storm, the woman running toward the road today with her toddler limp in her arms . . .

The shadow of the highest evil intermingled with the light of the highest good. Maybe all lives are filled with this. Maybe it is always a choice between embracing the darkness of one or the saving grace of the other.

I ponder the strangeness of it all as I try to keep Aunt Sandy from straining herself physically, but of course she insists on doing it anyway. I have no choice but to hover around, trying to take over the harder jobs, like removing the hurricane shutters, opening windows, taking the floodgates off the back doors so we can mop up floors and carry wet, dirty debris onto the deck. Floodwater stands under the boards, creating a dock that is only a foot above the out-of-place sea that reaches all the way to the sound. There is water pooled in Aunt Sandy's workshop out back too, but she's not as worried about that. The most important things have been raised or relocated, and years ago the old carriage house was lifted onto a block foundation in an effort to keep the historic frame building safe.

We mop, we rinse things, we do our best. We speak with neighbors and shop owners who pass by. I leave Aunt Sandy talking every chance I get, so she'll rest. Two guys in kayaks travel by on the sound, or perhaps they are in the backyard. It's impossible to tell. They wave, seeming to be almost enjoying the storm's bizarre aftermath.

A reporter from the *Charlotte Observer* comes by, working on an article. "This one will get special coverage in the *Washington Post* as well," he tells us as he walks with Aunt Sandy onto the back deck to snap a picture of her among the debris that is now drying in the sun. "We're doing everything we can to make sure that, in light of all the damage in New York City and along the Jersey shore, people don't forget you've taken a hit here as well."

From inside the shop, where I'm trying to finish some of the emergency cleanup Aunt Sandy insisted *had* to be done before we could possibly leave the store, I hear bits of the ongoing interview, but mostly all I can think is *My mother is going to kill us when we get home.* I'm surprised Mom hasn't abandoned the house and hitched a ride here by now. She expected us to be gone only long enough to check on the shop.

Outside, my aunt waxes nostalgic with the reporter, relating the challenges of living on a sandbar, and then she tells the story of buying the house and starting Sandy's Seashell Shop. "I guess you could call this my midlife-crisis store," she laughs. The sound jingles in the air like the tiny brass bells she attaches to the bottoms of some of her suncatchers so that when the window is open, they become wind chimes as well. "But I wouldn't have it any other way. It's some life, here on these Outer Banks. It really is."

Before he leaves, the reporter crosses through the store and snaps a photo of me down on my hands and knees, grubbing around behind the coffee bar. I'm horrified. I can just imagine how I look. "Don't print that."

His brows lower with a disappointed look. "Seriously?"

I sit back on my heels and wipe my forehead with the back of my hand. The weather is cool today. Technically the storm has been classified as a nor'easter, but I'm sweating like a pig in August. Those changing hormones Carol warned me about, perhaps. "No, it's okay."

He asks me for a bit of my storm story, and I share it. An outsider's point of view of surviving a brush with one of the most geographically far-reaching storms ever recorded in the area. *The perfect storm*, they're calling it.

He's putting the lens cap on his camera when I hear my aunt's voice outside. "No! No! No! *No!*" She sounds panic-stricken, and it stands me bolt upright.

The reporter follows me as I hit the back door in a dead run. I am on the deck before I catch sight of Aunt Sandy. She is waist-deep in the floodwaters of the backyard, almost all the way to the sound, reaching for what looks like a toy wagon floating by. The red kind that children play with. It's drifting along like a little boat.

The reporter's camera clicks as I hurry down the steps and splash into the water. *Mom's going to pull every hair from my head individually if she sees this* runs through my mind. Why in the world is Aunt Sandy wading out there to rescue a stupid toy wagon? There's junk everywhere. You can't tell what might be beneath the surface of this water, either. My aunt might trip over something and fall at any moment. She's not all that steady on her feet.

"Aunt Sandy!" The water resists as I plow through it like a water-aerobics student on steroids. "What are you *doing*?"

She catches the wagon, reaches for something inside it while I'm still ten feet away.

The wagon floats off as she turns around, and when she comes closer, I see that she's holding something small, black-and-white, and trembling. A little Boston bulldog. It's licking her face with ferocious gratitude as she tries to push its head away.

"Stop that! Hold still, you little scallywag. Cut it out."

The reporter's camera spins into high gear as Sandy draws within a few feet of me and holds up the prize for which she has risked the floodwaters. "Look at this little piece of shark bait. Saw him just floating by in that wagon. No telling how he managed that." She wobbles on her feet, and for a moment I think that both she and the dog are headed into the drink. Then she regains her balance, laughing and reaching for me. "Looks like we each saved a life today."

"Hey, cute dog!" the reporter cheers, and I have a feeling that the little Shell Shop castaway has just become part of the story.

CHAPTER 9

"I don't know . . ." Mom looks up from her suit-case, a half-folded shirt dangling from her hands. I'm not sure why she's folding it so carefully. It's dirty. All of our clothes are dirty. Water and effort can't be wasted doing the wash right now.

"Mom, it's time." The days have run together. Three? Four? It's a blur of dragging soggy inventory out of the shop, picking up water and supplies from the Red Cross station in a parking lot, delivering them around the island, checking on Aunt Sandy's elderly friends, helping with first aid where I can.

Mom casts a concerned eye toward the window. Outside, Aunt Sandy is headed down the driveway in the Jeep to go over to Fairhope and check on Iola Anne Poole one more time. The foundling bulldog is in hot pursuit, hopping like a rabbit, the little white spot under his nub tail flashing.

"I think she's trying to outrun him." I point toward the window, laughing as the Jeep squeals to a stop and my aunt exits with her hands on her hips. She comes at the dog, hunched over like a pro wrestler trying to intimidate an opponent.

She hates that dog. He scratches at her door every night, whines and cries, and doesn't stop until she relents and lets him in. Then the dog snores. Bad. She has started calling him Chum, not as in *friend*, but as in *shark bait*. She's careful to let us know that is not an official name. She's looking everywhere to find his owners, or at least some willing foster parents until his owners can be found. The story of his rescue made the newspaper, yet no one has come to claim him.

Even Mom can't resist the scene outside. The two of us giggle as we watch Aunt Sandy and the dog do their love-hate dance. Unless we physically restrain him, Chum pushes the screen door open and does this every time his new favorite friend tries to leave.

"I think I should stay here with her until George is back." Mom's smile fades and the concerned look returns as Aunt Sandy finally allows Chum into the passenger seat. Together they rattle off down the driveway and turn the corner, out of sight behind a bedraggled bayberry hedge.

I cram the last of my dirty, wrinkled clothes into the duffel bag that was supposed to last me a couple days. "He'll be home tomorrow, Mom. It's only one night. And if you don't come with me, you'll have to try to get a flight back to Michigan. With all the mess from the storm, that could be a problem." In reality, Uncle

George has told me it will be better if we go home now. On top of taking care of everyone else on the island, Aunt Sandy feels the need to treat Mom and me like houseguests. We've tried to set her straight, but you don't set that woman anywhere. She's like the value of pi. She just is.

My job today is to get my mother to come with me and stop butting in. Uncle George feels that there's less chance of Sandy digging in her heels if he can get home and speak to her about the health concerns calmly, one-on-one.

"Mom, there's no telling what will happen with the ferries and shoaling and the possibility of more bad weather coming. We need to get out while we can." I don't mean to sound selfish, but I miss my family. Other than a few short conversations on the Seashell Shop phone, we've hardly talked. I feel like I'm losing track of things at home, even though Robert has it under control.

Mom looks out the window, tearing up.

"Mom . . ."

"I miss my sister." Her voice quivers and breaks. "I can't believe all these years I've been so stubborn. I can't believe I haven't come out here and spent time . . . just because . . . I was mad that she moved away."

"You can come back again once things are normal. Now that you're retired, you could take an off-season rental and . . . stay for months each year if you wanted." Too late, I realize I have divulged the fact that I think the family needs to stop pressuring Aunt Sandy. This is her life, her second-half adventure.

"Something's going to happen. I just know it."

"If it'll make you feel better, we'll get one of her shop friends to come stay here tonight. Teresa, maybe."

"I just—"

Both of us turn toward the window at the same time. The barking has caught our attention, a wild, high-pitched *yip, yip, yip, yip, yip!*

I push to my feet. "What's he doing?"

Chum is headed up the driveway in a dead run, not bunny-bounding like he usually does but dashing flat and full-out.

I hurry from the bedroom and walk onto the front deck, then stand at the top of the steps and call Chum. He dashes to my feet, barking, but darts away when I reach for him. I walk all the way down and try again. He runs through the soggy yard, slinging water, comes my way, evades capture again, then bolts down the driveway, pausing at the end to see if I'm following. I go a few steps, call him again. For a minute, we're like a scene out of *Lassie Come Home*.

Mom follows me into the yard, and we stand looking at the dog. "Something's wrong." She frowns, clearly concerned. "Sandy wouldn't just let the dog out of the Jeep and leave him running in the street. She'd come back to check on him. She might be tired of him weaseling into her bed at night, but I know she cares about that little guy."

Chum barks three times and bolts for the road as if he realizes that we've finally caught on.

"I'm going to grab the car keys. . . ." Mom turns to dash back into the house. Fortunately we've moved her vehicle from one of the trailers to the driveway in anticipation of leaving today.

"She can't have gone far." I take off running after the dog. Down the driveway and the street, my legs pumping, the wet, brackish air seeming too thick to breathe.

I've gone a few blocks when I see the Jeep, cock-eyed in the ditch, the front end rammed against a tree. Strangely, the motor is still running, exhaust churning from the tailpipe and disappearing into the morning mist.

Mom and I arrive at almost the same moment. Aunt Sandy is slumped over the steering wheel, her arm hanging out the window in a stiff, unnatural position.

The door resists when I try to open it. I throw my weight against the handle, stumble backward when it finally gives.

My aunt's skin is coated with beads of perspiration as I lay her back against the seat and turn off the engine. A drop of blood falls onto the cuff of my jacket, leaving a small, round stain. She hit her head during the crash.

Aunt Sandy's teeth draw back in a tight grimace that seems more reactionary than intentional. She moans, the sound starting low in her throat and slowly rising. She is breathing, but I'm afraid the thing we've all feared has come to pass.

This looks like a heart attack. A catastrophic one.

"Aunt Sandy. Aunt Sandy, can you hear me?"

"N-n-not deaf. . . ." It seems like she's trying to force a smile, but it evaporates into a groan so guttural I ache inside.

"Are you experiencing pain in your arm? In your chest?" Again, the scripts come into my mind, clear, calming. I've been through this one so many times with callers.

"I . . . d-don't . . . h-have time . . . fff . . . for . . . a h-heart . . . 'tack . . . ," she assures me. If this weren't so serious, I would either laugh or cry. My aunt is still here with us, but this is bad. Medevac to a hospital will take a while, especially with all that's going on in the storm-damaged areas right now.

Mom elbows her way in beside me and takes her sister's hand. Tears fall next to the blood. "Don't you do this. Don't you do this, do you hear me, Sandra Kay?"

I push Mom away. "Mom, go to the neighbor's house. The one where Sandy used the landline phone the other day. Call in an emergency—tell them we have a heart attack in progress. We need medevac by helicopter. Now. The victim is conscious and responsive at this point. Give them her age, weight, and the address."

"N-n-not . . . th . . . the . . . w-weight . . ." Aunt Sandy groans.

"Ssshhh . . . You can stop trying to make us feel

better, okay?" I comb the hair from her face, look at the gash. "We're here. We're going to get you through this."

Mom pulls something from her pocket and presses it into my hand—a small foil packet of some sort. "Here, have her chew one of these. I'll be back as soon as I can."

I glance at the packet. It seems like a miracle in the moment. "Aspirin?"

"I always carry them in my pocket." Mom shifts the keys in her hand, preparing to run for the car. "It's a principal thing. All those teachers, dealing with stress and students. Never know when you'll need it."

"What . . . f-flavor . . . ?" Aunt Sandy coughs and spasms after attempting the joke.

"Shut up, Sandra Kay. *Now.*" My mother lays her forehead against her sister's as I struggle to tear the foil wrapper. "You have to make it through this, do you hear me? You are my sister, and I love you. We still have things to do together. You promised. We're going to walk on the beach and design sea glass jewelry, and you're teaching me to make those hummingbird suncatchers or *else*. It isn't time yet. It's not."

My aunt doesn't answer. I don't know if she's losing consciousness or merely obeying her big sister for once. A tear slips from beneath her lashes.

I stop my mother just as she is turning to run for the car. "You'd better help me move her out of the Jeep."

This is not the end of the sea glass sisterhood. Not if I have anything to say about it.

CHAPTER 10

The ferry landing is teeming with people. Red Cross trucks, National Guard caravans, and groups of aid workers in identifying vests or T-shirts exit the ferry in droves. Meanwhile, visitors who underanticipated the effects of the storm and residents who have decided to relocate to the mainland until things get better line up to shuffle their way onto the outgoing boat. Ferry attendants encourage everyone to be patient. The emergency transports are operating on a regular schedule, despite issues with shoaling and debris left behind by the storm. The commute across the water, two and a half hours under normal circumstances, will be slower than usual.

Arduous is what it will be. We have no idea of Aunt Sandy's condition. By now she has, hopefully, arrived at the hospital by helicopter and is in the hands of cardiac doctors and nurses. The Shell Shop friends have left their digging out in order to accompany us to the landing, as have members of Aunt Sandy's church and

Bible study group. We've gathered in a circle, joined hands, and prayed.

We hug and say our good-byes, and the ferry worker who was kind enough to move Mom and me to the front of the line escorts us on. There's no room for the rest of the Sisterhood of the Shell Shop to go. This ferry is full, and the wait right now is several hours.

"Let us know as soon as you hear anything!" Teresa yells.

We promise that we will, and then the crowd of weary, tired people closes in around us. I suddenly realize how much we all look alike in this condition. How completely desperation can equalize people.

It'll probably be a couple hours before we're close enough to the mainland to pick up a working cell tower and find out more about the medevac flight and Aunt Sandy's condition. We're fortunate that everything fell into place for her to be taken off the island so quickly, but even with the fast response, there's danger of a bad outcome. We know that. With a thready pulse and rising and falling from consciousness, she needed a top-notch cardiac team, sooner rather than later.

A man gives up his spot near the cabin wall, and Mom sits down, but I can't. I stand at the deck railing, hang over it, trying to let the sea breeze take away the feeling that I might throw up. Not far away, the pelicans swirl over the debris-littered surf, enjoying the buffet of floating treats offered courtesy of the storm. They seem to promise that all will eventually return to normal. The storm churns up food. The birds feast. Something good comes of even the worst events.

Is it possible? I wonder.

I watch the water slide by, and I do that thing I've mostly left out of my life these past few years, in favor of covering all the other bases. I pray and pray and pray . . .

I lose track of time. Maybe I doze off, standing there. I'm not sure. The adrenaline seeps out of my body, bit by bit, and I'm boneless and weary.

A guy I've never seen before hands me a protein bar and a bottle of water. "Here," he says, smiling at me. He can't be over twenty years old. Not that much further along in life than my own kids. A laid-back beach bum type. "They were handing them out from a Walmart truck. I figured if I took it, I'd come across someone who needed it. That's how it rolls, right?"

I nod and thank him and take the gift.

I figured if I took it, I'd come across someone who needed it. The wisdom of that strikes me in a new way.

I think of those weekends of advanced emergency training given to me by the county over the years. Of the relatives and friends who watched my children so I could go. The Red Cross volunteer who taught the classes. My long-ago high school health teacher who tested all the students to see who could react in a disaster. That teacher encouraged me to pursue something in the medical field, maybe think about becoming a doctor. When Robert and I made an immature decision on prom night and ended up coping with pregnancy, marriage, and the financial implications, that teacher helped me get into the 911 dispatcher training program with the county. Big dreams became smaller dreams, and life went on.

Sinking down against the railing, I rest my head and think of Aunt Sandy's advice to me about starting off on a new adventure in the second half of life. It comes back now, that long-ago dream of becoming a doctor. The idea resurfaces, dull and moss-covered, like something that's been trapped underwater for years. I pull it out, wipe it off, look at it from several angles, and think . . . *maybe* . . .

Could it be time now? Is this the time to reinvent?

Is survival sometimes about death and rebirth? Egg to caterpillar to chrysalis to butterfly? Is this, this ending of our family as I know it, not the death season but the birth of the butterfly season?

If a woman who's never owned a shop or lived by the sea can become Sandy of Sandy's Seashell Shop, what can I do?

If . . . *when* Aunt Sandy makes it through this scare, I won't try to persuade her to give up the Seashell Shop and move home, where the family can monitor and supervise and babysit her. A butterfly should live as long as it can in its natural habitat. This place of sand and water, of seasons and storms and challenges, has become who she is.

The thoughts seep through me, percolate like water

through coffee grounds, producing something new, thick with tantalizing aroma. What would Robert say if I suggested all this? What would the kids think? *You're not the only ones heading off to school. Mom's got plans. . . .*

I close my eyes and let the thought drift like a raft just floating wherever the current will take it. I doze and wake and feel the water swaying beneath me.

I'm surprised when I finally climb to my feet and we're within sight of land. I remember my phone and pull it out, but then I turn and catch a glimpse of Mom standing on her bench. She's already on her cell, waving at me, trying to give me the high sign.

I let out the breath I have been holding. The news must be good.

My phone chimes as the texts from the past few days rush in. There's Jessica in a cheerleading photo, smiling alongside the friend she'd been fighting with. *Miss you, Mom!* the message says underneath. Micah reports that he's pulled a B on his first calculus test. Robert must have made him send the text—Micah would never do that on his own. There's a note from Robert, offering the rundown of activities around home. *Knew you'd be wondering,* it says.

Another from Uncle Butch, several days old. He's worried about his sisters after the storm. He wants someone to send him more information. How dare the cell service not do his bidding. This is ridiculous. He just wants to know that everyone's all right, for heaven's sake.

Beneath that, Carol has sent an update, written during the graveyard shift as my mother, Aunt Sandy, and I huddled together through the heart of the storm. *TOD 6 hr b4 call-in. 10W mom and boyfriend. Wanted u 2 know.*

I close my eyes, take in a breath of salt and sand and driftwood drying in the sun. Tears squeeze out and trail along my skin, the breeze cooling the heat of sorrow. Little Emily was gone from this world six hours before her mother called 911. A bedtime battle, perhaps—that terrible hour of the evening when unstable homes erupt and unspeakable things happen. A plot by the mother and her boyfriend to stage a kidnapping to cover it up. Little girls should be safe in this world, in their own homes, but the fact is that sometimes they're not. By now that felony warrant for the mother and the live-in boyfriend has been executed. The baby still strapped in Trista's car that night is somewhere safe. Even though I ache with this news, there is that much to be thankful for.

Emily is safe now as well. I know it. She isn't cold or alone or hungry. She is not lost in the woods, running wildly as in my dreams. Seeking rescue.

She is home.

All around her, there is nothing but love.

A hand touches my shoulder, and I jump, then realize that Mom has pushed her way through the crowd to me. The lines have loosened around her eyes, and her brows have relaxed a little. "She made it there in good shape. They were able to clear the blockages with an emergency angioplasty and stents. They may do bypass surgery later, after she's had time to get better, but she's stable now and in recovery."

My mother stretches out her arms, and we fold together and cry and rock and breathe. I don't close my eyes but instead watch the sun specks through a watery rim of emotion. But for the floating debris, Pamlico Sound is beautiful today. A pod of dolphins plays in the distance. They seem jovial and untroubled, as if they're saying, *What storm? It's over. Let it go. Let's celebrate life.*

Mom finally releases me, then gives me a serious look. "I'm not going home after Sandy's surgery. I'm staying, and I don't know for how long. I already called and talked to George about it. Sandy needs someone to make her take care of herself the way she should, at least while she heals up." But there's something in her voice that tells me this relocation may be more than temporary.

I feel a sting of separation. As much as our rough edges may rub blisters on each other from time to time, my mother and I have never been more than a few miles apart since the Piggly Wiggly years. Now she will be halfway across the country.

I bite back a sudden wave of insecurity and the bleak but selfish thought that she will miss all the kids' senior-year milestones.

"I think you should." I have to force myself to say it.

"But I'll be home for all the kids' things. As many as I can catch." She reads my mind the way mothers and daughters do. "I have frequent-flier miles."

"The school will miss having you for all those volunteer hours." I'm searching for something innocuous that won't stir up more emotion. I know this is the right thing for my mother, and I don't want to mess it up.

She flips a hand in the air, swatting a man behind her, then turning to apologize before answering me. "Phooey on that school system. They should have appreciated me while they had me."

Her answer leaves me dumbfounded. This is the first time I've heard her actually let it go, not rehash all the reasons it was wrong for the district superintendent to make staffing decisions based on age and gender rather than years of experience.

Another milestone. Maybe we are both stretching our wings. Maybe this is a butterfly season for both of us.

Perhaps this rebirth from one thing to another happens repeatedly in a lifetime. Maybe life is a series of little deaths and rebirths, of passages and rites of passage, of God teaching you to stop clinging to one thing so you can reach for another.

A death grip doesn't reach very well.

I think of that tiny woman in her big white house in Fairhope. Aunt Sandy's friend, Iola Anne Poole—ninety-one years old, yet still surviving on these shifting bars of sand.

What she said makes sense now, as I stand shoulder-to-shoulder with my mother and watch the dolphins play in the sunlit water. *The storms come and it's water and wind as far as the eye can see for a bit. But winds calm and the waters drain. We find our feet again, and the ground under us sprouts a new crop of seed. That is always the way of it.*

I don't suppose this storm will be any different.

The Tidewater Sisters

CHAPTER 1

H e comes in summer, when the air is still and the bullfrogs sing in the sedges and the nightjars wail their quick, haunting calls: *Chuck Will's widow, Chuck Will's widow* . . .

He dances over the fog with the birdsong, feather-light. He is young and strong like a warrior crossing the Scottish moors, but the mist smells of Pamlico Sound and saltmeadow cordgrass and Spanish moss hanging like endless veils of torn lace.

He carries the scents of all these things—of the Carolina Tidewater and the earthy spaces beneath the willow trees and the high places atop barn roofs. He wears the melted asphalt of old country roads on the bottoms of his long, slim feet, and on the pads of his fingers there are mulberry stains.

That is the way I remember him. Always and forever in mulberry season.

The stains are the reason I know he isn't real. The reason I know he's only something conjured from old wishing aches, things left unsaid, and hopes that went unrealized. There are no sun-melted roads in heaven, no mulberry stains. He's come here again in a dream.

Part of me still believes there must be a way to change everything that happened. Part of me, the part that's well over thirty years old, knows how foolish and childish that is.

But you never forget your first love, no matter how much time passes. You never completely stop wondering, *what if . . .*

He smiles, and for a moment he seems more boy than vapor—sixteen, arrogant, silly, sweet, indestructible. He whispers my name, and I hear his voice.

Tandi . . . Hey, Tandi Jo . . . Tandi Jo from Kokomo . . . He tips his head back a little, his eyes a bright, sparkling blue, his body long and loosely muscled. Not quite a boy. Not quite a man. Newly licensed to drive and feeling his oats this year. Everything has changed since our last summertime visit to my grandparents' farm. The boy down the road has changed, and so have I.

I reach out to him. I want to say, *I thought you were gone. I thought you died a long time ago.*

Suddenly I am once again the thirteen-year-old girl who fell hopelessly in love, hidden amid the mulberry trees and muscadine vines. Hopelessly, innocently, unbreakably. *It's real,* my mind whispers. *All the rest was only a dream. A long, strange dream.*

Tandi, he says again, his voice deeper. The laughter is still there, but he no longer sounds the same.

I reach out to grab him by that old, sloppy T-shirt he loves. I want to hang on the way I would have while climbing the creek bank in the mud, taking advantage of his strength, his agility, using him as a towrope.

I feel his hand close over mine. He kisses it, says, "Well, hello to you, too. I guess you missed me."

I jerk awake, look up, and the eyes aren't blue but soft brown. The hair not silky golden curls, but reddish-brown. The skin not suntanned ruddy, but freckled, with a little burn on the end of the nose.

"Paul." I gasp his name like it's a surprise.

A wrinkle crosses his forehead, one eyebrow rising, the other lowering. "You were expecting someone else?"

Sitting up, I blink and look around, find myself in a rocking chair on the porch of Iola Anne Poole's big white house—the house where she left decades' worth of mementos from the Benoit shipping empire, along with eighty-one prayer boxes that contained the story of her long life here on Hatteras Island. The letters in those boxes changed everything. They're the reason I'm here on this porch.

"An electrician," I say, with one foot still in the dream. It feels odd, waking in this grown-up skin. Luke Townley has been dead for over twenty years. My grandparents' old farm across the Pamlico Sound in the Carolina Tidewater is long gone. The gummy tar-and-gravel road has probably been paved over with something better by now. Yet all of a sudden, I can feel its sticky warmth on my feet. "I was waiting for an electrician."

"And you didn't want to wait in the cottage?" Paul glances next door to the caretaker's cottage that has been home to the kids and me for over a year now, while I've supervised renovations on the big house. The cottage will be an office and gift shop soon, and the main house a museum and a genealogy center for those with ties to the long and colorful history of the Outer Banks and its families.

"Listen, the electrical guy has stood me up three times already." I rise stiffly to my feet, bracing my hands on my hips and looking down the driveway. "This time, I'm staying right here in plain sight until five o'clock so he can't claim that he stopped by and knocked on the door and nobody answered."

Paul leans close, threads his fingers into my hair in a way that momentarily distracts me, then kisses the little pout lip that's forming on my face. The Benoit House Museum is so close to being ready to open, much of the renovation done by volunteers. This snafu with work we're actually *paying* for is killing me. I need to be finished with all of this before the wedding, before Paul and I head off on the sort of honeymoon I never, ever thought I'd have.

"I can't imagine anybody standing you up," he whispers against my ear before pulling back to look at me.

"I know, right?" I hold up my paint-covered hands and display my gorgeous self. I can imagine what Paul is looking at—a stressed-out woman with bloodshot blue eyes and brown hair falling from a messy bun that's covered in Sheetrock dust. His future bride. If he weren't such an amazing guy, he'd be running for the hills. *I* wouldn't marry me right now. "I'm seriously about to commit mayhem today."

"Not on me, 'kay?" He backs away a step, grinning playfully, his mismatched Hawaiian shirt and camp shorts making him look like one of the Beach Boys on laundry day. His crazy fashion sense is a hit with his students. They wonder what the science guy will show up in next. "I've seen your mayhem. It scares me."

A laugh presses through and loosens the jaw muscles that are seizing up as I watch the empty driveway. Paul can always make me laugh. He's phenomenally unruffled, as if he has nothing—not one thing—to prove to the world.

I wish I could master that skill.

Through the windows of the rental cottage, I see Zoey and J.T. rummaging for food. They're probably worn out after a day of marking turtle nests on the National Seashore with Paul and the other Summer Sea Camp kids. It's not every activity that can occupy a fifteen-year-old and a ten-year-old equally well. They'll be ready to tell me all about it when we finally sit down to dinner later.

I remind myself that there are worse problems to have than an absentee electrician. Just over a year ago, a life like this one was hopelessly out of reach. Just over a year ago, we were on the run from a man I was terrified could find us anywhere. Just over a year ago, I couldn't have imagined someone like Paul, and a love that doesn't hurt, and plans for a beach wedding and a dream honeymoon with the one person who makes me feel perfect, just the way I am.

But I can't leave on that honeymoon until I've seen the Benoit House Museum project through. I owe Iola Poole's memory that much and more. I owe the people of Hatteras Island and Fairhope that much. After two devastating hurricanes, they're counting on the revenues Benoit House will bring in—tourist dollars plus the business from weddings, parties, and meetings in Benoit House's grand ballroom. The place is already booked solid for six months.

I have to make sure it's ready, but time is running out. We're opening in eight days.

A week after that, Paul and I are supposed to be nestled in a remote Smoky Mountain cliff house—part romantic getaway, part research trip for Paul, who's doing a study on native and invasive plants. We're looking forward to cool, crisp air and not another person for miles. Compared to the hot, crowded, crazy-busy summer months on the Outer Banks, our secluded honeymoon destination sounds like heaven.

The renovations on Benoit House *will* be finished on time, if I have to crawl up in that big, third-story attic and run the wires myself. Unlike some of the volunteers here, I'm not afraid of the attic. This house is like an old friend—the kind who wraps arms around you in your worst moments and never lets go. Despite the house's difficult and tragic beginnings, Iola Poole's kindly spirit seeps from the wood and warms every quiet corner and hidden space.

Right now, I have a feeling she'd like to wring the electrician's neck too.

"Can I do anything to help?" Paul asks, and knee-jerk resistance rises inside me. With Paul paying for most of the wedding and the honeymoon, and the girls from my part-time job at Sandy's Seashell Shop pitching in with planning, decorations, and supplies, I'm leaning on people far too much already.

I still feel like I don't deserve all of it. That's the truth. If I can see to it that the Benoit House Museum is finished and open on time, maybe it will make me worthy of all this . . . love. That's how I feel. Even though I know better.

Real love isn't a payment. It isn't a response to your accomplishments or anything else. It's a gift without strings.

I learned this from the letters in Iola Poole's prayer boxes, but it's still slowly converting from head knowledge to heart knowledge. I'm not quite *there* yet.

"You do too much already." I bite my lip and smile at Paul apologetically.

"There's no such thing as too much." He comes close, takes me in his arms, and a gush of love washes over me, honey-sweet and warm. "Tell you what—why don't the kids and I drive over to Buxton and forage for food? That way if the electrician runs late, we won't have to worry about supper."

"You think of everything."

"Yeah, I know. I'm good." He takes the time to kiss me for real then, and once again I find that I'm looking forward to the honeymoon. Maybe I'll just abandon the museum project altogether and elope with Paul.

"And humble," I add, teasing him. I watch as he strides off toward the cottage, stopping at the truck to snag his ever-present fishing hat and drop it on his head. An over-the-shoulder wink comes my way. He's proud of the hat.

I wave, cross my arms over my chest, squeeze them tight, and wonder why, as he walks away, all of a sudden, it's Luke Townley I see, crossing the patchy afternoon sunlight. Why is he on my mind today?

Why, when everything seems just short of perfect, has Luke come back to haunt me?

Is it pre-wedding jitters? Just me wondering how I could possibly be good enough for someone like Paul? Questioning whether, after so many bad choices and failed relationships, I should save Paul by just . . . running away? There's a demon in my head, and it sounds a lot like my daddy, and it's telling me there's nothing in me worth having.

Luke Townley hated my daddy. Maybe he's come to help me fight the demon. A battle against our common enemy.

I close my eyes and pray for the strength to let the past be the past. *You are not your mama or your daddy or your sister. You are you.* That's what Sandy says down at the Seashell Shop. She's been sensing the jitters when I'm there working my two afternoons a week.

A car pulls in and Paul hesitates on the cottage porch, then glances my way and yells across the lawn, "Hey, maybe that's your guy?"

I shade my eyes, watch the dark-colored vehicle come up the drive. It doesn't look like an electrician's truck, and it's awfully late in the afternoon to start on anything, but I hold out hope. *Borrowed his wife's car for the day, maybe? As long as he has tools in there, I don't care if he arrives by mule train.*

He hurries past the caretaker's house as if he knows he's late, and that gives me hope, but there's only one person in the car. How does he plan to pull wires without a helper? It's a two-person job, at least. Someone has to wriggle through the crawl spaces and climb around the attic while the other person feeds the wire.

My stomach turns as he exits the car. The sense of dread that has been nagging me since I woke roars like a dragon. He's wearing a white shirt and a tie, with some sort of official-looking nylon vest over the top. I hope he's not from the county, here to throw another monkey wrench in the plans. We've jumped through so many legal hoops already.

Paul leaves the cottage and starts my way.

I descend the mansion steps and meet the stranger

at the bottom. He's carrying papers. The patch on his vest reads, *Action Process Service*.

Maybe he's here trying to sell something? Or arrange a booking for a company banquet? Or put in a bid on the landscaping?

"Are you Tandi Jo Reese?" His manner is businesslike in a way that demands a quick answer. He's a big guy, with the air of a retired drill sergeant or a police officer.

"Yes, I am." The part of me that remembers a life of running from Child Protective Services, debt collectors, and drug dealers shrinks instinctively. But I have nothing to hide now.

"I've got some papers for you." He shoves them at me with enough force that I grab them out of reflex. I have a feeling that's all part of the plan.

"What . . . I . . . ," I stammer, blindsided. Paul reaches us and steps in beside me, hooking his thumbs in his pockets as he cocks his head to get a look at the documents now dangling in my hand.

"You are the Tandi Jo Reese who lives next door in the cottage?" the stranger confirms, backing away a step, intimidated by Paul.

"Yes, I am."

"Then those are for you. No signature required."

What's going on here? He's leaving the scene before I can even get the question out of my mouth. The dark car makes a hurried three-point turn in front of Iola's beautiful old house and speeds off down the oyster-shell driveway.

"What was that all about?" Paul watches the car disappear.

I stare at the papers, flip through them. Over the past year of supervising the museum project, I've practically earned my honorary paralegal degree. I can read through the official mumbo jumbo well enough to know what this document is saying. The problem is, it still doesn't make any sense.

"That was a process server." I look at Paul, and I'm relieved to the core of my being when I don't see suspicion or accusation, only bafflement. "Someone's taking me to court over . . . breach of contract, statutory fraud, and some other stuff I don't understand on a . . . real estate sale. But I don't even own any real estate."

CHAPTER 2

"Well, it looks like there was a contract to sell your land, earnest money and a down payment were exchanged, and then problems arose regarding a tax lien, some easements, and most importantly breach of the covenant to convey. The seller—that would be you—then promised to remedy these things and provide clear title within thirty days. The seller—you again—has failed to do so. The buyers don't just want their money back; they're filing a complaint for breach of contract, promissory estoppel, and specific performance, meaning they intend to force you to comply with your end of the deal, clear your title, and sell them the land," Vince says, sipping a tall frappe from the Sandy's Seashell Shop coffee bar. Kicked back with an ankle cocked over his knee and a flip-flop dangling, he looks as sure of himself here as he does in his ambulance-chasing legal commercials. Since moving to the Outer Banks, he's become one of Sandy's best customers, and I honestly can't think of anyone else to call. I definitely can't afford to hire a lawyer.

"Vince, I don't *own* any property," I insist again. "And I *didn't* steal anyone's earnest money. I have no idea what this is about."

Sandy frowns, her short blonde hair standing on end as she leans over the document. The fan of crow's feet around her eyes deepens ominously in the shadowy after-hours shop light. "This is obviously a case of mistaken identity. How do we get these people off our backs? How do we straighten it out?"

Suddenly *I* has become *we*. Seashell Sandy is ready for a fight, and apparently, so is her little shop dog, Chum. His tiny paws brace on the table, and he shows Vince some Boston bulldog teeth.

Vince lifts both hands, the evening breeze pressing through the screen doors and fluffing his comb-over. "Hey, don't shoot the messenger."

"So . . . what's the next step here?" As usual, Paul is the voice of reason. Steady, smart, confident. Completely certain that I haven't done anything wrong, and I *haven't*. Even so, I feel like there must be something I'm overlooking. I think of the man I was running from when I came to Hatteras, Trammel Clarke. Shady deals were his specialty. Could this have something to do with him?

"You have any enemies?" Vince seems to be reading my mind.

"It's a *case* of mistaken *identity*," Sandy insists again. "You tell us what we need to do, Vince, and I'll keep you in frappes for the next twenty years. You and Natalie."

Vince's smile turns a bit more tender. He appreciates the Seashell Shop girls for taking his much-younger wife under wing rather than giving her the reception a twentysomething woman with a middle-aged husband often gets.

"Washington County . . ." Vince reaches for his iPad. "Not much out that way, as far as I can remember. Sued a gas company there once when their pipeline blew up next to some lady's house. Good lawsuit. Brought the hammer down on 'em." The last part is a direct quote from one of his commercials. "Let's see if we can find out where this place is." He turns the pages and reads the property description again. "Sure you don't know anyone in Washington County?"

"I'm sure." But my mind is turning now. *Washington County . . . Washington County . . .* It rings a bell, but I can't quite figure out why. "Where is that?"

Vince homes in with his iPad. "Hang on a minute. I'll have it for you. Let me get the coordinates for this land entered."

Washington County Fair. That's what my mind was reaching for.

"Here we go. It's coming," Vince says.

I remember an old black-and-white picture . . . a shot of a prize-winning show steer posed in the victory circle.

"Wait for it . . ."

Vince's voice fades as the image in my mind clears and expands. There's a ribbon hanging beside the steer's photo. Once blue, it's now faded to pale lilac. *Beaufort-Washington Livestock Show, 1968,* the ribbon reads. *Grand Champion Steer.*

"Man, the Internet is slow tonight," I hear Vince complaining. "Okay, there it is. Let's zoom in on the Google satellite view and see what's down there. So . . . looks like a house . . . and some other buildings . . ."

I turn to the iPad, but in some way I already know what I'll find. Vince's short, stubby fingers glide across the screen, stretching the sky view of an old house and barn. My mind tumbles down and down and down, into the tiny world on the screen.

I feel the old shingles of the barn roof, know their scratchy surface and the network of pinpoint and scalloped imprints they'll leave on my skin when I rise . . . when Luke Townley takes my hand to pull me to my feet and we climb down the silo ladder, then hide in its thick moon shadow, where we're invisible, even to each other.

Someone yells my name from the house, and Luke just chuckles, tugs my hand, and whispers, *Come on. I've got an idea.*

I hesitate, he pulls harder, and the invisible roots holding my feet in place fall away, and we fly through the night dew into the cornfield, where no one can find us. I realize it's my sister yelling after me, not Mama or Daddy, and all fear leaves me. Gina can't hurt me.

Gina . . .

A gasp rushes from my lips, and Sandy, Vince, and Paul all look my way in unison.

My stomach clenches in a full-fisted grasp. I do, I realize, have an enemy.

"Gina," I whisper, rubbing my temples and squeezing hard, as if I can work her out like a charley horse. If only it were that simple. Anytime my life is stable, the cataclysmic downfall will in some way involve my sister. It's like she's radar-equipped for this sort of thing. Capable of knowing, from wherever she hangs out in the meantime, when to show up and do the most damage. Somehow or other, she's probably heard about the wedding. And given the way Gina and I left things the last time we saw each other, she's undoubtedly out for blood. "This has something to do with Gina."

Paul's eyes widen and Sandy's narrow. Vince just looks confused. My sister ended her short stay on the Outer Banks and disappeared before Vince and Natalie moved to Hatteras Village. Vince has no idea what we're dealing with here.

"If that witch gets within a hundred yards of this place, I'm gonna grab her by that blonde ponytail and sling her around until her eyes bug out." Sandy's lips tighten into a scowl.

In some weird way, her opinion of my sister stings. I wonder, will these bizarre family ties ever fall free? Gina is my last blood relative, true, but what does she have to do before I finally don't think of her as my sister anymore? Before I stop feeling like I owe her something?

"Gina? How so?" Paul asks cautiously.

"That's my grandparents' farm." I point at the screen. "It's in the Tidewater near Wenona. Washington County."

"That explains a few things." Vince nods as if this news is somehow satisfying.

"But my grandparents have been gone for years, and so has the farm." I stare at the image, trying to make sense of it. "My grandmother sold it to pay for Pap-pap's nursing care after his stroke." I struggle to remember how I know that. It seems like I found out sometime while I was in foster care as a teenager. Maybe Gina told me during a sibling visit.

"You can't sell property you don't own," Vince points out.

"My sister probably could."

"She probably *would*," Sandy agrees.

Vince returns to the legal documents. "Can't get any more details until Monday when offices open, but there's no secondary name on this complaint. Just yours. Could be they've gone after your sister in a separate suit."

"I really can't believe Gina would . . . use my name in some . . . some scheme. She doesn't even know anything about real estate." But the truth about Gina is, when she's either mad or desperate, she's resourceful.

"We'll just have to fight this thing. That's all there is to it." Sandy has her game face on. "Any of us can testify that Tandi hasn't been anywhere near Washington

County this past year. She's been with us on Hatteras, working."

"What's the procedure here?" Paul chimes in. "How long is this likely to take?"

I catch the look in his eye, and I know what he's thinking. Instantly, I think of it too.

The wedding. The honeymoon. Two weeks from now we're supposed to be standing before a preacher at sunset on the beach. We should be talking about flowers and finger sandwiches and the cute little starfish-and-sea-glass napkin rings Sandy wants to put on the reception tables. Instead, we're discussing real estate fraud.

I should be walking on air, but instead I'm tiptoeing on razor blades. The realization is sudden and stark. Even through all the planning and the talking and the napkin-ring making, I've never really believed that this wedding would happen. Deep down inside, I've known all along that things like this—dream weddings, friends who are closer than family, men like Paul Chastain—don't happen to people like me.

Who do you think you are, Miss High and Mighty? The voices are old, but they're still here, and still powerful. My mother, my father, my sister, my aunt Marney. *You think you're somebody special? That stuff's not for people like us.*

Guilt strikes my core, and I pinch my temples harder. I've dragged Paul and the shop girls into this mess, just by letting them care about me. By letting

Paul fall in love with me. By falling in love with him. He's a normal guy from a normal family. He doesn't know anything about this kind of dysfunction.

"I'll take care of it." I grab my purse from the table and start toward the door, the weak-kneed emotions of shock and disbelief quickly being forged into an armored suit of pure, white-hot anger.

How dare she!

How dare Gina use my name. How dare she involve the one place we were always loved and cared for and protected. That farm in the Tidewater is sacred ground.

"Hang on a minute." Paul's chair rattles over the uneven plank floor as he stands up.

"Where are you going?" Sandy calls after me.

"I don't know yet." But the truth is, I do. I know exactly where I'm headed.

And I know it's no accident that, just a few hours ago, I awoke from a dream of Mulberry Run Road and Luke Townley.

CHAPTER 3

Mulberry Run Road hasn't changed. The pavement is still sticky black tar that swishes like water beneath the tires. Quiet farmhouses, old barns, and hired-hand trailer homes look like they've seen better days. The fields, always ripe with tobacco, muscadine and scuppernong vines, and corn tassles towering head high, paint a patchwork of summer growth clothed in morning dew—short, tall, leaves, fringe, blooms, myriad shades of green.

Mailboxes still cling to leaning posts. Electric lines sag lazily. The canals, kept clean and in good repair by farmers, are still crisscrossed by occasional trails worn into the surfaces by livestock and kids on bicycles. Crossing a bridge that has been in place since long before my mother was born here, I slow, look down the trench, and remember pedaling hard toward it, then at the last minute throwing my feet out straight, waiting for the old Columbia 3-Star to fly for an instant before toppling off the edge, then careening down the slope and popping up the other side.

Now, bicycles like the ones we found in Pap-pap's barn are a hot item on *American Pickers* and *Antiques Roadshow*. I wonder what became of them. Was there an estate sale when my grandmother signed the farm over to a new owner, or was the farm purchased with the contents in place? Who lives there now?

For a moment, I fantasize that the bicycles are still in the barn where we left them during our hasty departure that final summer. I picture them propped against the wall in what was once a stall for plow horses.

I'm overcome with a sense of not wanting to go back and see that they're gone, that the house has a new family in it and there's nothing left but the ghosts of the past, still clinging to all the hidden spaces. But I know I have to return—to the farm, to what was, to the ghosts.

Sooner or later, the future always circles back to the past.

I've come full circle. All by myself. Against Paul's wishes and Sandy's protests and Vince's warnings that I shouldn't set foot on the land that's in dispute or talk to anyone about the lawsuit until he can make some more calls tomorrow when offices are open. In the meantime, he has promised to figure out what he can. I've convinced Paul that I need him to stay with the kids, and Sandy that I need her to look after the ongoing wedding plans, and Vince that I'd never dream of asking him to come over to the Tidewater with me pro bono.

The truth is, I have to make this trip alone. If it's

possible to prevent the past from spilling any further into the present, I have to accomplish that. I'll do whatever it takes—even confront the ghosts . . . and my sister. If I can find her. This fraudulent real estate sale could be something she's cooked up from hundreds of miles away. She could be back in Texas by now, but I doubt it. I have a feeling this is something she stirred up in person.

I clear a grove of Carolina pines grown up around what used to be a neighbor's double silo, and I see it ahead—the old white house with its three steep gables. Behind it stands the hip-roof barn that was always red. It's the color of weathered wood now. As I come closer, I notice that there are boards missing. In places, I can see all the way through to the sky on the other side. Along the side of the house, the roof of the wraparound porch leans, a post missing. The driveway is still in use, apparently. There's a layer of gravel atop the blackland muck and two clear tracks with a hump of grass between.

The orchard out back has grown into a forest, but I can see fruit trees here and there—pears, persimmons, figs, the little green apples Meemaw always used for apple butter in the fall.

Turning in the driveway, I wonder if the mulberry grove still lies beyond the old orchard. A few mulberry trees have sprouted in the fencerow at the edge of the yard, the seeds dropped by birds as they sat atop the wire. Pap-pap would have rooted out the saplings, back in the day. This place was always as carefully kept as an accountant's balance sheet. Everything in its proper place. Everything in working order. Nothing thrown away. The equipment and the furniture repaired, repainted, reupholstered, and used as long as it would hold out.

Now the farm is almost unrecognizable as its former self, a sad stranger as I climb from the car, shade my eyes, and squint up at the gables. It's like looking at a homeless person along the sidewalk and thinking for a moment that you recognize the face. Could this be an old friend you lost track of long ago? A part of you wants to pass on by without knowing.

Behind the wavy plate-glass windows, I imagine Meemaw in the pink room upstairs. *Gonna be a fine 'un today, mighty fine. Rustle up, child. The rooster's done sung and chickens been layin' for hours a'ready. . . .* Her Blue Ridge Mountain twang wraps me like music as I stretch bony arms against my pillow, hearing the creak of Pappap's old chair downstairs. He's shifted to one side, relinquished the newspaper, prepared the little warm space I'll snuggle into when I run to the day room. Together, we'll read the funnies while the scents of frying bacon, farm-fresh eggs, and biscuits waft from the kitchen.

We'll revel in this golden hour of the morning while my sister stubbornly sleeps in. I'll curl against Pap-pap's big barrel chest, wishing this time could last forever . . . and knowing it won't. Sooner or later, my mama and daddy will straighten out whatever issue has caused them to leave us here again. They'll come back for us, and we'll have that talk about making a new start somewhere. We'll all pile in the truck, and that'll be that for a while. Life will wobble around and around off-kilter until it crashes again.

The memory of those mornings tastes both bitter and sweet as I reach the front steps. They're intact, but the decking has been removed from the porch floor, only the joists remaining. Those have been exposed long enough to weather and gather debris of dead grass and leaves. Either someone began repairs here at one time and then abandoned the effort, or the house is under some slow form of demolition, perhaps being stripped for parts.

The second possibility makes me flinch. Maybe I really am better off not knowing. . . .

"Hello?" I call, though it's silly. Who would be living in a house with a five-foot drop outside the front door? "Is anyone here?"

I climb two more steps, crane to see through the dirty window glass. I'd swear I can see Pap-pap's brown recliner silhouetted beyond the entry hall, still resting in the day room, where it always was. It can't be there, of course. Undoubtedly, the house has been occupied since then, even if not in recent years.

"Hello?" An eerie feeling creeps over my shoulders. I pause on the top step, check the yard, the driveway, the farm field that appears almost ready for harvest. The land is still in use.

Something creaks rhythmically, and overhead, the weather vane groans as it turns. I remember the sound.

I cross a joist like a gymnast on a balance beam, my arms stretched the way they would've been when we traversed the sagging top rails of county-road bridges nearby. The higher the bridge, the better the dare.

This feels like a dare. My heart pounds. A pulse thrums in my throat. *Leave,* common sense pleads. *Don't do this. You don't need more trouble. There's nothing to be gained here.*

But I can't help feeling that the answers to my questions are hidden inside this house.

Maybe I just don't know where else to start looking.

I knock on the door, listen, knock louder. No one answers, of course.

The iron doorknob resists as I try to turn it. Locked. I feel along the top of the porch light almost without thinking. The key is right where it has always been.

An icy sensation walks up my spine as I unlock the door and let it fall slowly open. This is breaking and entering. I have no right to be here. But I can't stop myself. I need to know what's left. I won't stay long.

I step across the threshold, glad the floors inside are intact, but the olive-green linoleum sags beneath my feet as if it might give way too. I look down at it momentarily, test its strength, then survey the entry hall, gaze up the stairs, take in the pictures still hanging there.

Ancestors watch me from ornate frames—a farmer

posing with his hay wagon, my grandfather in his military uniform, my mother at two or three years old, my grandfather's family on their shrimp boat on the Outer Banks. My grandmother's people posed in front of a mountain cabin at a long-ago family wedding. How many times did I beg her to take down that frame and tell me one more time who those stern-looking faces belonged to? In the photo, my grandmother is the little dark-haired, blue-eyed girl posed with her hand on her grandfather's chair.

My baby picture is there on the wall too, and Gina's.

I blink, sweep over all of them, blink again, expecting them to disappear. How could this be after so many years?

It's all I can do not to run wildly through the place to see what else is left. Instead, I walk quickly from room to room, disturbing dust motes, sneezing at the mildewed smell, taking in with bewilderment the smattering of belongings that remain. Most of the antiques are gone. The old mantel clock, the iron bedstead in my grandparents' room, the beautiful hall tree Gina and I used as a princess throne—all have vanished. My grandmother's wedding china and Fostoria crystal are missing from the dining room cabinet. Her silver chest is gone. Her jewelry box is nowhere to be found.

The place has been scavenged.

Maybe Meemaw needed money after she had Pap-pap in the nursing home for a while? Maybe she sent someone here to remove estate goods and sell them?

It's hard to imagine, and the idea propels a wash of sadness and guilt that follows me up the stairs. I was just a teenager then, but I could've been some help to her. I could've helped both of them, if my mother hadn't concocted the terrible lies that prevented my grandparents from getting legal custody of us.

Meemaw's sewing room at the top of the stairs is practically untouched. It smells of musty fabric, and the air is warm and thick, but the cloud-muted light through the window is soft and inviting. Shelves bow beneath the weight of fabric and notions. The prints on the yard goods, now faded along the creases, read like a timeline of fashion from 1930 to the 1980s, when she retired from taking in alterations and creating custom prom dresses and bridesmaids' gowns for neighbors. I watched her fit garments to many a young woman in this room. She always kept the scraps. There were new outfits for Gina and me every time we came here.

I move around the shelves, testing the sags in the dusty floor, fingering a bridal veil left hanging from the edge of her bulletin board. The notes and pictures there make me smile—babies for whom she crafted intricate christening gowns, girls for whom she sewed first communion and party outfits, brides clothed in her beautiful wedding dresses.

There are books and boxes and stacks of patterns on the shelves all around the room. I want to open every one, look inside for connections to my grand-mother, yet logic tells me this is all a long, strange dream. The house couldn't still be here after so many years—a perfect time capsule in some places, pillaged in others.

An old J. G. Dill's tobacco tin atop the bookshelves catches my eye. It's roughly the size of a shoe box, almost invisible among the clutter, but I remember it now. I remember finding it buried in a drawer during one of my visits here and slipping my fingers under the lid, trying to pry it open.

I was fascinated by the image of a beautiful woman on the front. Etched in lines of black and red, hands thrown behind her head, she smiles in wild abandon, even now. Next to her the words *Cut Plug Tobacco* destroy the romance a bit, but I remember wanting the tin and wondering what might be inside. Meemaw found me with it and took it away. *Oh, pea pod, that's not for playin'*, she said gently. *Someday, when you get big, it'll be for you.* She set it high on the shelf. On that *exact* shelf, where it must have remained all these years, half hidden between a stack of patterns and a cardboard box.

I stretch toward it, but something shadow-moves in the corner of my vision. I gasp, slap a hand to my chest, wheel around so quickly that I'd swear the floor ripples beneath my feet like a paddleboard on a wake. There's a little boy standing in the driveway. Just standing there, staring up at the house with his arms hanging at his sides, the sun glinting off his honey-brown skin. His oversize jeans are bunched around bare feet, and his blue button-up shirt hangs askew, so he looks like something from *The Grapes of Wrath*. There was a hired-hand family that lived in a shanty house down the road, years ago. The grandfather still worked his little garden patch with a mule. We were never allowed to play with the kids. Could it be that the family still lives there?

Or maybe I'm only imagining the boy, remembering the past.

He seems to be looking at me through the window.

A toppled-over bike rests in the ditch nearby. It's modern enough to snap my mind from the haze. I've just been caught where I have no business being.

I hurry downstairs, wondering if he will still be there when I get to the door, and he is. He watches with consternation as I navigate the balance-beam porch and hurry down the steps.

"Y'ain't supposed to go up'n there," he says, and his directness surprises me. He's only nine or ten, around the age of my J.T., but he looks me in the eye, and his bottom lip squeezes upward into the top one.

"My grandparents used to live here," I offer, trying to appear calm, but inside the voice of reason scolds, *Good gravy, Tandi, what were you thinking? You could get arrested for this.*

Yet I want that tobacco tin, and other things that have been left inside the house. . . .

The boy looks doubtful. I don't blame him.

"Do you know who owns the place now?" It doesn't hurt to ask, I figure, since I'm already in trouble anyway. I do have a little money saved up—assuming I don't need to use it for a legal defense fund. Maybe I can buy the things I want.

"My daddy does the farmin' on it. Till they run him off, anyhow. You one a them people?"

I have no idea who *them people* are. "No. I'm not. Do you think I could talk to your daddy . . . or your mom? I'd like to find out who actually owns the place now." It'd be helpful information, considering that I'm being sued for fraudulently trying to sell it and stealing someone's earnest money, on top of failing to pay the property taxes.

"Reckon," the boy says. He's definitely not an excitable little scamp. He takes his time, moving toward the bike. "It's up yander a piece. We can walk it. I ain't allowed in no cars with n'body." He points in the direction I haven't been and didn't intend to go. Luke Townley's house was just a quarter mile up the road, barely out of sight behind a scrappy tree line of chokecherries and magnolias. I don't want to know if the place is still there. Better to leave it in my imagination, as it was before life took a heartbreaking turn that final summer here, twenty-odd years ago.

"Sure. That sounds fine." Walking will give me time to take in, piece by piece, the changes on the old farm road.

Eventually, you must stop running to something or from something and embrace where you are. Otherwise you'll never embrace anything. It's one of the lessons I drew from the letters in Iola Anne Poole's big white house. It has become my mantra in this midthirties time of finding my feet and myself.

I grab my purse from the car and we start walking, the boy keeping the bicycle between us and staying out of reach, just in case I have plans to nab him. He introduces himself as Bean, which he tells me is short for Beaudean. On the way up the road, I share information about Zoey and J.T. and how they're learning about sea turtles this summer. I mention that J.T. is about Bean's age.

"He can come o'er sometime," Bean offers. "We got lotsa kids usu'ly. One more don't make n'matter."

"I'm sure J.T. would like that." What exactly does *we got lotsa kids usu'ly* mean? I contemplate the possibilities and listen to the breeze stirring the fencerows. The sound is achingly familiar and so is the road, every step. It still feels the same.

"I'd like to see them big ol' turtles." Bean darts a hopeful look my way.

"Maybe you can come to the Outer Banks sometime."

"Ain't never been to the ocean."

I'm tempted to say, *Well, come visit. J.T. can take you to the marina to watch the boats.* But being a mom, I know better than to make an offer like that. Kids get their hearts set on things, and I don't even know Bean's parents. Still, it seems like every kid ought to have time by the seashore.

"If you're ever on Hatteras, look us up," I say innocuously. "Zoey and J.T. can teach you how to surf."

Bean's lips purse. Finally, he nods. "I might do that. I jus' might."

"If you do, come by Sandy's Seashell Shop in Hatteras Village and ask them where to find Tandi. They'll know."

We walk up the road a little farther, and despite the cloudy day, the heat swirling off the asphalt makes me regret the decision not to drive. It's melting right through my tennis shoes. I can't imagine how Bean walks it in bare feet, but he doesn't seem the least bit bothered. I can't help thinking of Luke Townley. The soles of his feet were like leather. He never wore shoes unless it was the dead of winter. His sister, Laura, was the same way. The Townley kids were always impressively rugged. Tough and wild and ready to try just about anything. My grandfather complained that their mama didn't have the word *no* in her vocabulary. His usual term for the Townley kids was *the hooligans*. Pappap didn't appreciate the fact that their parents were old hippies and their farm was a junkyard of loose goats, welded-together metal art, and broken-down equipment.

The place comes into view ahead, and I see that it hasn't changed a whole lot, other than the removal of the metal-art statues. It won't be making the cover of *House Beautiful* anytime soon, but the crops look healthy, and there's a harvester working in the fields. I'm a little surprised when Bean turns that direction to cut across the yard. I'd expected to go to a different house farther up.

Bean gets a running start at the ditch, jogging the bike down one side and ramming it up the other. "Come on. It ain't wet."

I follow him, feeling a little odd. I don't want to surprise these people or interrupt their day, but I need whatever information I can get about the goings-on down the street. I hope I don't surprise them at a bad moment.

I also hope they're not the ones Gina stole the earnest money from.

That idea ties my stomach in a gigantic slipknot as Bean announces our presence by yelling across the yard, "Mama! I found me a lady out here. She's wantin' you to talk to her."

The doors and windows are closed, of course, because this time of the year anyone not dirt poor is air-conditioning. The Tidewater in summer is sweltering hot, humid, and filled with mosquitoes. Today is unusually mild, or I would've been baked alive in Pappap's house already.

Bean keeps yelling all the way onto the porch, until finally a woman steps out, wide-eyed. She's holding a toddler on her hip, a little girl with curly blonde hair, who doesn't look anything like Bean. Neither does Bean's mother. She looks like the toddler. "Bean, for heaven's sake, what's wrong? You scared me to death." Still holding the screen, she stops, looks around the yard, and notices me.

"I got a lady," Bean reports again, offering me up as exhibit A.

"Oh." She blinks. "Oh . . ." Her gait wobbles slightly side to side as she advances onto the porch and lets the storm door fall shut. We stare at each other, and there's an odd, silent moment of minds thumbing through pages of memory. Sparks of recognition travel back and forth between us, slowly casting enough light to see by.

I recognize the eyes, the mouth, and the thick blonde hair, slightly curly like Luke Townley's. I recognize his little sister all these years later. "Laura?" It's clear that she thinks she knows me but can't figure out who I am. "It's Tandi," I fill in. "Tandi Reese?"

Her eyes blink, blink again, growing wider each time. "No!" Her mouth hangs open. "Get outta town!"

Her lips spread into a smile, and I'm reminded of childhood mischief the group of us cooked up over the years. I'm also reminded that the last time I heard Laura's name mentioned, she was in the ICU. She was never supposed to walk again, yet here she is, standing on the porch. I catch my gaze drifting toward her feet.

"Titanium," she preempts and leans over to knock on one of the legs just below her knee, then hikes the toddler back onto her hip. "Once I got into high school, I really wanted to run again, and the only way I could do that was to have the legs amputated and fit with prostheses."

"Oh . . ." Her matter-of-factness dispels the awkward feeling, but guilt hits me right after. It was supposed to be me in the truck that afternoon with Luke, but my mother, my sister, and my grandparents had been at odds all day. I'd stayed home to try to keep the powder keg from exploding again. The ice cream run that never happened changed everything. Laura rode along with Luke instead of me. Laura was sitting in the passenger seat of their old farm truck, where I would've been.

"You look so good," she says, seeming surprised. Shifting the toddler to the other hip, she stretches for a shoulder hug as if she means to reassure me. Either she doesn't remember that we didn't even attend her brother's funeral or she doesn't hold it against me.

"You do too." My breath ruffles her hair. It seems like she has a good life here, and somehow I gain an ounce of absolution from that.

"How's your health?" she asks, releasing me carefully.

"Fine . . ." What a strange thing to ask after not having seen one another for almost twenty years. Why do I get the feeling that she knows things about me? That she's not surprised to find me here? "Great, actually. I live on the Outer Banks now. For the last year, I've been supervising the renovation of an old Victorian house that's about to become a museum." I almost invite her to come to the opening and bring Bean to see the water, but that might seem strange after all these years.

Bean steps in and wraps his arms around her waist, the force knocking her off-balance a step or two. She catches herself on the porch rail just as I'm reaching for her. "Easy there, buddy," she says to Bean. Then she bends, kisses his sweaty raven curls, and sends him inside with the toddler to watch something that has just come on Animal Planet. I gather that there are other children watching too.

"We take in foster kids," she tells me, smiling after Bean. "The little one is mine. My youngest. But they're all mine after they've been here awhile."

"That's wonderful."

"Gosh, I'm glad you're doing so well." She runs a hand up and down my arm, her fingers scratchy and calloused, slightly sandy against my skin. There's a huge garden out back and a chicken yard with chickens pecking around. This place must be a lot of work. I wonder if her husband farms the fields, or if her parents still live here. "So I guess you got your miracle?" she asks.

"Miracle?"

"The cancer . . ."

"The what?"

Our gazes meet, and suddenly we realize we're

talking in riddles She crosses her arms over her chest, squints at me. "Your sister said you weren't well. That's why she'd always handled the property over the years. Dale and I hate to lose the lease on the land, although, really, with all the foster kids and our own farm, we've got just about as many acres as we can handle . . . but we've already got a crop in down on your grand-parents' place."

"*What* lease?" My mind runs a thousand miles an hour, but it's going in circles. Gina has been telling people we own this land and collecting some kind of rentals from it? How could she possibly get away with that?

Years . . . Laura said *years.*

"Laura, I'm sorry, but I have absolutely no idea what you're talking about."

We just stand staring at each other. Moments tick by.

"Whoa," she says finally. "Whoa. I knew there was something weird going on. I always told Dale things didn't seem right." She motions to the weathered metal rockers on the corner of the porch. "I think we'd better sit down. I have a feeling you're in for a bit of a shock."

CHAPTER 4

The fire runs rampant under my skin. It's like my body has been rolled in hot molasses, and I've stepped into a nest of warrior ants, yet I'm feeding on the venom. It's a strange, wicked, but sweet sort of pain, and the only way I can get through it is to fan the anger, clutch the steering wheel, and keep on driving . . . until I find my sister and wring every last droplet of the truth out of her. If that's possible.

Even then it won't do any good. The legal mess with the property is so complicated that Laura herself doesn't understand it. She just knows they've been warned of the dispute and told an injunction is imminent, which would mean they'd lose the crop they've planted there.

Sitting at Laura's table while foster kids ran to and fro, I took in so much information that now it's churning faster than the dust clouds in the car's wake as I race toward Greenville, where, according to Laura, my sister is dating the owner of a car dealership.

Gina has been keeping a secret all these years. She

and I *own* the farm, and we have since my grandparents'
passing. Years ago, when both Gina and I were far away
in foster care, my grandmother made the arrangements.
Meemaw, who'd never so much as balanced the checkbook, ensured that the long-term lease with Laura's
family would pay the taxes and yield a little bit each
year for Gina and me. My grandmother told Laura's
parents she planned to have the land legally divided as
soon as she could manage it—perhaps she didn't trust
Gina even then. Gina's portion was to be 120 acres
of irrigated Tidewater cropland. Eighty acres and the
house were to go to me.

My grandmother thought of everything, except the
fact that I might still be underage when death took her,
and Gina might be fully legal, out of foster care, and on
her own. And that Gina might be the only one to learn
of our inheritance. Who knows why the news never
reached me. In an overburdened Human Services system, channels don't always connect. Because the legal
division of the land never happened, Gina and I own
it as tenants in common, and she's been able to operate
the place all these years without my knowing a thing.

Of all the things Gina has ever done, including
dropping into my life on Hatteras last year and trying
her best to ruin *everything*, this is the worst.

She knows there has never been a place in the world
that meant more to me than this farm. She knows
that after my father ran off and CPS took us from
my mother, I pleaded for the social workers to bring

us here instead of moving us to an emergency foster home. Gina knows that I ran away three times, trying to get back to Meemaw and Pap-pap—that I told caseworker after judge after teacher that *none* of my mother's horrible claims about Pap-pap were true. No one would listen.

Gina knows that the scuppernong vines and the bayberry tangles and the mulberry orchard could have given me the healing I needed after the ragged patchwork of our childhood finally fell apart.

When my sister came to visit me in my future forever home the year I turned sixteen, she must have known we'd inherited the property. She never mentioned a thing. Instead, she marveled at the bedroom my new family had given me. She was impressed by the white board fences and sprawling horse barns, yet she tried to persuade me to leave it all and come with her. We were *sisters,* she pointed out, and sisters should stick together.

When I wouldn't leave with her, all she said was, *Oh yeah, by the way, the old folks are dead. He had a stroke a couple years ago, and they both croaked in the nursing home—just so you know. See ya. Have fun here at the Ponderosa . . . that is, till these people decide they're tired of their new toy, because that's always how it is. Nobody wants to just* get *a teenager, Tandi Jo. It'll wear off. When it does, come find me. I'll be around. . . .*

I could still picture my sister—tall, blonde, as beautiful as the models in *Seventeen* magazine—delivering the blow with a sympathetic smile.

The trouble with sisters is they know exactly where the tender places are. Gina has always known how to find all of mine.

I'm not sure exactly what I'm going to do when I catch up to her, but possible scenarios abound. In my mind, I'm everything from John Wayne to a ninja torture artist.

The phone rings, and for some crazy reason, I imagine it's her. That somehow she knows I'm headed her way at nuclear missile velocity. I grab my cell and bark out, "Hello."

"Whoa," Paul says on the other end. "You all right?"

"Yes . . ." Deep breath. *Don't say anything,* a voice inside me whispers, the usual instinctive reaction. Leftovers from a childhood of knowing that if you're too much trouble, people will walk out the door, or worse.

Tell him, I admonish myself. *Be honest. That's what love is—dropping all the barricades.* I know Paul loves me. I know I love him. Why is this still so hard? "No," I finally admit. "No, I'm not okay. . . ."

The story—what I know of it so far—spills out, and the anger that had been my power, my supply of venom, wanes. In its wake comes incredible pain. I want a sister who wouldn't do something like this. Ever.

"Honey, stop the car, okay?" Paul interrupts. "Pull over, stop the car, and calm down a minute. I'm afraid you're gonna end up wrapped around a tree."

He's right. I've been flying down the rural highway

like an idiot. I slow down and pull over by someone's gate. The SUV shudders as if it's trying to catch a breath of the muggy summer air. "I just . . . I just want to wrap my hands around her neck and squeeze right now."

"Are you sure that'd be a good idea?"

"Oh, it's a good idea. It's my *best* idea." My fingers knead the steering wheel like a stress ball, building muscle.

"I mean, not that I won't come bail you out of jail for the wedding, but . . ."

A grudging chuckle wrenches free, and a groan comes after it. I'm reminded that I should be home enjoying the wedding countdown. Paul and the Seashell Shop girls will make sure everything is ship-shape, but *I* want to be the one doing it. This is my once-in-a-lifetime. My forever. "Ohhh . . . don't make me laugh, okay? I'm just so . . . mad."

"I know, but what I meant was, take a minute to think things through. Right now, Gina probably doesn't have a clue that you're onto her. You still have the element of surprise on your side. Once you tip her off, she'll start into evade-and-escape mode, and you *know* where things'll go from there."

I pull in air, let it out slowly, feel my anger-stiffened limbs turning to rubber. "You're right."

"Yeah, I'm good that way."

"S-stop." Another chuckle forces its way out. I just want to be home with Paul, curled up in his strong arms, but I know I can't leave now. The farmhouse, the mulberry orchard, the eighty acres around it are mine. *Mine.* I want them. I have to save them somehow. I have to make someone—whoever has the power here—see that my sister has committed fraud and that she has been doing it for years.

Gina could go to jail for this. That thought hadn't even occurred to me until now. It comes with the weirdest stomach-stab of fear. Am I willing to take that route? To . . . prosecute my sister?

I feel myself shrinking away from the possibility, reconsidering my mad dash to the car dealership in Greenville. I sit staring across a farm field as another bank of clouds rolls in, casting shadow. The sharp edges fade.

"Honey?" Paul's voice presses through the paralysis. "You still there?"

"Paul . . . I just really need to think about all of this. And . . . and see what I can find out. I'm going to get a motel and hang around until tomorrow, when the tax office, the courthouse, and the lawyer's offices are open. Okay?"

I expect him to protest, but he says, "Whatever you need. Listen, I'll get Sandy to look after Zoey and J.T. for a couple days, and I'll come—"

"No, Paul, I'll be okay. I promise." Paul has Summer Sea Camp to teach, but aside from that, I still feel myself desperately seeking containment. A way to keep this life from spilling over into the one Paul and I have made. "But will you do something for me? A couple of things, actually?"

"Do you even have to ask?"

I have that sense of being gushy in love again. And with it comes the reminder that this is what love and family should mean. A covenant of protection and care and always wanting the best things for one another. Love doesn't *use* other people. It doesn't steal, kill, destroy. What has been passed off as love between my sister and me over the years has never been love. It's more like codependence.

"The neighbor told me that Gina's dating a guy who owns a big car dealership over in Greenville and that she apparently works there with him. Merritt Cars. It's on Sandpiper Road. That's where Laura sent the last rent check for the farmland. Could you call there and see if you can figure out when Gina works? Just in case she's the one answering the phone. She won't recognize your voice. Also, could you see if Vince can give us any more information about what comes next? What I have to do to straighten this whole thing out. . . . And what will happen to Gina if I do? She's apparently been forging my name on checks and legal documents for years, telling people I had cancer and she was looking after my affairs for me. If I turn her in for all of this, what are they going to do to her?" Guilt. I instantly feel *guilt*. As if I'm the one being cruel here.

"Tandi," Paul warns firmly, "you're not actually thinking of letting her get away with it?"

"I just . . . There's the wedding and the honeymoon and all of that to think about. The museum opening . . . Everything is finally good, you know? I don't want to mess it up for us."

"Nothing can mess us up, Tandi. I'm here, no matter what. I'm not going anywhere."

"I just don't want you to feel like you've invited Typhoid Mary into your perfectly good life." There. I've said it. I've done the thing that Brother Guilbeau over at Fairhope Fellowship Church has advised during our premarital counseling. I've trusted Paul with the ugly truth. Some of it, anyway.

I'm still afraid that I can never measure up to the wife he lost to cancer. The one he traveled the world with, made a dream list with, and lived as many of those dreams as possible with before it was too late.

"I don't," he promises. "We all have our baggage, Tandi. I mean, for instance, you'll probably be stuck playing Thursday night dominoes at the church with my grandma for the next thirty years, because she's not about to let you give *that* up. And then there's my questionable fashion sense. How many people would be willing to marry *that*, right?"

"You do have a point there." But he doesn't. He's just being silly, and he knows it. The kids and I love Thursday night dominoes at the church, and Paul's sense of fashion is what makes him Paul. He's famous for it.

Not *infamous* and certainly not *criminal*, which

makes our baggage completely different. But we exchange I-love-yous and let it go, and he makes me promise one more time not to do anything rash.

I agree not to rush into the confrontation with Gina. Not yet.

I tell Paul I'll call him later when I'm checked into a motel, but I've barely set down the phone before I'm staring in the rearview, thinking. Then action follows thought, and the car makes a U-turn in the deserted road almost by itself.

While I still can, I'm going back to my grandparents' farm to see what else has been left there.

I may not get another chance.

CHAPTER 5

T he house's shadow stretches long across the grass as I turn into the driveway again. I look down the road briefly, wondering if I should go tell Laura that I'm here. I don't want to scare anyone, and I doubt she would argue with my right to look through what remains and claim mementos before they end up in some sort of court-mandated sale.

But at the same time, there's that tiny bit of fear. What will I do if she tells me I shouldn't go back inside?

The decision is made before I exit the car. There's a black kitten lounging on the porch railing as I cross the exposed joists. Its wary amber eyes are the only ones to offer concern as I grip the handle, open the door, and disappear into the past.

At least, I reason, if I get arrested for this, Laura can honestly say she had nothing to do with it.

The search I begin this time is systematic. It seems more clinical that way, less like a potential criminal act. But in truth, the criminal act has already been committed here. Everything else of obvious value has been stripped from the place. I gather a small pile of keep-sakes from the kitchen—things I remember Meemaw cooking with, the little salt and pepper shakers she and Pap-pap bought on their honeymoon to the Grand Canyon, a platter with the invitation to their fiftieth wedding anniversary decoupaged on.

A wedding photo of the two of them has been shel-lacked to the back of the platter. Even through the crazed, yellowed coating, I marvel at how young they are, how happy they look, how beautiful my grand-mother is in her satin, 1940s-era wedding gown. The fabric hugs her body and cascades around her feet. *Always and forever,* a small brass plaque reads, *Daisy and Othoe.* A little silver pitcher lies tipped over on the shelf where the platter was. A mouse runs out as I reach for it, but I grab it anyway. This bit of treasure has escaped the looting, and it's going home with me.

The haul is similar in the other rooms downstairs. Mostly I find sentimental items. An afghan I remem-ber, a doll with crocheted clothing my grandmother made, a jewelry box with a crystal necklace inside. Mice scamper. The sun drifts from east windows to west windows. I make small piles in each room, decid-ing that in the long run I should see if the back porch is still intact. I could pull my SUV around there to load things. There's a bedside lamp and table and a stack of old framed pictures I'm determined to take.

The breeze rattles the front door and distant thun-der rumbles as I go upstairs. It's then that I remember the old tobacco tin in the sewing room. The one I wanted to open earlier. The one my grandmother always indicated would be mine someday.

I go in search of a chair to stand on so I can reach the shelf and I discover one in the bedroom at the end of the hall. The furniture is all still there, although the dresser drawers have been left askew. Strings of hand-tatted lace hang from the corners like chains of Spanish moss.

I stand staring momentarily, remembering two things. A vision of my grandmother's hands deftly moving the tatting shuttle in swirls and circles, winding thread into artful tangles, competes with a memory of my father in this room, tying yet another noose around our lives. Duffel bags, trash sacks, and cardboard boxes litter the bed, and he's throwing everything we have into them. My mother is downstairs screaming at my grandmother, who's begging her to leave Gina and me here until there's proof that Daddy's new oil-field job in Texas is even real.

Let us keep the girls until you're settled. Tandi Jo's havin' such a hard time a'ready, Meemaw pleads, and when that doesn't work, she begs Mama to at least wait until my grandfather gets back from visiting the Townley family at the hospital. *He'd gone to share in prayers and offer help with the harvest and give what little comfort neighbors can when a beautiful young daughter lies irreparably damaged and a handsome teenage son will never again open his eyes to this world.*

You think I don't know you're tryin' to steal my kids?
Mama shrieks, the sound so loud it travels up the stairs,
cutting through my numbness, my pain, the wave of
agony that has carried me since news of the Townley
kids' accident traveled in whispers down Mulberry Run
Road.

You stay too, Meemaw offers desperately, even
though every time we land here, my mother's presence
hits this house like an electric mixer on high. *Land's
sake, think of what just happened to the Townley kids.
That could just as soon be you and the girls. Is Wade
drinkin' again? Is that why he's in a yank to leave all of
a sudden?*

Turning from my grandmother's tatting, I sweep
the memory away like so much clutter. There's no
point in revisiting the drama of our last day in this
house.

On the way past the dresser, I snatch a piece of
her handmade lace and tuck it in my back pocket. She
made yards and yards more than she ever used, her
hands never idle, as she sat watching *Hee Haw* and
Family Ties in the evenings. Maybe I'll go through
the drawers, salvage some more, and look for her tatting shuttles, if there's time after I've checked all the
rooms. A display of those things would be nice in the
Benoit House Museum, along with a bit about how
the women of North Carolina's coastal areas passed
their time during icy winter downpours and howling
nor'easters.

My mind settles on the satisfying thought, finding peace there. Meemaw and her tatting preserved in the museum sounds like a fitting tribute. Perhaps I can even find a photo of her at work in her chair or her sewing room. I need a week in this house, not just a few hours. I need time to comb out the treasures that should be preserved, that have slipped through my sister's carelessly raking, greedy fingers.

But for now, it's the tobacco tin I want. I carry the chair to her sewing shelves, ignore the wiggling and groaning as I climb on top, and bring down both the tin and the box that's with it. A label scotch-taped on the tin reads, *For Tandi Jo.*

The cardboard box is labeled too. *For Gina Marie.* Acid boils into my throat, and I'm instantly furious again. Meemaw would be so heartbroken by what has happened in this house.

Leaning against the shelves, I set the tobacco tin in my lap, take a breath and exhale, and try to expel Gina from the room. This moment is just for my grandmother and me, as if she were handing me the mysterious treasure herself. I imagine that, from heaven, she's watching the opening of the lid. I can feel her all around me, smiling, her hands clasped over her baker's apron, her bright-blue eyes twinkling against her ruddy skin.

Inside I find what looks like a necklace of carved ivory beads, along with a rounded pendant, a piece of lace so old it's almost caramel in color, a filigreed gold ring with some sort of crest on top, and a note in Meemaw's handwriting.

I take out the note first and set it aside. A small gold locket hides beneath, the chain almost lost in the lace. I think I remember it from the trinkets I always admired in Meemaw's little heart-shaped jewelry box. She told me stories about the various keepsakes there. I think Pap-pap bought the locket for her. . . .

The other things in the tobacco tin I've never seen before, nor have I ever seen anything quite like them. The beads remind me a bit of the scrimshaw carvings we'll be exhibiting in the Benoit House Museum soon. There was a collection of them found in the attic, carved on walrus tusks and whalebone by sailors. Perhaps they were given to the Benoit family by various captains within their shipping empire, or possibly collected by the Benoits themselves on their seafaring travels. But the work on these beads is much more detailed and fine. They've been carefully shaped into land and sea creatures. A hummingbird, a sea turtle, a fish. Two oval beads bear the indented carvings of dolphins and boat oars.

The central pendant is teardrop shaped, with what looks like an ornate bottle stopper at the top where it's attached to the necklace. I would suspect that it's a snuff jar—I've seen some fancy ones while looking through potential donations for the museum—but there's a Maltese cross beautifully etched on the front. I doubt this was ever meant to hold snuff, but it was intended to hold *something*. I study it until I discern the location of a hinge. A tiny brass nail at the other end has been modified and notched to serve as a clasp. It opens with surprising ease, considering its apparent age.

The container is empty, but I sit and marvel at a lovely carving of a compass rose. Again, I try to imagine the carver, whoever he might have been. Did he create this work while lying in his bunk far out at sea, the ship rocking and groaning as it crossed from the old world to the new? Did he bring it home to a wife, or a son or daughter, who waited for his return? Or did he sell it in some foreign port to earn a few extra coins? I've always been a lover of old things, but these last months of working to reclaim Benoit House and open the museum have given me a new passion for their history.

Laying the piece carefully back in the tin, I pick up Meemaw's letter again. Where in the world would she have come by this odd collection? Did she know its origins?

The letter tells me immediately that finding out won't be so easy. Meemaw doesn't provide any answers. Just more questions.

Tandi Jo,
    You always been the one to ask me about
the old things around the farm, so you're the
one to have these. They been in my family long
as anyone can remember, handed down among

the womenfolk. My grandma give them to me when I married and left the Blue Ridge, but she couldn't tell me their story for sure. She thought they come over on the boat from the old country, which would mean they're pretty old. My granny always said she could've been in the historical society with the hoity-toities, if she wanted it.

I never tried to go back and find out. Seemed like there was always something better to do. Guess I've been more the practical sort all my life. I do know that the veil is called a mantilla, and that it's for the day you find the right man who'll love you all your life, and marry him. My granny wore it on the day she married, and I carried it on the day I married, and my granny told me that it had been wore by all the brides in the family before that.

I always hoped I'd give you this on your wedding day. But prayers sometimes aren't answered to our choosing. I can't really say why we always had so much trouble with your mama. I want you to know we tried our best for her. She was a good girl up until she got to running with the wrong kids and met up with your daddy. Seems like nothing we could do would fix things after that.

Be smart when you pick a man to settle down with, sweetness. Make sure he's a good one like your Pap-pap. Don't settle for one bit less.

Pap-pap and I always loved you girls to the end of the ocean and back.

Meemaw

PS: The locket is the first thing Pap-pap ever give to me, our first Christmas together. Not valuable, but it meant a lot. I want you to have it too.

There's no date on the letter, no way of knowing whether she wrote it shortly after my parents took us back to Texas or a few years later when my grandfather had the stroke that forced their move to the nursing home.

It doesn't matter, I suppose. What matters is that they never stopped thinking of us or hoping for us. After having largely messed up the first fifteen years of my adulthood, I'm finally living a life they would be proud of.

In some ways, I'm glad I didn't discover this letter before now. I wouldn't have been ready for it. But in less than two weeks, I will be walking down the aisle with a man who loves me in ways I never understood were possible. Now I'll be carrying a piece of my history, ties to my ancestors, a blessing from my grandparents.

This feels like an incredible gift.

I look at the box that has been left with Gina's name on it, and the usual anger bursts forth. Before

I have time to rethink, I'm lifting the lid, taking care not to let the dust fall inside. The contents are wrapped in faded blue tissue paper, and what I find only fans the burn. A wedding picture of my grandparents, and my grandmother's dress. The satin has aged to a warm eggshell color, and the light touch of beading around the draped neckline is a deep toffee shade. But the gown is in remarkable shape, a simple, sleek style with no petticoats and frills. There is also a pearl necklace, a folded note for Gina, and one of Pap-pap's harmonicas. Gina was always the musical one, the one with Pap-pap's beautiful singing voice. She talked about how she'd become a star and buy a big house for all of us.

I don't open her letter, but I can't resist taking out the gown. It unfurls as I stand, and I'm careful to hold it off the dusty floor. Unfortunately, I'm probably staining it green with envy. I've picked a simple dress to wear at my upcoming wedding, but I wish my grandmother had given me this special keepsake. It even seems to be about the right size.

I remember now that my grandmother sewed the dress herself. She told me the story of picking out the fabric and salvaging lace and pearls from a damaged ball gown given to her by a woman she worked for.

Without thinking, I hurry down the hallway to the pink room, where Gina and I stayed as children. The tall, oval mirror still stands in the corner there. In fact, the place is largely undisturbed. Maybe my sister didn't think there would be anything of value here. Maybe some spaces are sacred, even to her.

I hold my grandmother's gown over myself like a little girl playing dress-up, draping the shoulders against my body, leaning back slightly, hugging the waist with one arm, turning side to side and watching the satin swish.

I imagine what it would be like to surprise Paul, Sandy, and even the kids by walking over the dunes on my wedding day, not in the sundress with the tulle skirt, but in this amazing vintage creation, this garment that has in its very fibers the belief in a lifelong love.

Gina would've dropped this thing at a Goodwill by now if she had it, I tell myself. *She doesn't want it. It means nothing to her. Besides, she's already taken more than her fair share here. . . .*

I know I'm rationalizing. Guilt creeps in. My grandmother left this for Gina. It doesn't belong to me.

I can't start my new life wrapped in a lie, no matter how precious it is to me.

Tears crowd in as I take one last look in the mirror and imagine what might have been.

Pulling out my phone, I think of at least snapping a photo to keep, and the phone rings in my hand. Paul is on the other end with information. He asks how I'm doing. My attempt to sound fine isn't too convincing. I'm looking at the dress again, wanting it. I imagine Zoey someday wearing it at her own wedding.

My mind is only halfway on the call as Paul offers

up the latest. "So, your sister works at the car dealership, Monday through Friday. She comes in at ten. You
wouldn't have caught up with her this afternoon if you'd
driven there, anyway. Their lot is closed on Sundays,
and there's no one there but an Internet shopping spe-
cialist, answering the phone. I tried to poke around for
personal information like where she lives, but I didn't
get anything. Didn't want to tip anyone off."

"That's good, I guess." Angel and devil are at war
on my shoulders, tugging at the dress.

"Hon?" Paul says. "You all right?"

"Yes. Sorry." I'm not sure why I don't tell him where
I am and what I'm doing. I guess I'm a little ashamed
of myself. I suddenly feel like a looter, no better than
my sister.

"Vince has been trying to make some contacts,
to see what we can do about dealing with the people
on the other end of this lawsuit, but it's tough on the
weekend. He says it'll help to show that you weren't *in
knowledge* of the contract if, first thing Monday, you
file a complaint against your sister."

"Ohhhh, I hate this . . ."

"A few hours ago you were ready to choke her with
your bare hands."

Air escapes in a long sigh. The dress falls from my
shoulders and hangs over my arm. "I know."

"Second thoughts?"

"I don't know."

He laughs softly. "Maybe you should sleep on it."

I nod in agreement, even though he can't see me, and turn to look at the pair of twin beds, with their dust-shrouded pink chenille spreads. The place where two little girls slept side by side.

My head swirls, and I realize I haven't eaten a thing all day. I'm thirsty, too, and exhausted.

More than that, I just have no idea where to go from here. Should I load the car with all the things I've gathered? Should I leave them and come back for them later?

Gina won't be at work until ten tomorrow. I could come back in the morning and finish up.

"Can you tell Vince I'll call this evening, but I don't want to do anything official until I've actually talked to Gina? She . . ." I'm about to say she may have some explanation, but that's a waste of words. Gina *will* have an explanation. Many of them, most likely. Every one will be as slick as the polished silver that has disappeared from the china cabinet downstairs.

"Seashell Sandy says she's ready to get the widow maker from behind the store counter and come take care of business over there." That's Paul's way of warning me not to be drawn in by my sister.

"I'm sure she is." Sandy, who loves her own sister like crazy, has no illusions about mine. She probably would take out the baseball bat she keeps for protection and go after Gina. "Is everything okay at the museum?"

"Shipshape. The kids and I tracked down the electrician today, and he'll be here tomorrow. Told him if he didn't show to finish up his work, Vince was going to bring the hammer down on him and get our advance payment back. I don't think we'll have any more trouble. Other than that, your little college intern seems to be doing a good job holding down the fort."

Relief seeps into me, but another wave of light-headedness hits at the same time. The filthy bed looks tempting suddenly. I really need to go to town and get some food.

A dog barks outside as Paul and I say good-bye, and I jerk away from the mirror with a start, then look through the wavy, dirt-streaked plate glass, still holding the wedding dress looped at my waist.

My chin drops and I can't move for a moment.

That's old Boomer. I'd know the black lab mutt anywhere. After all the days of watching him nip the salt air in the bed of Pap-pap's truck, dig tunnels in the dunes, chase ghost crabs on the beach, and ride with Pap-pap in the tractor cab, I'd never mistake another dog for him.

A wave of excitement fills me, followed by over-whelming warmth and joy. Boomer was my friend and confidant, my comforter each time my parents split and we landed here with Mama. Boomer was always willing to run to the mulberry orchard with me and lie patiently across my lap for hours, licking the salt of my tears.

Now there he stands by the yard fence, gazing up at the window as if he's beckoning me. *Come and rest,* he seems to be saying. *Come sit under the mulberries.*

The illusion bursts as quickly as it has formed. It's gone like a soap bubble. Boomer would be ancient by now. That can't be him. Maybe the hunger has gone to my brain.

But everything's there. Even the peanut-shaped white patch on his chest.

Maybe I'm . . . hallucinating? Maybe I've passed out on the floor and I'm dreaming all of this?

There's no clean place to set the wedding dress, so I hurry to the hall and run down the stairs with it still folded over my arm.

The back door sticks, and I'm sure Boomer is a figment of my imagination anyway, but when I finally rush out, there he is. Still standing in exactly the same place, calmly watching me from the fringes of the orchard.

"Boomer?" I whisper.

He wags his tail slightly, as if the name has meaning . . . but how could it?

His head lifts, jerks toward the barn.

I hear whistling. A man's whistling. It echoes off the house and outbuildings, seeming to come from everywhere and nowhere.

My heart leaps up and pounds in my neck.

The breeze lifts the wedding dress, folding the satin around my legs as if to hold me there against my will.

The dog and I stare in the same direction, and the whistling grows in volume and narrows in focus. A form melts from the shadows of the wide barn door

. . . worn work boots, long legs in dirt-stained jeans, a faded blue chambray shirt, a face hidden beneath the brim of a straw cowboy hat that's seen better days.

He looks up, and the misty light reveals him, and all at once I realize I knew him already by his lanky, loose-jointed walk.

But it can't be. It's impossible.

My mind screams against it, the farmyard swirls, and I do something I've never, ever done in my life.

Blackness closes around the vision of him, and I let it swallow me whole.

CHAPTER 6

I wake to a dog licking my face, and at first I think it's Chum, from Sandy's Seashell Shop. He comes home with us sometimes when Sandy is away. The kids have been campaigning for a dog of our own, after Paul and I get back from the honeymoon.

My mind slips into the thought that the wedding has already happened and we're settled in at Paul's grandmother's, helping her take care of the rambling I-style house on Hatteras.

Then I hear a man's voice, and it's not Paul's.

"Boomer, cut it out. Get back."

I blink at an expanse of sky, wide and blue and empty. Then I see the dog's face and the man's, side by side, and my mind is lost in time and space.

I'm left powerless, floating from one idea to the next.

Am I dead? Maybe a blood clot or an aneurysm? Heart attack? Something that kills silently and without warning?

Heatstroke? But it's cloudy and mild today. . . .

Who'll tell the kids? Thank heaven they have Paul and his family.

But *I* want to raise my kids. I want to be alive. *This isn't fair,* my mind screams. I zero in on the face above me again. He seems so real. I try to remember, did he and his older brother look this much alike? Could that be who's hovering over me now, trying to elbow the dog away?

But I know one could never be mistaken for the other. The older brother had brown hair. The eyes staring down at me now, the knitted brow with curls of blond hair hanging over it, the up-and-down quirked mouth . . .

This is Luke. *My* Luke.

Maybe I'm still out cold on the lawn, caught somewhere between heaven and earth.

Luke? I try to say, but my voice is barely a croak. He smiles the wide white smile that once came with double-dog dares—that later convinced me to sneak out the window and climb the silo ladder with him, to lie on the roof of the barn counting a million stars and watching a distant sea storm, billowing toward the Tidewater flatlands.

"You had me worried." His voice is just as I remember it from that last year, when suddenly it had become a man's voice. The person crouched above me is older, world-worn in a way I can't define, but this *is* Luke.

I try to sit up. "I . . . think I . . ."

"Ssshhh. Hold on a minute. Not so fast." He slips

an arm beneath my shoulders, gently supporting my weight.

I feel the wedding dress slide across my arm. I need to keep it off the damp ground.

The worry is quickly eclipsed by the sight of him.

"You look like you've seen a ghost," he laughs, but it's not funny. There's nothing funny about it. I feel the blood draining from my head again.

"Easy there. You're not quite yourself yet."

"Luke?" Finally, I speak the name.

"You were expecting, maybe, the Easter bunny?" He uses the exact line from that last summer together, when he had changed, and I had changed, and I barely recognized him, a foot taller and almost a man.

No one else would quote that silly Bugs Bunny cartoon to me. No one on this earth.

"I didn't mean to scare you." A concerned look follows his apology. "My sister told me you were down here when I came in from disking the field a while ago."

"Your sister?" I speed-recycle the conversation with Laura. Mostly we were preoccupied with the property issues, but she mentioned that her brother was helping with the work around the farm. I'd assumed she meant her older brother. How could it be anything else?

I must be dreaming all of this. I'm probably back home on Hatteras, still asleep in my bed, and none of this—the farmhouse still being here, the treasures Meemaw left in the tobacco tin, her wedding dress—is real. It's all just a figment of hope and regret. The conclusion brings a stab of disappointment but also a conscious decision to go along with it. I want to live in this dream for a while, see where it leads.

There are things I want to say to Luke. A million things.

"I've missed you." It seems all right to admit that in a dream. But afterward, I feel awkward nonetheless.

His smile falls, and sadness darkens his features. There's a haunted look in his eyes. The dog nudges him, concerned. Boomer always had a sense of people's emotions, an innate desire to comfort and protect.

My mind begins to clear on that thought. I start trying to compile logical answers again, but I really can't come up with any.

Luke scratches the dog's head, looks toward the mulberry orchard as if he's remembering all the times we selected tree castles and played Robin Hood there. His blue eyes are clear and contemplative. "I always wondered if you'd ever come back." A flush steals into his cheeks. "I've seen your sister a couple times over the years . . . when I've been home. I've lived a lot of places."

I wonder if Laura has told him that Gina's story about my having recurrent leukemia was a complete hoax. One she kept going for years.

Reality seeps in a little more. *I've seen your sister a few times . . .* Has he?

Has Gina been here and seen Luke, *my* Luke, walking and talking and fully alive? And never told me?

Is he alive? Is all of this real?

He looks at me a moment, his gaze seeking mine, almost as if he's wondering the same thing. "You're two shades of pale, Tandi Jo. How about we go sit on the porch a minute until you get your feet under you?"

"That's probably a good idea." As he half lifts me from the ground and walks me to the porch, I admit to him that I got wrapped up in looking through the house, and I haven't eaten all day. He offers to grab the leftovers from the lunch his sister packed for him when he headed to the field this morning, then jogs off. I'm almost reluctant to let him disappear into the barn. I'm afraid he'll never come out again.

I keep my hand on the dog, hoping he'll stay as proof—something not made from smoke and wishes. Boomer *feels* real enough. His ribs rise and fall beneath my hand, and his heartbeat flutters against my fingers, yet he must be dead by now. Part of my mind insists this must be a dream.

I notice my grandmother's wedding dress lying on the grass, and I wobble over to retrieve it, lay it gently across the porch railing, where the wind has swept the wood clean.

If Luke thought it odd at all to find me in the yard, holding a satin gown, he didn't say anything. But it must've looked strange.

In a minute, there he is again, crossing the yard on long, unhurried strides. Just as always.

He opens a lunch sack and offers up a peanut butter

and jelly sandwich, some chips, a banana MoonPie, and a juice box. "Sorry. She feeds Dale and me the same things she feeds all the rug rats."

"Are you kidding? It looks delicious." Silence settles over us, and I would be embarrassed to eat in front of him, but I'm too hungry to care. He waits until I've devoured the sandwich and half the juice before he starts the conversation again.

"So . . . tell me where you've been all these years?" he asks finally. I'm conscious of the fact that he's watching me intently as I open the MoonPie, pinch off a bite, and savor it. MoonPies were Pap-pap's favorite.

I wonder if Pap-pap and Meemaw will eventually come into this dream too. I would love to see both of them again.

"Well, I live on Hatteras now. For the last year, I've managed the renovations on one of the biggest historic houses on the island. Benoit House. The community is turning it into a museum, and people will hold weddings and occasions there. Long story about how I got into that, but I was in the right place at the right time with the right skill set. You know my dad always did construction, and I helped a lot with his business." We're both aware that *helped* is a strangely innocuous term for it. From the time I was nine or ten years old, I was driving my father to and from jobs when he was too drunk to get behind the wheel. "I moved to Hatteras not long after the hurricane, so one thing sort of led to another. I also work a couple days a week at

Sandy's Seashell Shop and sell some of my driftwood art there. I have a daughter who's fifteen and a son who is ten. Zoey and J.T. They're great kids, if I do say so myself." For some reason, I hesitate, intending to add, *and I'm getting married in less than two weeks,* but Luke responds in the pause.

"Wow . . . kids . . ." He draws back a little. "You have one who's fifteen?"

"I got pregnant my first year in college. It's not a real pretty story." So many things aren't, but if this last year has taught me anything, it's that God has the capacity to make incredible things from our mistakes. Zoey is incredible. "That's enough about me. Tell me about you. Tell me where you've been." I try to imagine what he'll say. Will he describe heaven? Or in this dream, has he gone on and lived a regular life? He did say he'd been lots of places. What does that mean?

A bank of clouds further dampens the sun, and he turns his shoulder to me, resting his elbows on his knees and letting his head fall forward. His shoulders hollow out an arc, the chambray fabric settling over them.

I want to lay a hand there, and I don't even know why. The dog circumvents me and curls up beside Luke on the porch step, his face resting on the black dirt stains that tint Luke's work jeans.

"It's not the prettiest picture either. You know, after the accident, when they finally dialed back the meds and I came to, Laura was in a wheelchair, and my parents had spent almost everything they had, paying the medical bills, and it was all my fault. I just couldn't . . . deal with what I'd done."

A long breath shudders out. He strokes the dog's soft coat, studies the field. "I didn't make very good use of the second chance at life. When you're running from things, you never do. You spend all your energy on pointless movement. You don't have anything left to build with. I moved here and moved there, worked on a shrimp boat, did some seasons at ski resorts and national parks, went through a stint as an Army Ranger and tried my best to get myself killed, came home off and on and helped with the farm. I wanted to do what I could to make it up to Laura, not that she ever told me I needed to. But I was the one driving the truck that day." He casts a sad look my way, as if he desperately wants to know what I'm thinking, as if he *needs* to know. "I was always glad you weren't in it."

My head reels so wildly that I can't even answer. Reality doesn't just seep in, it floods. I'm underwater for a moment, gasping for air. "They told me you died" is all I can manage.

Bright-blue eyes blink, stare, and blink again. "They what?"

"When we left here that summer, you weren't expected to survive." The news had been all over Mulberry Run Road. I can still hear my grandparents talking about what a tragic thing it was. "Sometime after that, my father told me you were gone. My parents were in a custody fight with my grandparents by then, and Daddy wouldn't even bring us back here for the funeral."

His brows rise and hover. I can see his thoughts moving. "Well . . . the doctors did tell my parents to be prepared. They'd had the talk about organ donation. But you know, doctors aren't always right. Sometimes it doesn't happen like they expect. By the fourth or fifth day, and the fourth or fifth surgery, they thought I might make it after all."

He goes on and describes what he survived as a sixteen-year-old and what his family went through, with two kids facing months and years of follow-up surgeries and physical therapy. I try to imagine as if it were Zoey and J.T., but I can't.

I keep thinking, *By the fourth or fifth day . . . they thought I might make it. . . .*

It was well after that when my father, frustrated with my tears and professions of love for Luke and pleas to return to the farm, said something like, *Shut up about it already. That Townley kid died a couple days ago. I didn't tell you because I knew you'd be all broke up. You're thirteen. You don't even know what love is. I don't wanna hear about that Townley kid no more, you get me? Just leave it go. . . .*

By the time Luke's story ends with his leaving home at seventeen, the dog is chasing the leftover banana MoonPie down the steps. I must've dropped it.

"Boomer," Luke scolds. "Get away from . . . well,

too late." He aims a shrug my way, seeming ready to lighten the gravity of our conversation.

"Boomer," I repeat. "That's not *the* Boomer?"

"Of course not. He'd be, like, twenty-five by now. But your grandpa's dog *got around*, if you know what I mean. You could say his legacy lives on." Luke's lips quirk in a way that is so familiar. I suddenly remember that first kiss in the mulberry orchard. I remember everything about it.

That kiss both rocked the world and changed it in the way that first kisses so often do. When Luke Townley kissed me, I thought I knew, right then and there, what my future would be.

We planned it all out together, lying side by side beneath the mulberry trees.

Now, looking at him, I wonder . . . Does he remember the promises we made?

CHAPTER 7

"Well, I've definitely never seen anything like it," Luke says, closing the lid on the tobacco tin and handing it back to me. We're standing in the backyard, just sort of hovering near my SUV.

He's helped me carry things from the house, then wrap and pad and pack them into the cargo area. Together, we've sorted through the last few rooms—and through a hundred different memories. He has reminded me of so many moments I've forgotten, and I've unearthed touchstones he'd lost as well. Our off-and-on childhood friendship feels as real as if we had just seen one another yesterday. Perhaps that is where its magic lies. The misty, impractical hues of childhood sprinkle glitter over everything.

Neither of us talks about the bad parts. We don't discuss my father, roaring drunk in the yard, as he and my mother have yet another shoving match, and she tells him once again to get out, and Pap-pap bursts onto the porch with his rifle. We don't discuss Luke and me making plans to run away together, promising each other forever as mere teenagers, having no concept of how complicated forever can be.

Neither of us mentions that volatile, sweet-then-bitter last summer at all. We've just spent the last hours of daylight sorting, carrying, and reminiscing back and forth from room to room, sometimes laughing so hard we're in tears.

Even Boomer looks at us like we've lost it. It's true, we have. We've lost all the intervening years, all the pain and disappointment, all the adult worries that weigh us down and keep us from launching into flights of fancy.

A few times I've let my mind stray into *what if*. What if my parents hadn't dragged me away that first week of August? What if hopes and first love could've taken care of me the way Luke promised they would? What if, instead of running from his pain, Luke had gone on to college and become the thing he always said he would be, a veterinarian?

What if Zoey and J.T. were *his*, and we had lived all our lives together in some little house in the Tidewater or by the shore?

But I curtail the wondering each time it comes, and I close the door on it again as we stand beside the car, neither one of us seeming quite ready to leave. I know I should. Just being here, just thinking these thoughts, feels disloyal to Paul in some way. I know the only reason he hasn't called to check on me is that he thinks I'm in a motel somewhere, catching up on my sleep. He's being what he always is—a protector, a best friend, a hero, the first person I've ever known who loved me just for me.

Even Luke's love *wanted* something, back in the day. I'd overheard Pap-pap warning Gina about what a boy's love could want, after she was caught sneaking around with Luke's older brother. *You watch out for that Townley boy. Not a whole lotta difference between a young rounder and the yard dog. You stand in front a one with steak on a plate, he'll be your best friend, long's the steak's still on the plate. You let him empty the plate, and he'll be gone soon's some other girl walks by with a platter in her hand.*

The analogy makes me chuckle now, but it also makes me wonder. Did Luke mean all the things he said back then, or was that just teenage hormones talking?

Maybe it's a mercy that there was never a chance for my illusion to be shattered. Maybe it's good when a first love remains the fairy tale you always believe in.

Opening the car door, I set the tobacco tin on the passenger seat by the box with Meemaw's wedding dress. In the morning, I plan to see my sister face to face. Sometime before that, I'll have another conversation with Vince, get more details about what could happen to Gina if I take her to court, load up on ammo. I want to make this sound official. To let her know she can't walk all over her baby sister this time.

"You know, it's still there," Luke says, seemingly out of the blue. He's looking off across the yard.

"What is?"

"Our spot." His lips curve playfully. "Up on top of the barn by the silo. I was up there the other day. It just crossed my mind all of a sudden. How much we used to sit out there, I mean."

I feel the link between us again. He remembers those times on the roof too. A smile tugs the corners of my mouth. "I loved the fact that Gina could never figure out where we went."

Climbing the silo ladder and hiding in that place where the barn and hay shed rooflines met was our special secret. Somewhere high enough that no one could hear us as we shared thoughts about life and dreams, and we painted fanciful wishes. We hatched a million plots to convince my parents to leave Gina and me here at the farm permanently. Everything from unexplained illness to seeing if we could find a job for my father in town. One of the times we'd actually stayed long enough to enroll in school, I'd even tried out for the school play. For some reason, Luke and I thought my parents couldn't possibly take me away if I'd committed to a part in the fifth-grade Christmas musical. The music teacher, Mrs. Vilmer, was a veritable dragon lady. If nothing else, we were sure she wouldn't let it happen.

I can't help reminding Luke of the Mrs. Vilmer scheme, and suddenly we're reclining against the car again, laughing together.

"Hard to believe we ever thought it would be that simple." He shakes his head ruefully, shrugging toward the barn. "Want to see it one more time? The old place, I mean? First star oughta be out soon." There's a challenge in his eyes, the same one that convinced me to ignore my fear of heights and make the first climb out the silo hatch at nine years old, and many times after.

But there's something deeper in Luke's face also. I wonder if it's longing. That's what it looks like.

I realize I might be leading him on. I don't mean to. But I haven't said anything about my wedding. The sharp needle of conscience pokes a soft place, injecting an IV dose of mature reality. You can't go back in time and grab the past, no matter how much you'd like to believe it's possible.

"I probably shouldn't."

His disappointment is quick and evident, but he also seems to understand. "Got places to be, I guess." The statement somehow points out that he doesn't. He's not trying to coerce me. Rather, he just seems sad.

"I really should get on over to Greenville and check into a motel. I need to take some time to plan tomorrow's full-frontal assault on Gina." I've already filled Luke in on all the details, including her working hours. He's offered to go with me, and I've wisely told him no. "I have a ton of things at home to check up on too. Not only is the museum opening in a couple weeks, but I'm getting married." The last words are dry on my tongue. I taste the salt of what feels like a broken promise, but that's silly, of course.

He hides his reaction by watching Boomer prowl

the twisted scuppernong thicket along the orchard fence. The vines have gone wild, taking over three times their old territory, too tangled and knotted now for anyone to groom or sort them. "That's really great. Congratulations." His voice is flat.

Fortunately, a phone chimes in his pocket before I have to answer. He goes to it as a welcome distraction. I watch his profile in the soft pink light as he reads the message.

"Laura says come on down for supper. She was hoping to get to see you at least a little more before you go."

"That sounds nice." I'm thankful for the reprieve. I don't want to leave, but I know I can't stay here like this, alone with Luke and the thinning clouds and the first faint star testing the horizon. It's too familiar.

I'd like to talk to Laura a bit more anyway, find out what sort of money Gina has glommed on to while stealing the farm rent over the years.

A whistle calls Boomer from his hunting place. "Why not walk?" The melancholy is gone, and there's that boyish hint of double-dog dare again.

"Yeah. That sounds nice." One more journey down Mulberry Run Road with Luke Townley and Boomer. Just about perfect.

We slip into the past again as we set off, talking about bike rides and frog gigging and the time we put a black racer snake in Gina's purse. "My daddy whipped the fire out of me for that. But it was kind of worth it."

I've said it before I realize that talking about Daddy

and whippings is a potential conversation spoiler, considering how much Luke actually knows about my family. The comment slides away as we turn into Laura's yard and a gaggle of assorted kids runs out to greet us. They make a human jungle gym of Luke. I can't even tell which ones are family and which ones are here for foster care. He seems to love them all. It crosses my mind that it's a shame he's not a father.

The melee travels inside with us and continues as Laura and her husband, Dale, do their best to get a meal served. It's sloppy and messy and chaotic, but you can feel the love in this house. As we pause to pray over the food, I'm thankful that Laura has all of this. After what she's been through, she deserves it. I'm awed anew by the power of a single, ordinary life—one the rest of us would think of as broken. Here she is, with no legs, and she's giving these children wings.

I'm more determined than ever to save the old farm, to retain possession of it. I want to bring Paul and the kids back here to spend time. I want to show them all the old childhood places. I want them to get to know this amazing woman and her cornucopia of kids.

But as the prayer ends and conversation flies, I look across the table, see Luke, and wonder how it would be to introduce him to Paul. To bring together these two men who saved me at different times in my life.

Maybe it wouldn't be the right thing to do at all.

It's likely that it'll never happen, anyway. I don't have to listen to the chatter long to realize that Luke's not kidding when he says he's moved around a lot. He never stays here very long. He never stays anyplace. The kids ask for stories, and he tells them about one home after another, one person after another, but they're all temporary in Luke's life.

I'm still trying to form a complete picture of his wanderings by the time supper ends. He and Dale go outside with the kids to feed scraps to dogs, gather eggs from the coop, and do the barn chores for the night. I stay in with Laura to help clear the dishes, even though she insists that I don't have to. She tries to urge me to go with Luke. I have a feeling she's hoping to set something up, so I make sure to tell her, as we're washing and drying plates, about to the upcoming wedding.

Her reaction is a little like Luke's, but she says, "Oh, that's awesome. I'm so excited for you!"

"He's really an incredible guy." Why do I feel strangely like I'm justifying myself? "The best."

"Good for you. Congratulations."

The focus drifts to easier subjects as we finish the plates, then stack them in green-painted cabinets that look the same as they did when Laura's parents lived here. It's easy to tell by looking that Laura isn't much on decorating. The house bears the evidence of constant, semi-chaotic activity. It is what it has always been—the sort of place where there's no need to worry about damaging anything. The sort of place that's meant to be lived in.

Laura lets out a soft laugh as she closes the cabinet. "You know, when Bean brought you here, and I realized who you were, I sort of wished Luke wasn't out in the field. After the kids saw you there at the house again, I sent my brother down on purpose. I guess I just thought . . ."

A preschooler runs through, and Laura grabs a towel and does an expert whiplash swat, making the little boy dodge and squeal. Laura finishes the thought finally. "I don't know, I got this wild feeling that maybe you and Luke . . . that maybe something would change for him because you came here. I've told him over and over that I don't blame him for the accident and what happened. But no matter what I say and no matter where he goes, it isn't quite what he needs. He just seems . . . lost. I don't understand why. I've committed a lot of hopes and prayers to that over the years, but so far the answers haven't come."

I feel an odd sort of pressure to somehow be the answer to those prayers, but I know I'm not. I have a life of my own on Hatteras, and it's full. It's happy. There are a hundred selfish reasons why I don't want to take on Luke's problems. I can't, anyway. I've finally come to fully understand that you can't fix another person. You can't fix the past. You can only change your way of reacting to it.

You have to wait for other people to fix themselves.

"I'm sorry." I can't think of what else to say.

"Oh, goodness, don't be." Laura waves the regrets away like smoke. "That's just me being dreamy eyed. There's a lot of my mother in me." She abruptly moves to a new question. "So listen, did you talk to your sister today? What did she say? Did you find out anything more about what's going on? We'd sure like to know when we're going to be locked off the land and whether we'll be able to bring in our crops first."

It's the perfect segue into asking her about the farm rentals over the years, and the conversation drifts naturally. But in the back of my mind, the other track keeps playing. It repeats to the point that I don't stay for ice cream after dinner when the men and kids tumble back in from the barn.

I purposely say my good-byes while Luke's outside, taking one of the kids to the shed to return a smuggled kitten. But he walks around the house just as I'm about to put the vehicle in reverse.

I roll down the window and wait while he comes to the car. "Gotta go?" he asks.

"Yes. Have to plan my strategy. Laura gave me some good ammunition." I pat a stack of copies of rental checks and lease contracts from years past.

A worry line curves Luke's forehead. "Call if you need anything, okay? A little muscle . . . electric cattle prod . . . accomplice. We could kidnap her and lock her in the old granary again."

The picture makes me laugh, and of course the thread pulls up with several other memories attached. I don't mention them because I know where we'll end up if I do. "I'll keep that in mind, thanks."

"I mean it. Anything you need." His eyes meet

mine, as compelling and sky-blue as ever. I wonder what he's seeing. Does he see the girl he used to know?

I want to say the same thing back to him, but I can't give Luke what he needs. "Take care of yourself, okay?" Tears press unexpectedly and my voice trembles.

He shrugs off the request. "You know me—wherever I end up, I always land on my feet." Something about the way he says it tells me that whenever I do come back to the Tidewater blackland, he'll be gone again. His gaze strays down the road as if he's already thinking about bolting.

"You should stay here. You're so good with these kids."

Again he shrugs it off. "I'm feeling the itch. Too hot and sticky here this time of year. Maybe time to head for the mountains . . ."

Without even meaning to, I reach out and lay a hand alongside his face, turn it toward mine. "Don't be so hard on yourself, Luke. Everyone's okay here." I indicate the house, where Laura has her sweetly unconventional life under control.

"Yeah, I know." He lifts a hand and gently slides my fingers away, rubs them between his palms. "Take care of yourself, Tandi. Tell the groom he's a lucky guy."

With one last, soft squeeze, he lets go and walks away, and somewhere deep inside me the years since that thirteenth summer turn tissue-thin, then shred and disappear. Luke Townley has come back to life, but I also know I'll probably never see him again.

CHAPTER 8

I wake up in the motel room, confused at first about why I'm here. I think I'm on a business trip for the museum—another journey to pick up Outer Banks historical items and old documents too valuable or fragile to be shipped through the mail.

Looking at the clock, I remember where I am and why all at once. Heat boils up, and I'm instantly ready for war. I lie there, recounting all of my sister's sins, not the least of which is that she knew Luke Townley hadn't died in that car crash and she never told me. Sweet whiffs of yesterday's memories drift by, but I don't turn my head to capture the scent. Instead, I focus on how angry I am—on all the wrong that's been done.

I think through my game plan. Since leaving Mulberry Run Road, I've talked to Vince and Paul again. They've made some progress on their end. The buyers are skittish of the idea that I could prove I had no knowledge of the sale plans to begin with. It's really Gina's portion of the land that they want, anyway—the farm fields. Vince is working to persuade them that it's best to give up on going after the house and surrounding eighty acres and settle for getting their down payment back on that part. Of course, beyond that, the tax lien has to be satisfied.

I'm fully prepared to threaten my sister with all that can happen if I file a complaint against her. If she doesn't find a way to make this right. I know how much money is needed to clear my portion of the land and pay to officially divide it. It's over fifteen thousand dollars. I can't imagine how Gina will come up with that.

I tell myself again that Gina is resourceful, if nothing else. I silently promise that this time I won't back down. I'll send her to jail without a second thought, if that's what it comes to. But a part of me wonders what will happen when we're face to face. A part of me remembers the times she dragged me under the bed and held my body against hers while Mama and Daddy waged war. Part of me remembers how she protected me from older boys and the letch next door during our first months in emergency foster care.

Part of me still cries out, *But this is your sister. This is not the way things are supposed to be.*

Lying in the motel room, still miles away from her, I'm tearing in two.

Finally, I sit up, take the tobacco tin from the nightstand, read Meemaw's note again, and finger the necklace with its carefully carved bone beads. I sent pictures of it to Paul and to the Seashell Shop girls last night. Nobody has ever seen anything quite like it.

They all agree that, based on the motif, it was probably carved by a sailor. How it ended up in Meemaw's family is a mystery.

Thank goodness Gina didn't find it before I did. It undoubtedly has value, and it would probably be in a pawnshop somewhere by now. This mysterious inheritance from my ancestors in the Blue Ridge Mountains both intrigues and saddens me. It's one more thing Gina tried to take away. One more keepsake she cares nothing about.

This treasure was entrusted to me. I'm thankful that it's safe now.

The worst part of today will be offering Gina the box that Meemaw left for her. The wedding dress. I hate even the idea of it, but I know it's the right thing. It was what Meemaw wanted.

"No time like the present," I tell the empty room and get up to make ready for the day. Before turning out the lights and leaving the motel, one last look in the mirror provides a final delay tactic. My sister will no doubt look like a million bucks. She always does. I don't want to be outgunned.

In the parking lot, I trade texts with Paul, who has called the dealership pretending to be a repeat customer, to make sure Gina is there. She is.

My sister has no idea what's headed her way, and that leaves a wickedly satisfying taste in my mouth as I drive the five miles to the car lot. Unfortunately, the taste turns bitter and burns going down. Revenge often does. I think of a verse about vengeance being God's portion, and again I wonder, am I doing the right thing?

Is that God knocking on my conscience right now saying, *Stop this. Don't let her turn you into a mirror of herself?*

Or is that just me, being the second-born, the baby, the peacemaker, the wimp?

Maybe I'm supposed to finally stand up for myself. Otherwise why would I have been brought here and bombarded with all the things Gina has kept from me?

Strangely enough, when it's decision time, I don't hesitate. I park in front of the dealership, grab the box that's Gina's, march right past the reception desk, and follow the directions Paul was given on the phone. She isn't hard to find. She has a glassed-in office down the hall from the showroom. High-quality digs. Just the kind my sister likes and usually manages to score until the jig is up.

She's sitting against the corner of the desk in a smooth-fitting miniskirt, her long, tanned legs attractively crossed as she talks to a young guy dressed in a button-up shirt, tie, and khaki pants that look like they've been around the car lot too long.

They're joking about a customer. Gina frowns and examines her gold-manicured fingernails. "Yeah, tell him you came in here and begged me. And then tell him we'll take $19,599, but his old truck isn't worth squat to us, so it's Blue Book or nothing. But hang out in the break room for fifteen or twenty minutes before you go back and talk to him. Let him think you worked really hard trying to get your mean old manager to come down."

She gives the salesman a perfectly practiced pout lip, then sucks it back in immediately when she sees me in the doorway. Her eyes fly wide and her nostrils flare. "Okay, Ramon, we're good." Suddenly she's turning off the flirt and giving Ramon the bum's rush. "Don't come back to me without a deal."

Her mouth squeezes tight, her chin lifting as the salesman and I brush by each other in the doorway. He slants a curious look over his shoulder, and my sister skirts me to move a wooden wedge out of the way so the door can fall closed.

"What in the *world* are *you* doing here?" It's like Gina to attack first, to act like I'm the one who's up to no good.

I was prepared for that. "Funny you should ask. It looks like we have something we need to talk about."

Her gaze narrows curiously as I set the wedding dress box in a chair. She crosses her arms over her chest, the tank-style dress gaping, showing cleavage. What looks like a nice-size diamond dangles from a chain there, but it's probably fake, like everything else about my sister. "I hope you're not here to beg me to be in that stupid wedding of yours. Yeah, I know about that. I saw it on Zoey's Facebook page. Seriously, just how long do you think you're going to be happy, married to Mr. Science Teacher Nerd?"

"I didn't come here to talk about my wedding."

Something flits across her face, then hides. Disappointment? Trepidation? Has she figured out why I'm here?

"A courier showed up at my door the other day. He had a notice about a lawsuit and the sale of some property. Only I don't *own* any property. Nothing I ever *knew* about, anyway."

Her jaw clenches and a vein pops in her forehead. Turning her focus to the desk, she makes a show of putting some loose pencils in her pencil can. "Oh, *that*. I was going to get all that straightened out and surprise you with a check for your wedding, but now you've ruined it."

"I'll bet." Did she come up with that on the spur of the moment, or has she been thinking about what she'd tell me if I ever found out about the farm? "That's why you lied to me all these years? That's why you never told me Pap-pap and Meemaw left the land to us? That's why you collected thousands of dollars in rental fees and kept it for yourself?" I snatch the folder off the top of the box and wave it at her.

Her response is a tired eye roll. "Oh, for heaven's sake, there never really *was* any money. It was barely ever enough to pay the taxes and fix stuff around the place. I don't know *what* you're carrying on about."

"You stole from me!" I shriek, and two glass walls away, heads turn in one of the offices.

Gina's lashes flare. "Be quiet!" she hisses under her

breath, her gaze darting around. I can almost see the sweat glands opening on her forehead. "This is a *business*. I'm at *work*."

"Gina, I'm through being quiet. I don't care if the whole world knows." I consider stepping out the door and shouting the entire story at the top of my lungs. I want to so badly.

She reads the thought, shifts a bit, like she'll block the exit path if I try it. Sadly, it wouldn't be our first wrestling match. "Don't you *dare*. If you cause trouble for me here, Tandi, I'll make sure you're sorry you *ever* walked into this place."

I take a breath and rein myself in. Getting arrested for disorderly conduct in a car dealership won't help me seem like a sane and completely innocent person if this thing goes to court. It also won't solve our problem. I hold all the cards here. But I need to play them strategically.

I measure the next words, keep them level and fairly emotionless. "I've been to see Laura. I know how much money the place made each year. You never told me we had it because you wanted to keep the checks for yourself."

An indignant cough answers the accusation. "I did you a favor by not telling you. First, when I found out they'd left us the farm, you were just a kid, and I didn't want you to have to worry about it. You were living in Niceville on the big horse ranch with your swanky new parents, remember that? You were all settled into your bed of roses. And you didn't *want me* in it. You said you just needed to forget Mama and Daddy, forget everything that happened, and make a new life for yourself. What good could the farm have possibly done you? It's never been anything more than an albatross anyway."

"I love Pap-pap's farm. I've always loved it. And there were times I could barely feed my kids and keep a roof over our heads, Gina. And still you never told me."

There's a hint of emotion again. It looks almost like guilt. It's quickly gone. Like vapor. "Well, I knew you'd just get desperate and sell the place because you were in a mess. And then later you'd feel all guilty about it. Because that's what you do, Tandi. You go around obsessing about what's right and how things are supposed to be. You drive yourself crazy because you can't ever just accept the way things are."

There's a shred of truth in what she says. I *want* to believe in things. I want to believe in a world where family means more than money. Where sisters love each other and sacrifice for each other.

Gina wants me to believe that world doesn't exist.

Hatteras Island, Paul's family, the Seashell Shop girls, and the prayer boxes of Iola Anne Poole have taught me otherwise. A life can be blessed without your ever deserving it. You can be loved by people just because they choose to love you.

I spew out some facts and figures on the rental income, wave invoices in the air, and Gina and I argue back and forth, and I produce Laura's paperwork, effectively nailing my sister to the wall.

"Oh, for heaven sake, all of that is fake." She huffs dismissively at the copies on her desk. "Laura and Dale probably made that up for their accountant."

"Yes, and I suppose she made up the tax lien, and the lawsuit, and the fact that you put together some shady deal to sell the property and then stole their money."

She huffs again. "That isn't my fault. I used a guy I met. He had a real estate license, and he said he'd handle the place, cheap. He's the one who ran off with the up-front money on the deal. Jerk. Anyway, I've got it all worked out, so you can just simmer down. I found another buyer, and they're primed and ready. When the deal goes through, I'll take care of the stupid lawsuit and the taxes and send you the money for your part. My little wedding gift to you and the nerd. You're gonna need it. Teachers don't get paid squat, you know."

My hands clench tightly enough to drive the fingernails into skin. I want to tag Gina with a hard right cross, but I'm not the type, and if I did it, she'd probably sue me anyway. "And I guess you're going to bring me a check for the things you stole from *inside* the house too?"

She slaps a hand to her chest. "I *never* took anything from inside the house. The place has been sitting there for years. Who knows who's been in there? It was probably some of those kids they take in down at the Townley house." She sneers when she says it, as if we were never *those kids* ourselves.

"And what about Luke Townley? Were you ever going to tell me he actually recovered after the accident? That you'd seen him over the years?"

Gina's brows shoot skyward. Perfect red lipstick hangs in a lopsided O, framing parted teeth. Slowly, she reels it up, forming a sly smile. "Oh . . . so *that's* what's really behind all of this. You're still nursing some silly schoolgirl fantasy that you and Luke Townley are star-crossed soul mates. You know what? I did you a favor there too. The last thing you needed in your life was Luke Townley. He's got issues of his own. Believe whatever you want, but that's reality, Little Sister."

I wonder in a brief, stomach-turning way whether Gina and Luke could have had something going on over the years. Just the idea makes me sick, but something about the way Gina reacted to his name seemed personal. Maybe she's just doing it to get to me. And it's working.

I feel the cork on my self-restraint slowly wiggling toward the rim of the bottle. If it pops free, something ugly and acidic will flood the entire place. "I'll tell you *what*, Gina. Let me give you a dose of reality." My last bit of ammo comes from the bottom of the folder. I bring out a fax Vince sent to me at the motel. It has his letterhead on top, and basically it says he's representing me. Slapping it on my sister's desk, I point a finger at her and go for the jugular, just as Vince has advised me to, whipping out the rather impressive arsenal of legal terminology along with my demands. "Either you find a way to give me the money I need to clear the house and eighty acres that Pap-pap and Meemaw intended to leave to me, or I'm pressing charges. Statutory fraud, breach of fiduciary duty, theft of property—how does that sound for a beginning? You push me on this, Gina, and my lawyer won't just go after you for the fraud on the land sale. We'll be taking you to court for what you've stolen from me over the years. Every *single* cent."

The sideways tilt of her head says she doesn't believe me. She probably thinks I typed up the letter myself. "Seriously. You know, if you'll just wait a couple weeks, I'll have this all taken care of, and you'll have a nice, big check to show for it. We've got a month before they docket the tax sale on the place, and those lawsuit people know it'll cost them more to go to court than if they just work with me. In a week, maybe two, the property sale will be signed, sealed, and delivered to the new buyer. The debts and taxes get paid off as part of the sale. They're giving us a good price on the land, too—something about the government wanting off-site plots for the Tidewater Research Station. See? Win-win. So you can put your little lawyer letter away and get out of my office. I try to do something good for you and this is the thanks I get."

"I am *not* selling."

"That's what I knew you'd say. That's why I didn't

even tell you about all this. I knew you'd get some stupid idea about keeping the farm. You can't *afford* to, Tandi, and you know it. Even if I take care of the earnest money thing, how are you going to come up with the chunk of change for the taxes? We both know you don't have that kind of cash lying around."

My molars grind so hard I'm afraid I'll need dental work after this. Gina can twist a conversation until it's like spaghetti on a plate. "*You're* going to come up with the money to pay the taxes and return the earnest money on my part of the property. *You're* the one who *stole* the farm rental checks and didn't pay the taxes in the first place."

"I got a little behind last year after you kicked me out of your casita there on Hatteras," she says vaguely, shrugging as if she's done with me. "Anyway, I don't have that kind of cash lying around."

That's the first truthful thing she's said, and of course I'm ready for it. "Come up with it, Gina. Now. Or I'm having my lawyer go forward with this." I look around at Gina's posh new digs and take in the clothes she's wearing. "Sell your car. That shouldn't be too hard, considering." On the way in, I noticed her tricked-out Jeep—the one she had on the Outer Banks last year—parked around the side of the building.

Her posture softens. I can see her switching tactics. She sinks against the corner of the desk, meets my gaze, sister to sister. "Listen, Tandi, just chill, okay? Merritt doesn't know anything about . . . my past. He doesn't know about the property or the tax mess. He's a really great guy and he's crazy about me. I can't screw this up. Just give me a couple weeks to—"

"No. Gina. *No.*" I'm resolved not to fall for any of this. Where Gina is involved, promises are made to be broken. "Whatever you do with the acreage Meemaw and Pap-pap wanted to leave to you is your choice, but my wedding is in twelve days, and the museum opens this weekend, and I'm *not* having this hanging over my head, or Paul's. You and I are settling up *now*, or else."

She tries to stare me down, but I don't flinch. Her lower jaw juts outward, and I can see another firestorm brewing. In under thirty seconds, she's sending off a new shot. "You need to work with me here. It'd be *terrible* if something happened to screw it up for you and Mr. Wonderful . . . wouldn't it?"

"You stay away from Paul, Gina." My fiancé can take care of himself. I know that on one level, but fear gnaws deep in my stomach, chewing holes. I have no idea what Gina is really capable of. Over the years, I suspect I've only seen the tip of the manipulative iceberg.

She tastes the rim of her teeth, one weapon stroking another. "I mean, it'd be such a *shame* if someone called that school he works for . . . or say, CPS . . . and said they'd seen him cuddling up a little *too much* with one of those lonely teenage girls he teaches, wouldn't it?" A falsely innocent sigh regrets what mess an accusation like that would create. "Just a *concerned* citizen, of course. Someone who'd *seen* something that didn't look right. They'd have to investigate. Can't take any chances. *Better to err on the side of safety.*" Her voice rises falsely high as she repeats the overheard words of a social worker from long ago—the words that inadvertently promised we'd never be going back to Pap-pap and Meemaw's house. "CPS might need to look into it for J.T. and Zoey's sake too. Make sure you're not moving your kids in with a pervert. What a hassle, huh? Once a rumor like that gets around . . ."

She stops there and lets me conjure the consequences on my own. My head swirls. I want to turn tail and run. My life with Paul, our happiness, our *peace* is worth more than any possession on earth. Even the farm.

I hear myself silently praying. Begging God to tell me what to do. To make order from chaos.

Words come. "You're not Mama, Gina. You're *not.*"

Our gazes lock, and we stare at one another for what seems like minutes, but undoubtedly only a few seconds tick by. My mind races with images of her face next to mine, the two of us forehead to forehead as we hide beneath the covers or in the closet on nights when storms raged—within the house or outside it. *Ssshhhh,* my sister whispers. *Go to sleep. I'll watch out.*

She's in there somewhere. I know it. *Ssshhhh,* I hear myself thinking.

Finally, she sinks to the desktop with an irritated sigh, her thin frame collapsing inward. "Fine. Be a jerk about it. I'll get your money for you. But I have to go back to work right now." She points over my shoulder, and I see Ramon waiting in the hall. "You'd be a lot better off my way, you know. We both would, but of course all you care about is what *you* want."

Despite everything, that sticks a knife in a tender spot. A lump rises in my throat. I swallow it and say, "I wish we weren't at this point, but I guess we are."

"I guess so." She returns a cold look. "Come back after five and I'll have your money, but if this ruins things for me with Merritt, I'll never forgive you."

I don't respond. I can't think of anything to say, anyway. I just gather the rest of the rental invoices, scoot the letter closer to her desk chair, close the folder, and turn toward the glass, where Ramon stands bug-eyed.

"What's in the box? More goodies from your lawyer?" Gina stops me before I can open the door. I've forgotten all about the box. Looking down at it in the chair, I'm overwhelmed with sadness. I consider picking it up and taking it with me, pretending it contains nothing more than paperwork.

"Meemaw left it on the shelf in her sewing room. She put your name on it. Her wedding dress is inside . . . and a few other things. She wrote you a letter." I turn to my sister again, seeking her reaction. Does she know the box was there? Does she care at all?

There's no hint of emotion. She's just . . . perfectly cool. Her gaze flicks past me. A middle-aged man has stopped to talk to Ramon in the hall. I recognize him from the larger-than-life photo on the billboard. This is Merritt Walker himself.

Worry lines crack Gina's cool exterior.

I take one last look at the box. "If you decide you don't want the dress, I'd like to have it . . . to save it for Zoey, at least." I hate myself for asking, but not as much as I would if I didn't try.

"Pppfff!" Her response chases me toward the door. "Of course I want it. Merritt and I are getting married too. You think you're the only one who can land a guy? At least I found one who's got something to offer."

I don't even answer. I can't. I just yank open the door and walk out, leaving my sister and the wedding dress behind.

CHAPTER 9

I'm sitting in the bookstore and Internet café across the street, just waiting, as I have been all day. I feel like a detective on a stakeout, only in a sad sort of way, since the fact that I'm here means I don't trust my sister. I circled the dealership before I left, and all the exits lead onto this one road. If I see her making a break for it, I'm not sure what I plan to do. Follow her, I guess. Make certain she's headed to a bank, rather than the nearest highway out of town.

Maybe she believed my threats and the letter from Vince, but in spite of the knock-down fight in her office, it feels like she gave up too easily. Part of me says she must have something up her sleeve. Part of me says she has a cushy deal here at Merritt Cars and she doesn't want to blow it by having me march in there and make it known to everyone what a shyster she is. She clearly wants to take care of this quietly.

That's to my advantage.

But Gina doesn't like to lose, especially to me. Aside

from that, I wonder where in the world she will come up with the money. Maybe she really will sell her Jeep.

The hours have been endless. I've read two books and talked on the phone with everyone I can think of, just to pass the time.

Fifteen more minutes go by. The five o'clock deadline looms close. What is my sister doing over there? Worrying away the minutes like I am, or loading up on ammo and excuses, so she'll be ready when I come back?

A sweat breaks over me, travels from head to toe, a kind of walking dread.

That's it, I text Paul. I've promised to let him know when I leave the coffee shop. I'm going over. I reason that it'll take me at least ten minutes to pay my bill, get in my car, and find a break in the rush-hour traffic.

Unfortunately, it doesn't. There's no one in line at the checkout counter and traffic parts miraculously, like the Red Sea. I'm in front of the dealership six minutes early.

When I step inside, it feels like the receptionist and everyone else are watching me. Is that my imagination?

I cross the showroom, turn the corner, and Gina is standing in her office with her chin held high and her teeth clenched. Behind her, her backup is none other than Merritt Walker. He's an imposing figure, at least six foot four, 280 pounds, and in middle-aged good shape. He eyes me with his arms crossed, a stern frown on his face. I can only imagine what my sister has told him about me. Gina has an amazing way of convincing people she's the victim.

It doesn't really matter what Merritt Walker thinks, and Gina doesn't introduce us, of course. She merely snaps the check off her desk and extends it my way. "Here. Maybe this will help you *get by* awhile."

I take it from her hand, notice it's written straight from the car dealership. Merritt Walker's signature is on the bottom. That's a relief. At least I know it won't bounce.

"You mean it'll take care of the taxes that weren't paid on the land. And the rest of the money due." An angry, wounded part of me yearns to say more, to spit out the truth in a great gush that would undoubtedly knock her boyfriend right out of his fancy Italian-leather loafers.

"Whatever you want to do with it," Gina says sweetly, but the tight-lipped smirk Merritt can't see is far from sweet. *Don't say anything more,* it warns.

There's no point, anyway.

I tuck the check into my purse. "Okay, well . . ." I'm a little stuck for a graceful closing line. Certainly not *thank you* or *I'll see you later.*

None of the things that should be said between sisters in parting.

The familiar regret tugs, like the pain of an old scar that won't let the skin stretch. Pap-pap and Meemaw would've hated the idea of our fighting over the land.

"Good-bye, then." I don't look at her. I really can't. She'll see that she still has a hold on me.

"Yeah, see ya. Take care of yourself." She continues the performance for Merritt's benefit, making *me* sound like the one with the screwed-up life.

"I wish you would've just told me about the land and paid the taxes, and it wouldn't have come to this." I can't help it. The sentence slips out. My voice cracks at the end.

"I really did think it would be better if we just sold it." For some reason, Gina's words ring true. "It's time to move on, and the offer on the property was good. I think you're going to be sorry you went this route."

"Well, at least now I can make the decision for myself."

It's time to end the conversation, so I square my shoulders, settle a hand over my purse, and walk away.

Curious glances follow me across the showroom again. People in Gina's new world clearly know *something* has happened. Maybe they all think I have leukemia, too.

Strangely, I feel both lighter and heavier as I reach my car. I'm just standing with my fingers on the handle when the dealership door swishes open behind me, and I catch a peripheral glimpse of my sister's blonde hair swirling on the wind.

I turn, and she's carrying the box from Meemaw's house. "You might as well have this." Nose crinkling, she shoves it my way. "I kept the pearl necklace that was in there, but I'd never wear this old thing at my wedding." She releases the box so that I almost have to catch it in midair.

An awkward stalemate holds us in place, neither party willing to fly the white flag or fire another cannonball across the battlefield.

My sister studies me as if I'm an alien life form she no longer recognizes. "Thanks for not saying anything more to Merritt."

"You should tell him the truth yourself."

A head shake indicates that I just don't get it. "You know, Merritt is a really decent guy. The past just needs to stay in the past, that's all."

I think of what Luke said about never being able to make a good life while you're running. "I hope things work out for you, Gina. Thanks for letting me have the dress."

"You're welcome." She says it begrudgingly, but then our gazes meet and she softens. "*You* need to leave things in the past too, little sister. Don't let Luke Townley screw it up for you and Paul. You're lucky you found somebody who really loves you, even if he's not sitting on a fat checkbook."

"I know I'm lucky to have Paul." And then for some reason, I feel the need to call it what it is. "Blessed."

Looking down at her red, high-heeled shoes, she hugs her arms around herself and glances back toward the dealership as if she knows we have an audience watching through the glass, and she feels the need to wrap up this conversation.

Yet there seems to be something more she wants to say. "Listen, I didn't keep it from you about Luke Townley because I was jealous. I mean, I *was* always jealous that he liked you the way he did, but . . . I wasn't trying to hurt you by not telling."

Again, there's possibly some underlying truth in all of that. Just enough to make the words burn soul deep. "How long have you known?"

"Always."

"Since we left Meemaw and Pap-pap's?"

"Since not long after."

"How did you know?"

"I heard Mama and Daddy fighting." She sighs, seeming to suffer a pang of regret. "I couldn't tell you. You were better off letting the Luke thing go. We were all better off."

"Why?"

For the first time, somewhere in that pretty shell, I see the sister who protected me when she was just a child herself. Who fed me when Mama was too drunk or stoned and Daddy was off doing whatever he did every time he walked out on us.

I feel like I'm standing in front of a firing squad blindfolded and waiting for the click of the trigger. What secret has my sister been keeping all these years?

Gina's expression suddenly deepens. The cool, glassy shield is gone. "Daddy told Mama the Townley boy's eyes were as big as baseballs when he saw our truck coming at him that day. Daddy didn't even see Laura in the truck, so she must've been bent over in the floorboard right before the accident happened, but he knew Luke saw who it was . . . and Luke knew our truck, anyway. Daddy and Mama were both afraid that if Luke did make it through all the surgeries, he'd remember what happened. They figured the less the Townleys were reminded of us, the less chance there was."

My stomach feels like one of the dishrags in Laura's kitchen, filled with dirty water and discarded food, slowly being squeezed dry. Filthy streams run everywhere, but through them comes clarity. Now everything makes sense. "The accident was Daddy's fault? Daddy ran them off the road?"

Even Gina seems to feel remorse over this disgraceful piece of family history. "After the DUIs, you *know* what would've happened to Daddy if he got caught again, Tandi. He would've been in prison. For a long time. And where do you think we'd have ended up then? Mama'd never held down a job, and she sure wasn't going to come back to Pap-pap's again when she knew they were trying to get custody. I couldn't tell you about the accident or Luke. I had to keep it secret."

You should've told. It would've been better if Daddy had gone to prison. But I don't say it. I understand the warped logic and misguided loyalties of a messed-up childhood. I know exactly where my sister was coming from. I've been there.

Instead of going to prison, my father ran out on us a few months later and eventually drank himself to death. I wonder who else he may have damaged before it finally happened.

I think of Luke, of what Laura has told me about him, about his life, and I'm overwhelmed with guilt. If my father had faced up to the truth, if my mother had told, if my sister had set the truth free . . . so many things could have been different.

"At least now I know," I say numbly, and then open the car door. The box with the wedding dress goes on the passenger seat beside the tobacco tin.

I tell my sister good-bye and back away, and she's still standing in the parking lot when I leave. I wish what has been broken between us could be fixed. Not all things are so easily made right, but the anger slowly cools. I feel it chipping off and falling away as I drive mile after mile, racing toward the Tidewater while the sun rests on long, lacy clouds near the horizon.

Some good can come of this, even now, even after all these years, if I can find Luke Townley. If he hasn't disappeared into the world again.

I try to call him, but there's no answer on his phone or Laura's.

I hold my breath as the scenery grows more and more familiar, and I cross marshes, sedges, and Tidewater irrigation channels. All around me, crops peek from the soil. Fresh, green leaves. New things from old.

A rebirth.

And then, up ahead, in the field across the road from the one where my grandfather grew long, straight rows of corn and sweet potatoes, there is Luke on the tractor. Boomer sits in the cab with him, the two of them turned around and watching the cultivator cut the soil.

I think of an old sermon my grandfather quoted from time to time—something about not looking back when you're plowing a field, but instead finding a mark in the distance and focusing on that. Otherwise, the rows won't come out straight.

I understand the meaning now in a deeper way. Both Luke and I have spent far too many years looking back, wondering if something could have been different that bittersweet summer when everything changed.

But it's time to look forward. Hatteras Island, with its storms and its recoveries and its hardy, determined people has taught me one overarching lesson, and I know I must not only remember it but live by it. The past must be let go before the future can be grasped.

I feel the burden lifting as I hurry from the vehicle and step over the ragtag fence to flag Luke down before he turns to plow another row. He sees me and waves. My heart beats fast as he stops the tractor at the edge of the field, releases the hydraulics, and turns off the engine. Quiet settles over the field after the tractor wheezes to a stop.

The evening Tidewater sun silhouettes Luke's form and Boomer's as they cross the grassy margins, but I am only lost in time for an instant. Just a heartbeat in which he and Boomer are what they used to be, and the future is still an expanse of sand, waiting for the tide to deposit things upon it and ripple it with the coming and going of days.

And then I am back in these shoes. My shoes. I am thankful for this life in which ashes become second chances.

"Hey." Luke slips his hands loosely into his jeans pockets, that wide white smile creasing his face, showing that he is both surprised and glad to see me here. "Thought you might be headed home to the Outer Banks right now."

"I was afraid you'd be gone already," I blurt.

He surveys the field. "Couldn't leave the job half finished. I'll be done in a couple days. Soon enough to move on."

"Maybe you shouldn't."

His gaze catches mine, and there's a strange hope there. I open my mouth to tell him why I've come back, but he preempts me with a question. "How did things go with your sister?"

"Good and bad. She had a lot of reasons, or excuses, depending on how you look at it, for what she did. But she managed to get together the money to pay what's owed on my part of the land. I'm keeping the house and the eighty acres, at least for now. Until I've had time to think it all through and decide what's best."

"Laura and Dale might rent the eighty from you.

With Dale working full time, and all the foster kids, the whole two hundred was a little much for them, but they probably could take on the eighty again and look after the house. The kids love the orchard. They pick the berries and the scuppernongs and set up a stand down on the highway, just like we used to. Remember that?"

The memory is as clear as yesterday. The image of us, sun bronzed and dirt covered and knobby kneed, separating our bounty into crates and pints, arguing about who picked the most—this will always be as sweet as the ripe fruit of the mulberry trees.

Its lingering syrup tempts me, but I settle for only a taste. "Luke . . . Gina told me something you need to know." I don't wait for him to answer, but rush through repeating what I've learned from my sister about the accident. Each word is like a brick, settling on my shoulders, mortared together with heavy globs of guilt. If we hadn't come home that summer . . . if I had ever admitted to a teacher, a neighbor, a social worker, that my father was frequently too drunk to navigate, and Gina and I drove him around, maybe he would've been in jail that day, not weaving down Mulberry Run Road.

Maybe I could have prevented everything that happened.

But if that thought ever occurs to Luke, he doesn't let it show. He looks down at the ground, as if he's combing the blades of grass, expecting to dig up answers. "I don't remember any of that. I just . . .

the last thing I remember was Laura and me goofing around in the truck. We knocked over the sodas, and Laura was bent down, trying to throw napkins on the mess, and I reached to grab one of the cups before it spilled any more. That's the last thing I knew. We all just figured I ran us off the road and the truck flipped."

"You were avoiding my *father*," I tell him again, but he still looks as though he doesn't believe me. "Gina heard my parents arguing about it. Luke, if you hadn't veered into the ditch, it would've been a head-on collision, and you'd probably all be dead." My throat swells, and I can't say everything I want to say. I finally manage to whisper, "I'm . . . I'm so sorry."

"It's not your fault, Tandi."

I swallow the thorny mass of blame and regret. "And it's not your fault either." My arm bridges the space between us as I touch his shoulder. Boomer sits at his feet, resting against Luke's leg, sensing the tides of pain that still ebb and flow within this man. "My father's damage has to end here, Luke. *We* have to end it. I want you to be happy. I want both of us to be happy. It's the only way we stop living as his victims and start owning what's ours."

Luke nods but doesn't speak. Instead, he reaches for me, and we share the embrace of old friends, while the dog leans burrows close.

"You go make a good life, Tandi Jo Reese," Luke whispers into my hair. "A really good life."

He softly kisses the top of my head before we part.

"I will if you will." I reach out to cup his face and smile into blue eyes where the clouds seem to be parting . . . or I hope that's what I see. "I need you to be okay."

"I think I am." He nods and grabs a breath of the warm, wet air, his body expanding with it. Taking my hand between his, he holds it a minute, then lets go. "I think I will be."

We say good-bye, and I turn away, walking down and up the ditch we once crisscrossed on bicycles and red wagons and farm tractors, Luke Townley and me. This land bears the tree castles of childhood dreams, the blood of skinned knees, the imprints of bodies gazing at stars, the sweat of summer days, the tears of broken hearts, the fairy dust of first love.

I feel all of it as I slip into my car, buckle the seat belt, and take one last breath of the old home place before turning the key. Outside, the tractor rumbles to life and Boomer's excited yips cut the air, but I don't turn to watch Luke and the dog as they disappear into the dust of the rich blackland soil.

I'm through looking back.

There's incredible freedom in that, and now I realize that a chain I didn't know I still carried has been cut free. I'm fully ready now. Ready to become Paul's bride. To start this new life with no shadows in it.

I touch the box with my grandmother's wedding dress inside, and the old tobacco tin with its strange bone beads and ancient lace, a link to Meemaw's people far off in the deep hollows of the Blue Ridge Mountains. A thread somehow tied to my past. A mystery I'll carry with me into the future.

Passing by the old farmhouse, I smile at reflections in the windows, imagine bringing Paul and the kids here to spend time, to learn the stories, to harvest the scuppernongs and the mulberries. I think of Meemaw and of Pap-pap. I realize that those who have loved us are never really gone. They live on in all the ones we love and all the ways we love.

They are the reason we know how to love at all.

The Sandcastle Sister

CHAPTER 1

"Paris," he says, and his blue eyes slant my way, accompanied by a contemplative smile as a few almost-black curls whisk his forehead. His tongue touches his teeth, as if he's sampling the idea and likes the taste of it. "Springtime in Paris, Jen. It has a ring to it, you have to admit."

"Evan . . ." I give him *the look*. It's meant to be a gentle reminder to focus on business. We're at the Bath Literature Festival in the south of England, for heaven's sake. Home of Jane Austen. Setting of *Northanger Abbey* and *Persuasion*. The crowds here are huge. The books are many. Evan's readers have come in droves. It's literary paradise. Is there a better place to be fully present in the moment rather than thinking ahead?

Yet there he sits, on the other side of the table in a sidewalk coffee shop, his mind on Paris. Of course I know why, but I'm trying not to bring it up. I don't want to argue. Not here. Not in this gorgeous place.

He sulks in his seat, and for a moment he looks like a little boy who's been told he can't have what he wants at Toys"R"Us—the sort of boy who's *used* to getting what he wants and doesn't take no for an answer. If I didn't fully understand that about him before Vida House Publishing sent me along on this three-month book tour—which has somehow stretched into an off-and-on six months—I know it now.

When Evan Hall wants something, he pursues until he gets it.

And he wants me.

The feeling is mutual. I'd have to be crazy for it not to be. He's the devastating trifecta of talented, gorgeous, and smooth. Not to mention rich, famous, and nice to be with.

For all those reasons, he scares me to death.

I suppose I convinced myself that the chemistry brewing between us as I edited *The Story Keeper*, the novel for which he's now on this multinational book tour with only short breaks back home, was a passing distraction. I saw it as a misty, nebulous thing, thickened by too many after-hours talks about the manuscript. I thought it would dissipate once the book hit the shelves and Evan left on the tour, vast distances separating us. The completely unprofessional attraction would then stretch thinner and thinner until it finally broke. Evan would be busy with crowds of adoring readers. I'd be in my small, safe corner office at Vida House, looking for my next bestseller and telling myself we were all better off this way.

Then my boss sent me on the tour—flat informed

me that, if I valued my editorial position, I'd go. Evan wanted me along for the ride; he felt I deserved it, after all the hard work to bring the book to print. I wasn't given the option of saying no, so I packed my suitcase and told myself that the stresses of travel and book events would kill this romantic undercurrent deader than a fly at a state fair bake-off.

Put two people together in a pressure cooker long enough, and they'll get tired of one another.

Yet here we sit.

He's waiting for an answer, and I know the question without his having to repeat it. He's suggesting that, as soon as he's done speaking at the lit fest's "Afternoon Tea with Evan Hall," we blow off the evening cocktail soirees and hop on the Eurostar. In just over two hours, the high-speed train could deposit us in the City of Love.

The perfect place for a wedding.

Something romantic and wildly impulsive.

"Come on. Don't overthink it," he urges, and his eyes twinkle, curls falling over them again before he leans closer across the table. "Say yes this time."

My heart hammers. I can't catch my breath. "I'm scheduled for the Jane Austen walking tour tomorrow," I blurt.

He cocks a brow, trying to make light of the excuse, as in, *Seriously? Did that just slip out by accident?* But there's something deeper in that look. He's disappointed. And hurt. He desperately wanted me to jump on board the train this time and leave all the baggage behind.

The baggage is exactly the problem. No matter how hard I try, I can't let go. I can't make the commitment he's asking for. I've backed myself into a corner, and I don't know how to get out.

"*That's* your excuse? The Jane Austen tour? That's all you've got?" He says exactly what I thought he'd say. He's joking, but he's not. A twitch of frustration tightens the muscles between his neck and jawbone. "Come on, Jen." He takes my hand, folds it between both of his on the table, so that our fingers intertwine, flesh to flesh. "What's *really* going on here?"

His gaze pierces me through, searching for an explanation. He popped the question in Florence a month ago, at the top of the campanile, as we stood taking in the ancient city in all its glory. There's magic in a sunset view of Florence. I was mesmerized by it. By him. I turned from the cityscape, and there he was, down on one knee with an antique sapphire ring he'd bought while I wasn't looking. *Marry me, Jen,* he said.

Yes, I answered in that dreamlike moment and then panicked before we made it down the 414 stairs to the ground. By then, Evan was already talking about the tour schedule and when and where we could slip off and make it official.

I started tossing out the road spikes to slow things down and haven't stopped since. In my family, marriage represents the death of every far-flung girlhood dream a woman has for herself. It's the end of planning for college or thinking about your fantasy job or deciding what you'd like to become. In the Church of the Brethren Saints, a woman's role is to mind her family, *keep pleasant* at all times, have children as fast as possible, and submit to everything her husband may demand of her, no matter what kind of man he is. Growing up, I'd never even *seen* a marriage that didn't include threats, intimidation, and abuse.

How can I possibly know how to create one?

Evan deserves so much more.

Letting my head fall forward, I exhale a long breath, shuddering without meaning to as long, wavy strands of dark hair fall over my shoulders and draw lines between us. Close up, they seem solid, like prison bars.

Just explain. Tell him. It's not like he doesn't know some things about the Church of the Brethren Saints. Evan Hall has lived in the Blue Ridge Mountains all his life. Of course he's aware that the Brethren Saints are cultish, odd, exclusionary, that they practice a perverse, twisted form of religion. Evan has seen my sisters in their old-fashioned, handmade dresses and carefully plaited hair and black stockings. He knows how worried I am that, while I'm away on this book tour, the Brethren Saints and my family will reclaim my youngest sister, Lily Clarette. I'm terrified that they'll steal her from her first semester in college and spirit her back to the holler and the church.

The picture taunts me even now—Lily Clarette, with her bright golden eyes and long dark curls. She looks like me as a teenager, and she's teetering on the same precipice I was at her age, after a scholarship to Clemson offered me an escape from our life in Appalachia. From where Lily Clarette stands right now, it's either fall back into the pit of all that is familiar or walk the hard road to the outside world.

If I marry Evan, it'll stir up a hornet's nest. The family will be that much more determined to lure Lily Clarette home, to march her down the church aisle, re-baptize her, and marry her to a man of the Saints before she can follow my example and permanently break the faith. I can't protect her from half a world away. If Evan and I wait, take a while, hopefully I can ease things along when the time comes.

"There's so much to think about, Evan. So many decisions to make." I chicken out, settle for the easier issues and use them to eclipse the harder ones.

"For instance?" I can feel him analyzing me. His doubt is palpable. He's adept at speed-reading people. It makes him a fabulous writer . . . and a frustrating fiancé.

"Okay, for instance: You've got Hannah to raise." Following the DUI prison sentence of his black-sheep brother, Evan has assumed responsibility for his niece, which has made this book tour that much more trying. Long-distance parenting isn't ideal, even with the dedicated support of extended family. "It's her first year in middle school. She's excited about softball and about going out for cheerleading this spring. You can't move her away from Looking Glass Gap, not when she's finally starting to open up and make new plans. But my job is in New York. I *love* Vida House. I love the publishing business. I love being in the middle of it. I'm a New York City girl." These things are all true, but they're so far from the heart of the problem, an arrow through the middle of them would barely be a flesh wound.

He scoffs softly, his fingers toying with mine. "Jen, you can work remotely. And you can go to New York anytime you need to. Or want to. There are these things called airports. . . ."

"Very funny." I look up at him, bite my lip against a smile. He has a way of making me laugh, then skillfully catching me off guard. I love and hate this about him. He's just so bloomin' . . . good. "Yes, there are airports."

"Exactly."

Touché. He knows he's just rendered that argument dead on the field of battle. Several team members at Vida House cyber-commute. Editors and literary agents all over New York are doing it now.

"Jen, it's not like I can't afford—"

"And there's that, too. Evan, I bring almost noth-ing to this marriage right now. Financially, I mean. It's all *yours*. The house in Looking Glass Gap is yours. If I move there, even the vehicle I'll be driving will be yours. I don't own a car. After putting the money aside to help Lily Clarette with college, I can't buy one, either. I can't even pay for a wedding. And it's not like my family's able to do it . . . or would if they could."

He gives me a look that's older and wiser. Every once in a while our ten-year age difference bothers me. He's been through so much, had so many experiences, traveled the world, been a superstar since he wrote his first novel in college and hit it big with the Time Shifters series. We're at completely different places in life.

"Jen . . ." The single word envelops me, and I'm struck with one undeniable fact. I love Evan Hall down to the marrow of my bones. "Do you really think I care about any of that?"

"No."

"Is it that you want to take the time to plan a real wedding—big church, guest list, flowers, the whole nine yards? If that's what you want, Jen, we can do it that way. I understand how important all the pomp and circumstance is on the female end of this thing."

"Evan Hall, you know me better than that. I am *so* not a girly girl."

"Good. Then let's go to Paris and get married in jeans. We'll say our vows barefoot. In the park. That's how my mom and dad got married. We'll follow the hippie tradition."

"I probably have relatives who got married barefoot too . . . but not because they were hippies."

The two of us laugh together and fall back in our chairs, breaking the tension. A tug on my hand pulls me close again, and he kisses me, and when the world finally stops spinning, I whisper against his lips the one thing I know is true. "I love you, Evan."

"I *am* going to marry you, Jen Gibbs. It might as well be tomorrow. In Paris."

My cell phone rings on the table, and I bolt upright as if it's a tornado siren on a windy day.

Evan rolls a look my way, recognizing the diversionary tactic.

Can he see that *yes* is on the tip of my tongue? Can he sense it in the lingering taste of the kiss?

"What in the world?" My mind clears, the mist vanishing like fog on a windshield as I push the button and answer. "Lily Clarette? What time is it there?" The real question is, why is she calling?

Even Evan registers a note of concern.

"How is every-thang?" My baby sister's Carolina mountain drawl seems so out of place on the streets of Bath. It's a reminder of home. I realize how much I've missed Lily Clarette these last few months during the European tour.

"It's good. Really good." I hurry through a few details about the book tour and the sights we've seen, but I'm barely conscious of what I'm saying. My mind is conjuring reasons for this call. *Please don't let her tell me she's dropping out of college and moving back to Lane's Hill.* Last I heard, she was having a tough semester and was too shy to haunt her professors' doors for help.

"I miss ye-ew." She stretches the last word, sweetens

it in a way that's suspicious. During the year she lived with me in New York, I came to know the baby sister I'd barely seen since I left Lane's Hill at eighteen. I've spent enough time with her to know when she's trying to broach a subject I won't like.

"I miss you too. How are things looking at Western Carolina U today?"

Evan kisses my hand, folds it in his lap, looks toward the café railing and notices a knot of fans standing there, comparing him to the photo on the back cover of one of his Time Shifters books. He gives my fingers a last squeeze, stands up, and walks to the barrier to oblige an unofficial book signing.

His smile is arresting. He chats and teases. Women swoon.

The heat of jealousy rises beneath the collar of the swaggy wrap sweater I've donned with my jeans and boots on this unseasonably lovely March day in Bath.

I want to walk over there and stand beside Evan, rest a hand in the crook of his elbow, and stake out my territory. The urge catches me by surprise, but it's potent.

You're the fool who hasn't married him yet, a voice whispers in my head. *What if he decides he's tired of asking?*

Would he? Could it happen? If I can't get over these irrational fears and trust that he really loves me and that it's possible to leave past family patterns *in* the past, will Evan just . . . move on eventually?

Lily Clarette is chattering about her history class, telling me that the teacher is her favorite prof and she's been working like crazy on what will be her end-of-semester research paper. "He said we could write anything about North Carolina history, so I ask him if I could do my paper on Mama's people, the Melungeons, and the carved necklaces like the one Mama left for us girls." Evan's new novel has created something of a firestorm involving the possible origins of the "blue-eyed Indians" of Appalachia. It's a mystery with ties to our family, but we don't know in exactly what way, and my mother isn't around to tell the tale. Lily Clarette is naturally curious about it. "Some readers who liked Evan's book have sent information to Vida House about the Melungeons in their own fam'ly roots. A couple of them have story keeper necklaces in their fam'lies, just like we do. I thought if I could track down those folks, it might help us find out more about Mama's people, since we don't know anythin' about that side of the fam'ly. . . ." My sister is talking a million miles an hour now, spilling information about her discoveries as she's tunneled into the murky sludge of our past.

"Listen a minute," I interrupt her finally. Alarm bells are going off in my head. As the eldest, I know the most about the background of the mother who left us not long after Lily Clarette was born. The sum total of my information doesn't amount to much, but what little I do have scares me.

"Did you know that Mama had a brother?" Lily Clarette bursts out.

I need some sort of transatlantic reach. I want to grab my sister and turn her squarely in another direction. "Yes, I knew that. Mama's brother showed up at the farm once when I was little." I remember the ragged-looking teenage boy with caramel-colored skin and stark hazel-gold eyes. My mother hugged him until I thought he might break. She called him Robby. "He wasn't there very long before Daddy came home and kicked him out. Mama and Daddy argued over it." I don't go into the gory details of my father taking up the long rod and using it to properly subjugate my mother for letting someone into the house without his approval. Lily Clarette doesn't remember any of that, though the rod didn't leave the household when my mother did. The rod is part of life among the Brethren Saints. Long rod for major transgressions. Short rod for minor ones.

"His name's Rob. I sent him a letter."

"Lily Clarette!" I gasp, and by the railing, Evan glances away from his fans, one eye narrowing warily. I lower my voice, turn a shoulder, and hunch over my chair. "That's not a good idea. People around the church used to talk about Mama's family, okay? There was some scary stuff." I hate acquainting my innocent nineteen-year-old sister with this part of our history, but it's better than letting her be lured into something she can't handle.

"I know that, Jennia Beth." She uses the double name I grew up with. "Folks around the church *still* talk."

"Then you understand why you should stay away from Mama's family."

"Just because I send the man a letter doesn't mean I'm gonna invite him over for Sun-dey dinner," she snaps. I'm surprised. That isn't like Lily Clarette. "Anyhow, he answered me."

"What did he say?"

"He's in prison for drugs . . . and for breakin' into a convenience store."

I feel sick. "Oh, Lily Clarette, please don't—"

"Just listen a minute, 'kay?"

"Okay." *Please, God. Please let this be some sort of strange dream. A nightmare. I wrestle my little sister away from my father's family, and now she's in touch with my mother's? How can this be happening?* "But I don't like it at all."

"Did you ever hear that Mama had a sister?"

"No. The only person I ever saw from Mama's family was the one brother, Robby."

"The sister was lots younger than Mama and Rob. Her name's Rebecca Christine. She's just a few years older than you, really."

A fist is slowly tightening around my throat. There's more going on here than Lily Clarette doing a little research for a history project. She's digging up the family graves, sorting through the bones and the relics. She's trying to figure out who she is. Who *we* are.

"You learned all this from one letter to this . . . this Rob? Are you even sure you've got the right person?"

She could be writing to some creep, some con man, pretending to be my mother's brother.

"Yeah, I'm sure. We talked on the phone a couple times."

"You're sharing *phone calls* with this guy?" How much does he know about my sister? Are there return addresses on her letters? There must be. He could track her down . . . or have someone else come for her.

I have to stop this. Now.

"I wrote to a lady I think is Rebecca Christine." My sister adds fuel to the fire. "Rob didn't know for sure where she was livin' now, but he said she works on boats and stuff and lives over on the North Carolina coast somewhere, and this lady I wrote to has a boat shop in Elizabeth City. I found it on the chamber of commerce website. I figure it's gotta be her."

"What did she tell you?"

"She didn't answer. I called and left a message the other day. She didn't answer that either."

"Maybe she doesn't want anything to do with all of this. Or maybe it's not even *her*. Or maybe this *Rob* is making up the whole thing, just to pull you in." Has he asked Lily Clarette for money? Care packages? Help getting out of jail?

How long until he's released? Is that scheduled to happen anytime soon?

"How many Rebecca Christines can there be in North Carolina by the water?" my sister persists.

"More than one, probably." The name strikes me

now. *Rebecca* and *Christine* are the saints' names of my two middle sisters, Coral Rebecca and Evie Christine.

My mother named my sisters after a sibling she'd left behind when she married my father?

"I'm gonna drive over there and try and find her next week durin' spring break. I might stop by the prison and see Rob, too. I gotta ask him about something face to face. I need to know if what he told me's true."

I have to go home. Now. I have to take control of this before something terrible happens.

My mind begins rushing through flight schedules, international airports, paid vacation days. What will the big boss say about my abandoning Evan for the last leg of his tour?

There's only Paris left. He can handle Paris without me.

Paris . . . the wedding question. Will Evan think this is just another excuse?

The sapphire ring glitters up at me, asking questions. *What if Evan finally gives up on you? Could this be the breaking straw?*

"What? What did Rob tell you, Lily Clarette?" A chill slides through the weave of my sweater and crawls up my arm. I realize there's a shadow blocking the sun. Evan's.

"That Mama had a baby when she was thirteen. Rob said Rebecca Christine *isn't* really Mama's sister, even though she was raised like it. She's not our aunt. She's our *sister*."

CHAPTER 2

Heathrow Airport is a madhouse, travelers with luggage whizzing by, flight delays flashing on overhead screens, cell phones ringing, ticket agents calling, "Next, please. Next in line, step up." Voices, shuffling feet, luggage wheels, and conveyors mingle in a deafening hum of white noise.

Outside the glass, it's a dank, foggy London evening. The lonely, mournful kind that's perfect for curling up by the fire with a cup of tea and someone special. I feel hollow and guilty, leaving Evan here like this. Alone.

"I'm sorry." My eyes sting as he sets down the bags and sighs, looking as miserable as the wet London weather.

"I know." He hasn't complained about this. Not once. He's been a trooper through all the scrambling around, the looking for flights, the mad dash to Heathrow so I could catch the most direct one.

He hasn't once argued about abruptly ending the talk of Paris in the springtime.

Yet disappointment radiates from him like heat from an ember—invisible evidence of something smoldering. Does he really understand?

All those women following him around today . . . the superfans. There will be just as many in Paris. . . .

He whisks a glance toward the lines nearby. We both know I need to get in one, *now*, if I'm going to make my overnight flight across the ocean. "I really don't like the idea of your doing this alone."

"I'm not going there to join in on Lily Clarette's crazy plan. I'm going there to talk some sense into her. It's a bad idea. I can feel it."

"Me too," he agrees. "Call me when you land in the US."

"I will."

"And when you get off the commuter flight to Greenville too."

"Okay." Evan has already made arrangements for his farm manager in Looking Glass Gap to take a car over to the airport. It'll be waiting when I get there.

His hand cups my face, his long fingers sliding into my hair. I lean into his palm. A lump rises in my throat, so that I can't speak. Instead, I grab handfuls of his nicely pressed shirt. It's a casual blue color that matches his eyes.

Someone bumps me from behind, and I barely even feel it. Neither of us looks away. Evan's voice is soft and intimate, almost a whisper against my hair. "I didn't realize how much I'd gotten used to having you around."

"Me either." As happens so often, he has mirrored my thoughts. After weeks of nonstop interaction on this European leg of the tour—planes, trains, automobiles, and appearances—it has just hit me that tomorrow morning I won't glance across the table over coffee and scones and find him there, giving me *that look*. "I love you, you know, Evan. I really do."

Does he know? Does he believe it? Does he understand how much I want to figure out how to love someone the *right* way, even though it scares me to death?

"I'll take that as a yes."

"Yes to what?" Is he teasing or serious? I can't tell.

"The question I asked in Bath . . . and in Rome . . . and in Florence." He lists the cities of our discontent—the ones where he suggested something impulsive, but fear held me rooted right where I was. "Don't go falling for some mountain man while you're up there in Cullowhee with your sister." A smirk and a wink tantalize me.

"I've already fallen for a mountain man." It's a bad time to be heating up the conversation, but I can't help it. I tug the handfuls of his shirt like I'm threatening him. "You watch out for those Paris women, mister."

"Those Paris women can't hold a candle." He kisses me long, then turns me toward the terminal, holding me by the shoulders as if he's bracing me up. "Go. Before I change my mind."

CHAPTER 3

Fifteen hours, two connections, and one parking lot shuttle later, I'm calling Evan from the driver's seat of a red Jaguar F-type convertible. His drowsy hello makes me laugh. I know that sleep-deprived voice. The man is a night owl. I can't count how many times, while working with him on edits for *The Story Keeper*, I paced the floor, waiting until what I thought was a decent hour of the morning to call him, only to discover that he was still out cold, having worked most of the night.

"Hi, sleepyhead. I just wanted you to know I made it to Greenville. This is some car, by the way. I thought you'd have Mike bring me one of the SUVs."

I actually wish he had. The Jaguar intimidates me a bit. I know this car is Evan's pride and joy.

He yawns, and I drink in the cozy sound of it. I try to imagine what it would be like to wake up with someone morning after morning after morning . . . every morning for the rest of my life. "I thought the car would be a nice surprise."

A warm feeling sprinkles in. Suddenly I'm no longer tired, sore, and neck-stiff from plane sleeping. I feel giddy and light-headed. "It was. Thanks."

The line goes quiet, and I wonder if he's fallen asleep. "Evan?"

"What? Huh?" The words are thick and slow. "Sorry. Late night."

The jaws of insecurity bite down hard, teeth sinking in. He didn't have a book event last night. I purposely sent a quick text instead of calling when my first flight landed—the layover was short, and besides, I didn't want to disturb him if he was sleeping in. Apparently he might've still been up. Why? "You made it to Paris okay?"

"More or less. Can't remember what time the train got in. Had something on my mind, anyway, so I stayed up overnight and worked on it. Just crashed a few hours ago."

"I'm sorry I woke you up. Go back to sleep. Get rested for your event this evening. Don't sleep through it, okay? If you're AWOL, my name will be mud for leaving you there." It's easier to talk business, but what I really want to say is, *I miss you. I miss you already.*

"Yeah, yeah," he drones.

"Evan, I'm serious. Set an alarm or something. Now you're scaring me." The editor-slash-handler in me takes over.

I hear bedsprings squeaking, imagine him settling in at some swanky but charmingly antique Paris hotel.

He loves places with history, so that's what the publicist has booked for the most part. "You just take care of my baby. You. Not the car."

I stop with some quip halfway to my mouth, choke up a bit. Can all of this really be happening to me? *Me?*

Evan Hall is the kind of dream that doesn't come to girls from the deep hollers of Lane's Hill.

It's *I love you, I love you,* and a good-bye. Then I'm off to Cullowhee to find my little sister and stop a collision of past and present that's more likely to bring about disaster than anything else.

The drive in the thick morning fog takes longer than it should. On the way to Cullowhee, I wind along through the rustling river valleys and over the craggy peaks of Appalachia. I mentally review all the good reasons my sister should *not* be involved in this thing she has planned. As always, the Blue Ridge swallows me whole. The mountains are quiet and bare, still wearing their winter cloaks of brown. Only the pines add color. This early in the year, even the redbuds and dogwoods haven't bloomed. Here and there, a few wild daffodils offer splashes of paint along the roadsides. The rivers are swollen with snowmelt, icy water bubbling beneath fog.

Memories ferry me along, the way the currents would carry a leaf, tossing it, tipping it over, swirling it round and round and round until it's drenched and shapeless. I think about Mama, though on the plane last night, I vowed that I wouldn't go there, even in the private darkness of my own mind.

It's time to give up wondering about her, I've told myself over and over. *You can't blame her for what she did. She had no resources, no one to rely on or ask for help. No one who wouldn't take her to the elders of the Brethren Saints to cleanse the devil from her . . .*

It's not like anybody would have helped her get treatment—recognized the symptoms of postpartum depression in danger of becoming postpartum psychosis. By leaving, she probably saved all of you . . . and herself.

She wasn't in any shape to take six kids with her. . . .

I've accepted this rationalization—for her disappearance and for the fact that we never heard from her again and have no idea where she went after she left us. We don't even know whether she could be out there somewhere yet. We probably never will. None of us have ever had the courage to dig very far into it.

Until Lily Clarette. Studious, plucky, incredibly smart Lily Clarette. The one who loves science and now plans to become a pharmacist, so she can graduate and move back to Looking Glass Gap to keep the old Mountain Leaf Pharmacy open. It's the only pharmaceutical outlet left within an hour's drive, and locals need it to be there. Lily Clarette wants to be the one to save the day.

It figures she'd also be the one to attempt dissection of our past. She wants to know the truth, and she's not afraid to go after it, even if the truth may hurt. Even if the truth may be that, after Mama left us, she formed another life, a good life somewhere else, and never gave us another thought.

Apparently she'd done it once before—left a baby behind. She gave that child to her parents to raise and kept it a secret when she married my father. A child born out of wedlock would have made her unacceptable as a potential bride for my father. It was trouble enough that she didn't come from the Brethren Saints, but merely joined in order to marry.

Could there be more half siblings who were born after Lily Clarette? Others out there who've never been told about us? Does this mystery half sister, this Rebecca Christine, know what happened to my mother? Did Mama go back to Rebecca Christine when she abandoned us?

In truth, if this woman was raised by Mama's family, or anyone close to them, chances are she's as much a mess as my mother was. If our situation was bad growing up, my mother's upbringing was absolutely unthinkable.

I lose track of the road and suddenly realize I'm taking a switchback curve way too fast. Evan's words whisper through the cab. *Take care of my baby. . . .*

Fortunately, the Jaguar is as nimble as its namesake. It hugs the pavement as trees rush by, and I take my foot off the gas and focus on the way ahead, not what lies behind. Around the bend, a black bear prowls by the mailbox of a sagging trailer house. I slow as I pass, feeling vulnerable in the tiny convertible. The bear could rip the top off this tin can in a heartbeat, but I creep along nonetheless, in case the animal startles and bolts into the road. I can just imagine telling Evan I ran his man-toy into a black bear.

"Yeah, that's the kind of thing that can test a relationship," I joke, grabbing my phone and pausing long enough to snap a photo for Evan. I can already see a caption in my head: *He said your car tasted delicious.*

Evan's deep laugh rumbles through my thoughts, and I chuckle along, deciding I'll send the text later in the day, so as not to wake him again. Before long, I'm almost to Cullowhee, anyway, and my tired mind refuses to call up the layout of Western Carolina University, where Lily Clarette is taking basics before hopefully transferring to the pre-pharmacy program at Clemson.

Rather than wandering around, looking for flags, stadium lights, and the clock tower, I let the GPS guide me in, then find visitor parking and call my sister to surprise her with the fact that I'm no longer half a world away.

CHAPTER 4

Lily Clarette slaps a pair of tennis shoes into her duffel bag and jerks the lid shut. I've never seen her so red-faced or this close to petulant. The whole time she lived with me in New York, we didn't even come close to having a fight. I've never heard her get forceful with anyone. Apparently my little sister has grown up in these few months as a college girl. She's become a woman. A woman who does not appreciate her big sister showing up unannounced in her dorm room.

"I'm not some dumb little child," she complains. The soft, complacent voice trained into women and girls of the Brethren Saints has disappeared. She sounds like any other local kid, her heritage evident in the Appalachian twang. "I'm makin' it through all my classes with straight As and Bs. I drive back to Lookin' Glass Gap every other weekend and work at the pharmacy, and I get there and back all by my own self. I can find my way to Elizabeth City and home without somebody babysittin' me."

"And to the prison to see Rob?" The idea of her walking through prison gates makes my blood run cold, not to mention all the other risks of her involvement with our supposed uncle.

"I decided that maybe wasn't a good idea." She sits down on the edge of the bed, lets her hands fall into her lap. Slump-shouldered, she looks more like the submissive girl I remember. More like she has been reminded that women must *keep pleasant* or else. I don't want to break her newfound spirit. I only want to protect her. How can I make her see the difference?

"You shouldn't be driving to Elizabeth City all alone. You've only had a license for six months, and you've never driven more than a couple hours from here. Elizabeth City is all the way across the state."

"Well, who was I gonna ask to come with me? It's not like I could call Marah Diane or Coral Rebecca or Evie Christine. You know how they all feel about Mama's family. And even if they wanted to go, Daddy wouldn't let it happen."

She reminds me that, not far from here, my father is still in charge of everyone and everything. Even now that my sisters' goat's-milk soap business brings more income into the family than the labors of most of the men, the women still have little say in the decision making. It's not a woman's place.

"So the family doesn't know anything about this?"

"No." She stares at her hands. "I wasn't even gonna tell *you*. I shouldn't've, but I thought if anybody remembered somethin' about Mama's people, you'd be the one. I didn't think you'd come running home all the way from Paris, France. Evan's probably mad at me now."

"Why would Evan be mad?"

"He was gonna marry you in Paris."

"How did you know that?"

"He told me." A blush colors the olive skin of her cheek. She looks so much like my mother right now, so much like the young Melungeon girl in Evan's latest novel. Our family ties to those mysterious mountain people show most in my youngest sister. In her, I can see the triracial mix rumored to have long ago created the Melungeons, who were known as neither black nor white nor Native American. The descendants of lost sailors, escaped slaves, and indigenous peoples—all three. There is still no one who can conclusively tell the story of Appalachia's "blue-eyed Indians" and how they came to be here before the first recorded European explorers pressed in. It's no wonder my sister is curious about that mysterious heritage and how it ties to my mother's family.

"Evan *told* you that?" I didn't know Evan and my sister ever talked, at least not since we'd left on the book tour, and no more than casually before that. Occasionally when Lily Clarette would answer the phone at my apartment, he'd tease her a little or something. . . .

The idea bothers me a bit. What other secrets is Evan keeping from me?

Then again, I've been keeping secrets too. I never mentioned my mother's family . . . until Lily Clarette's plan forced me into it.

"He called to ask me what size dress do you wear and stuff. If you said yes to Paris, he was gonna have everything ready there for y'all."

Two things strike me at once—intense guilt because I spoiled Evan's plans and amazement that he never said a thing about it when I told him I needed to fly home. He just . . . let me go.

How many men would do that?

Once again, I'm aware of how different he is from Brian, my one serious boyfriend in all those years in New York. With Brian, the relationship was a toxic mix of competition and control. When Brian wanted something, he laid on the pressure, the criticism, the silent treatment, the guilt trip—whatever it took to break me down until finally, I doubted myself and gave in.

Eventually it occurred to me that, yes, I was *living* a thousand miles from Lane's Hill, but I might as well be right around the corner, still under threat of a caning if I stepped out of line. Old patterns are hard to overcome. The easiest way to take care of the issue was to end the relationship and not seek another one. Problem solved.

Lily Clarette frowns, her eyes narrowing as if she's looking right through me. "You oughta go back. Tell him you're gonna meet him in Paris after all. His book tour's done in less than a week. Y'all could have a big ol' honeymoon there and probably charge it off to Vida House, even. Heck, George Vida would probably pay for it anyhow, he's so happy about how Evan's book is selling."

"Lily Clarette . . ."

"It's *Lily* now. Just Lily. Meagan says Lily Clarette sounds like one of the Beverly Hillbillies."

I'm gathering that much of my sister's bold new personality comes from her roommate, Meagan, who has already headed to Daytona for spring break.

"Lily . . ." Should I? Should I fly back to Paris? Get married on a whim?

I feel my feet rooting to the spot again. Hesitation tunnels downward from my toes, pressing through the cement and into the rocky soil of the Blue Ridge with impressive speed.

"Lily, we're talking about *you*. About this quest you're on. Digging into Mama's past is a bad idea. Do some research on the story keeper necklaces and the Melungeons if you want to and write about that. There's a museum over on the coast—I can't think of the name right now, but I can ask Evan. Anyway, they're working on the history of the carved necklaces, like the one in Evan's book and the one Mama left for us. Evan got an e-mail from the museum director there. They were interested in his research for the novel."

"I know. Evan already sent me the e-mail. I ask him about it when we talked about y'all and Paris. I was gonna go over there and visit with the museum people, dependin' on how long I ended up being in Elizabeth City. I've gotta get back here to school at least by tomorrow-week, so I can study for tests and stuff."

I run the timing in my head. Today is only Saturday. It's less than an eight-hour drive to the North Carolina coast, all of which means that my sister thought she might spend up to six days in Elizabeth City. She's been anticipating an extended visit—or hoping for one—with this mystery half sister. Either that or she's lying about plans to spend time visiting the prison. . . . Maybe she really was intending on a reunion with "Uncle Rob."

How in the world was she going to pay for all this travel?

"Do you have a hotel booked?" I fish for information.

Dark lashes lower evasively, hooding her eyes. "I figured I'd just . . . do somethin' when I got there."

"Do you have money for a room? And gas . . . and food?" Then it becomes completely transparent. It shows in her face. She's pictured that she'll knock on this stranger's door and be invited to stay. She's dreamed up a warm reunion with Rebecca Christine, just the way I'd once imagined tracking down Mama. In my childhood fantasies, I'd always found her settled into a little white house where there was a room waiting for me. I wasn't all that much younger than Lily Clarette when I'd conjured that glittery scenario. It had buoyed me through the awful years of taking on my mother's place in my father's household.

"Some," Lily Clarette mutters, suddenly dismal. Reality and I are crashing her party.

I cross the room, sit down beside her, smooth her long curls away from her cheek and tuck them behind her ear. There's not a stitch of makeup on her face, and she's so beautiful. I wonder if she has any idea. The world in front of her is an open highway to a million wonderful places. There isn't any reason to travel the dirt roads and rabbit trails of the past.

"Lily Cla—*Lily*, you know I admire how well you've done these past months, taking on the move to Cullowhee and living here in the dorm with someone you didn't know and learning to drive and . . . well . . . everything." Coming out of the Brethren Saints lifestyle is like stepping into a new universe. "But if you're determined to do this—to go to Elizabeth City and look for this woman—it's something we need to do together."

A tear seeps from her lashes and draws a trail down her cheek. Sunlight glints against it. "I just wanna know about Mama," she whispers.

I clutch my hands so tightly they hurt, tuck them between my legs, as if they're covered with some form of contamination.

"It's not a pretty story," I begin.

CHAPTER 5

We sit side by side as the Jaguar's engine sighs into idle. "You think this is it?" Lily sounds doubtful. All the young-adult bravado that brought us here has faded. She looks as meek as a kitten, huddled in the passenger seat. Maybe that has something to do with the fact that I've spent the last eight hours telling her everything I know about Mama's history and what our family life was like before she left us. None of this should make Lily feel any more confident in her quest to excavate the past.

The building in front of us doesn't help either. It's nothing but a small frame house with a squatty metal shop out back along a canal. We've had to ask around Elizabeth City quite a bit even to find it. The GPS directions took us to a dead-end road that led past some decaying trailer houses and into a bog appropriately labeled as part of the Great Dismal Swamp.

This place doesn't look much more encouraging. The windows are dark and grass has grown up in the gravel driveway, as if no one has been here in a while.

The sign out front does promise that we've made it to the home of J & R Marine Service. Some old outboard motors and boat parts lounge along the shed wall, but judging by the rust, they're nothing but relics.

"Maybe . . . they're just gone for the night," Lily suggests. "Maybe we should come back in the morning."

"I think so." I'm only too happy to leave, but not so enthusiastic about returning tomorrow. Elizabeth City is a friendly town—touristy and accustomed to outsiders—but I picked up a strange vibe when we asked around about the boat shop. People seemed a little reluctant to tell us where to find it. I'm still wondering what that meant.

"Let's get some supper and sleep on it." Maybe by tomorrow, I can talk Lily into a nice shopping day by the water and then a return trip to Cullowhee.

"Okay." Her face falls. Even after hearing the sad bits I was able to relate about Mama's family, Lily can't let go of something Uncle Rob told her in his last letter from prison—that Rebecca Christine will be so glad to meet her. Apparently Rebecca Christine has taken Rob in a time or two when he was down and out. She also helped him arrange some legal help on the robbery and drug charges.

I shift the car into reverse to back out of the driveway and at the last minute look in the mirror. A gasp wrenches out when there's a man blocking our way. No more than a silhouette against the setting sun, he's standing with his feet planted and a tool dangling from his hand. It looks like a scene from *Deliverance*. I decide that the tool is an ax.

I reach for the window button, but I'm too late to close us in. Avoiding a mud puddle that blocks the way to the driver's side, the stranger rounds our car and is standing by my sister's door in a heartbeat.

I lean across Lily and crane to see all the way to the top of the man mountain. He's at least three hundred pounds and six foot five, wearing overalls and a shirt with the sleeves ripped off. It would be funny, if it weren't for the small matter of mortal fear.

"Excuse us," I squeak, as in, *Dude, you've got about 2.5 seconds before we bolt. I'll run you over with the Jaguar if I have to, dent or no dent.*

"You need somethin'?" His voice is thickly accented and gruff, his face shadow-cloaked beneath a taco-shaped straw cowboy hat.

"We were just turning around. Sorry." *Out. Out of the way. Now.*

"We're lookin' for the lady who owns the boat shop. Rebecca Christine Fields," Lily interjects.

I can't *see* the man scowling, but I can feel it. "Ain't here. Don' know when she will be. Don' know if she's even comin' back."

"Thanks." *We'll take you at your word. See ya.*

"Do you have any idea where we might could find her?" My little sister is like a coonhound on a tree. And this man definitely qualifies as a tree.

"Lily!" I snap.

"He might be able to tell us somethin'." Trying to elbow me off her lap, she pushes her sweet face closer to the window. We stare at the axman side by side, like guppies in a bowl.

I wonder if he likes guppy. For dinner.

"We're relatives." Lily stretches out the last word, so that it has all the proper Southern syllables. About eight of them.

The man looks the Jaguar over from headlight to back bumper, resting the ax and a meaty fist on his hip skeptically. We probably don't look like relatives of anyone who lives in this place.

Lily's bony shoulder pokes into my neck as she strains to be free of me. "We drove all the way over from Cullowhee. I go to school there." She's laying on the backwoods charm so thick I can't help but think, *Who is this child?*

The hefty stranger softens some. "Relatives?" he mutters. "Thought you might be one of them people from the bank. Been a tough year for RC and Johnny."

"Oh, I'm sorry to hear that." What other choice do I have but to join the conversation? "Maybe we shouldn't bother them, then."

"Imagine she'd wanna know ya come all this way. She ain't here, though. Won't be back yet 'til a few weeks yander. Gone to the Outer Banks. Her and Johnny's got the maintenance contract on some boats over there. Get 'em all cleaned up and tuned this time of the year so the boats is ready for the rich folks when season comes. I keep an eye on their place for 'em." He motions across the street, swinging the ax as if it's a child's plastic plaything. Then I realize that it is. There's a little barefoot boy padding across the road from a house hidden in the pines. He's asking for his toy.

A laugh pushes up my throat, and I have to bite down hard to stifle it. I can't wait to tell Evan this story.

Lily Clarette whips out a piece of paper and we take down the name of the marina where the man thinks we can find Rebecca Christine. "Tell RC I said hey."

We thank him and abandon the driveway, watching out for kids, who are popping one after another from the brush. They stand in the road, ogling the Jaguar.

"Whoa, it's a race car!" A little boy beams. "I'm gonna have me one a them someday! Race car driver!" He adds steering motions and engine noises. He and his siblings, muddy-faced and barefoot, their hair tangled with dry grass and leaves, remind me of us when we were young.

I wave out the window as we leave, then gun the engine to give them a thrill once we're a safe distance away. The kids jump up and down in the rearview mirror, and race-car-driver boy waves an invisible checkered flag.

We wind back to town, grab supper, then go spend the night in a hotel. For a while, it's just like the good old days in New York. We discuss Lily's college plans. We talk about the publishing business. We talk about

Lily's favorite TV shows and campus activities. We discuss Lily's roommate, Meagan, an Army brat who has lived on three different continents. She has opened my sister's eyes to a whole new world, literally. We scroll through my iPhone and I show photos from the book tour, and Lily tells me what she knows about those places.

"You should've got married in Paris," she says finally. "Meagan says it's *so* romantic."

"Well, coming here was more important." I burrow into the Chinese takeout bag, dig up a fortune cookie, and crack it open, seeking a diversion. The fortune is an innocuous one about today being my lucky day, but I pretend to be interested.

Lily is having none of it. "So did he ask you about Paris?"

"Sort of."

"Did you say yes?" Her amber eyes grow wide with girlish fascination.

"We never finished the conversation."

Even at nineteen, naive and prone to taking things at face value, she recognizes an excuse when she hears it. No girl in love would pass up a proposal like that from a guy like Evan.

I search for a simple response. One that will stop Lily from asking all the questions I've already been horsewhipping myself with. "Look, Lily, both Evan and I know that we'll get married eventually. We just haven't found the right time yet."

"*He* thinks it's the right time." She breaks open a fortune cookie, reads the fortune, smooths it between her fingernails. I've never seen them manicured and painted before. The roommate's work, no doubt. "You wanna know what *I* think?"

Not really.

"I think you've got *trust issues*."

"Did you learn that in your psychology class?" As soon as it's out of my mouth, I realize the comment was snippy. I'm jet-lagged, exhausted, and all of a sudden I miss Evan in the worst way. "Sorry. I'm just tired. I think I'll get a shower and read a little while, okay?"

My sister nods, still looking down at her paper fortune. "Sure."

I stand up, clean my mess, and drop it in the trash can. Lily's words catch me as I move away from the table. "I didn't learn that in psychology class, though. I learned it from the college counseling office."

I blink, surprised. "You've been going to the counseling office? As in *counseling*, counseling, or just help with picking out classes?"

"The first kind. I needed to talk to somebody about stuff."

I lay a hand on her shoulder, lean down and hug her. "Lily, I'm so proud of you." My sister has found the courage to do what I haven't done in all these years. Face our past head-on.

She rests her hands on the table, picks at the nail polish as if she's still not quite comfortable with its being there. "I don't wanna live all my life messed up, y'know? I wanna be normal. To be happy."

Her hair feels like silk beneath my fingers. I remember the moment the midwife placed her tiny body in my arms, her skin still so hot from Mama's body, it seemed to melt right through the blanket, joining itself to mine. "I hope that for you, Lily. I do." She is so strong. She may be the youngest of all of us, but she's also the toughest. The only one with this kind of courage.

"You oughta hope it for *you*." She turns the fortune around, lays it on the table in front of me so that I can't help but read it. The advice is short, but applicable. A single line of type that sums up reality:

Everything you want waits on the other side
of fear.

Those words cling to me as the evening goes on, and I fall asleep thinking about them, taunted by a smattering of print on a bit of fortune-cookie paper. A scrap, really, but it identifies the part of myself that I like least. My one fatal flaw.

In the morning, the truth is still there, teasing the tip of my mind. I am a person who hides everything. Growing up, I learned to conceal myself behind a placid exterior. Stillness gives the appearance of confidence. I keep the inner voices hidden. I don't want the rest of the world to hear what they say.

But *I* can't stop hearing them.

How can I marry Evan if the outside is all I have to offer? He senses it, I know. Maybe that's why he's been pushing so hard on the impromptu wedding idea—he suspects that impulsivity is our only hope.

But I *can't* be impulsive about this. Not when the hearts and futures of others hang in the balance. Evan has already been through enough tragedy in his life, and on top of that, there's the little girl he's now raising. Hannah desperately wants a mother figure. She wants her uncle Evan and me to settle down together, create a family. She prays for it daily. I know that because she tells me at least twice a week, either in person or via Skype, depending on our locations.

"Oh, what is wrong with you!" I growl, running my fingers roughly into my hair and tugging until it hurts as I wait for Lily to finish grabbing a bagel at the breakfast buffet and make it to the car.

The hotel door swishes open, and I find my composure so my sister won't see the ongoing battle of self versus self. Outside input doesn't help, and I already know Lily's opinion anyway. She thinks I'm nuts for being here, rather than across the ocean. Maybe I am.

In short order, we're headed toward the Outer Banks. The day is clear and beautiful. We chatter about the sights, and Lily gasps in awe as we cross the bridge. The water looks inviting, even though it's only March. Looks can be deceiving. The waves will still be chilly this time of year.

As we reach the islands and begin the drive south and south and south, the scenery runs in direct conflict with the turmoil in my head. We pass seaside stores, massive beach houses towering on stilts, and rows of dunes that dwarf the sleek red car.

Lily suggests we put the top down, so we do, even though it's cool. The wind streams through our hair, and we look like we belong in this vacation paradise— as if we could be the owners of one of these monstrous, multistory beach homes.

Evan could buy one without even blinking an eye. Even that bothers me. There will be people who talk behind their hands. They'll say I used my position as his editor to worm my way into his life. There are already rumors around the industry that *I* was the one who insisted on joining Evan's book tour, not the other way around.

I shouldn't care, but the insecurities sneak in anyway. Growing up, being snickered at by the schoolkids because of my plaited hair and long, homemade dresses, I cultured a habit of worrying about what other people think. What they whisper just out of earshot. It's a terrible habit, but it's hard to stop.

As we draw near Hatteras Village, I leave off thrashing around in my own issues and begin wondering about this long-lost sister of ours. Is she really here on this island? Will we find her? What will happen if we do?

"Can't be much farther, I guess." Lily points as we

wind through Hatteras Village, surveying sleepy souvenir stores, water-sports rental stores lounging in the
early spring sun, a library, a fire department, a welcome
center. A sign indicates that the ferry landing is close.
One more mile and we'll drop off into the ocean.

We pass a few more tourist traps, most sitting dark
and quiet in the off-season. All of a sudden, the ferries
and the marina lie just ahead on the right. Both of us
lose our nerve at once. We decide to grab lunch at the
quaint shopping center positioned at land's end near
the docks. While we're eating, we watch boats of all
sizes come and go from the marina. Is our sister on one
of them? The place is larger than I'd imagined. What if
we're not even able to track her down?

Yet I know it's really the reverse I'm worried about.
I'm afraid we will find her and open a Pandora's box
we won't be able to close.

"I keep lookin' at everybody that goes by and won-
derin' if it's her." I barely hear Lily at first, but as I'm
tuning in, I can't miss the hope in her voice. She's been
building the meeting scene in her mind as we silently
watch the water, lost in our own thoughts.

"Lily, you have to be prepared for—"

"Don't say it, okay? I know it might not work out
like I want." She pushes back from the table as if she's
afraid I'll contaminate her.

The next thing I know, she's at the counter, asking the clerk for information. He's friendly and forth-
coming.

"Yeah, you might still catch RC." The guy gives her the flirty once-over, and I want to cross the room and shake a finger at him. It's still hard to think of my little sister as a full-grown woman. "RC kinda comes and goes. Sometimes she's out taking a boat into the shop, or she's at the house with Johnny." He continues on, telling us which slip number she was headed to when she came by for coffee this morning, then pointing us in the correct direction. "If there's not a thirty-eight-foot Contender in the slip, she's gone. If the boat's there, she's either on it working or she's gone home for the day."

The clerk looks at me as I come closer, then squints at Lily Clarette again. Is he seeing a family resemblance to RC or just wondering why we're here? He doesn't say, but he does watch us intently as we go out the door. I'm left wondering if it's just a flirt or if it means something.

The March wind gives us a bracing shove as we round the corner on the boardwalk. Far in the distance, there's weather rolling in. A nor'easter, maybe. I wrap my arms around myself as the breeze needles through my sweater, and beside me, Lily zips her jacket. It's as if the island has changed moods while we were in the café. Now it feels wet, cold, and uninviting. Even a little threatening.

My heart lurches as we find the right row and walk along it. Breath hitches in my chest and turns shallow. I strain to see around the hulls of other crafts, wondering if the thirty-eight-foot Contender is, indeed, in its place. At this point, I'm not sure what I'm hoping for.

And then, there it is ahead—the slip we're after, and it's not empty. A sleek-looking fishing boat rocks softly in the choppy water. The name painted on its stern seems almost an omen. *Discovery Girl.*

A pile of rags and a bucket rest on the dock near the boat's mooring lines. Bottles of Star Brite marine anti-freeze sit on the hull. Metal pings echo from the cabin.

Someone is inside.

My heart knocks against my breastbone like a wood splitter's ax, trying to open me up.

I hear Lily Clarette take in a breath. She flashes me a wide-eyed look. I wish I were as positive about this as she seems to be. Hope and dread are like Rock 'Em Sock 'Em Robots having a grudge match in my stomach.

"Hello?" Lily Clarette calls before we're very close. The use of mountain etiquette is completely natural to her. In Appalachia, you never approach a stranger's house unannounced. You're liable to get shot that way. "Hello in the *Discovery Girl?*"

The metal pings stop. No one comes out. Lily Clarette repeats her greeting, but this time we've stopped just a few feet away. I feel the dock rocking beneath my feet, or maybe that's the world shifting off center.

A silhouette bisects the sunlight at the base of the open cabin door.

Lily grabs my hand, but I barely feel it.

My mind stumbles through time, then loses its balance and tumbles end over end as a woman in jeans and a sweatshirt emerges. A shadow hides her face until the muted sunlight slips beneath the red bandanna tied over her dark hair. Other than the clothing, she's almost exactly as I remember her.

I see my mother.

I know it can't be her.

I have a feeling the woman on the water is thinking the same thing.

CHAPTER 6

C louds boil across the sky and thunder rumbles, not so distant now. We've been here on the dock, talking, forever. With the sun hidden in a thick blanket of clouds, I have no idea what time it might be. Other than finally sitting down, none of us have moved. RC is propped on an overturned bucket on the boat, and Lily Clarette and I are cross-legged on the dock. It is as if we are three dreamers, afraid to move. Each of us fearing she'll wake and the other two will vanish into thin air.

But this woman's life is hardly the kind of thing I would conjure, even in my worst nightmare. I doubt if Lily could have imagined that pasts like Rebecca Christine's exist. My little sister is getting an education in the sort of darkness that lives far off the beaten paths in the backwoods. By comparison, our twisted upbringing among the Brethren Saints seems routine, strangely sane, and almost cosmopolitan.

Where our half sister grew up, among my mother's family and actually just a few hours from our hometown, drugs were a staple and food was an occasional visitor. The ragged cabin in which my mother birthed her first baby without the aid of a doctor was home to any number of relatives and "business associates" who came to flop, hide out, or trade for drugs. One of those visitors was probably the man who got my mother pregnant at barely thirteen, but RC has no idea who her biological father is. She grew up thinking that my mother was her older sister and didn't learn the truth until years after Mama left the household.

As RC reached adolescence, she might have shared the same fate as our mother, if not for the intervention of an aunt who didn't do it out of concern for her niece's future. In reality, the aunt saw RC as romantic competition—she'd caught her husband peeping at RC, just twelve years old, in the outdoor shower. The aunt then spirited RC away, drove her down the mountain, and dropped her at a group foster home.

"That's when I found out who my mama really was," RC says as matter-of-factly as if she were reporting the weather forecast from twenty-five years ago. "Robby tried real hard to get me out of the foster shelter. He even tracked down your mama and asked her to come talk to child welfare and tell them she was my mother. He thought he could get me out that way."

"I remember the day Robby showed up at our farm," I admit. I was little then, but the encounter is still clear in my mind. I was old enough to be shocked that my mother had a brother, and then to wonder what my daddy would do if he came home and caught Mama with a teenage boy there. Likely as not, I figured, it wouldn't be good. "Mama sent us out of the house before I could hear what they were talking about and why he was there."

"I was the reason," RC tells me. "He came about me—to try to convince her to go after custody and spring me from CPS care."

According to RC, Mama begged her brother to vacate our place before Daddy saw. She couldn't let Daddy find out about the illegitimate baby she'd left behind. She must've known what kind of punishment and purification would be required by the Brethren Saints for a transgression like that. And it wouldn't only have happened to Mama. Such a revelation would've rocked the entire congregation. There was literally no telling how the elder council would have reacted or what would've happened to us kids. We were already walking a thin line because our mama was an outsider.

"I don't hold any ill will over it." RC picks at a ripped knee in her jeans and shrugs. "Here's the thing. If you keep looking backward, all the obstacles you think are behind you are actually still ahead of you. If you're bumping across the same things over and over, it's a sign that you're stuck in reverse." She winks and nods, tucking flyaway strands of wavy salt-and-pepper hair under her bandanna. She has the relaxed countenance of a woman who's made peace with her demons. I gather that she and her husband, Johnny, have lived all their adult lives around the sea. They've worked on boats, set up housekeeping on boats, traveled to some of the far corners of the world.

Lily hugs herself and shivers, blanched and shell-shocked by the family revelations. "I'm so sorry." Her teeth chatter, the words shuddering with the cold. "I feel like, if Mama hadn't had *our* family to worry about, she would've come back for you."

"Well, most people do what they can with what they have," RC observes. "I'm sure she was just trying to get by. And things worked out for the best. Those years in the group home weren't great, but they did give me a little taste of normal life. I knew enough to realize I didn't want to go back to what I came from . . . which might've been what led me to run off with Johnny when I was seventeen, but that's a whole other story. People said we'd never make it, but we were young and in love, and we thought we had it all figured out. God protects the foolish, I guess. Good people helped us because they could see we needed it. We worked hard. We did okay. I can't complain."

I look at this woman, my half sister, her hands red and raw from scrubbing boats so other people can enjoy them this spring, and she radiates contentment. Where does that sort of stillness come from? I wonder.

"I'm glad," I tell her. "I'm sorry we've never had the chance to meet before now. We never even knew about you."

She studies me, then smiles, the wrinkles around

her eyes testifying to many years in the sun. If Mama
birthed her at thirteen, RC is roughly four years past
my age, but she looks and seems older. I doubt she worries about it. There's no makeup on her face, and her
hair hangs from the bandanna in a long, loose braid.
"I knew about y'all, of course, but when your daddy
caught Robby at the house, he made it clear that none
of his wife's family were welcome there. Robby said he
felt lucky to get out with his hide, basically. I figured
things were better off left alone after that."

A puff of wind wafts by. Lily shivers again, and I
fold my arms tighter, tremors rattling my ribs. A fine
mist has started to fall. We need to abandon our spot
on the dock before we freeze to death. No doubt we're
interfering with RC's work too. Maybe she'd like to
meet for supper tonight? I do want to know her. I want
to grasp at the opportunity that has been denied us all
these years.

She seems to read my mind. Checking her watch,
she looks over her shoulder at the boat. "Tell you what.
I've got an hour or so left on the *Discovery Girl* here,
and then I need to run to the house and check on
Johnny. He was feeling poorly this morning. Why
don't y'all two enjoy the shops or whatever? I'll finish here, look in on Johnny, and then meet you up
at Sandy's Seashell Shop for some coffee in . . . say an
hour and a half? You'll love Sandy's place. It's an island
tradition."

We agree to meet at the shop later. Lily and I hurry

to the car and sit in the parking lot for a few min-utes with the heater cranked. We talk about what a strangely wonderful experience it was, meeting RC.

"She seems real nice. I just knew she would be, from what Rob said." Lily brims with excitement. "It's so sad how she was brought up, though. I thought things were kinda tough for us, what with Daddy like he was, and the church, and us never havin' much money, but we didn't go through anythin' like RC did. We're so lucky."

On any random day in the past, those words would've brought a protest from me. Now they feel like truth. I've spent so much time resenting the things that happened in my childhood—the abuse, the con-fusion, the fear, the manipulative twisting of religion, the constant berating and threats—that I've never con-sidered being thankful for the empty half of my cup. For things that *didn't* happen. I didn't go hungry. I wasn't forced to live in a drug den. I wasn't targeted by some pervert. I wasn't taken away by a jealous relative and dropped in a strange place.

I survived, and good people took an interest in me, and I was given opportunities. I got out.

Thank you, I whisper in the silence of my own mind as we pull out of the parking space to start back to the village. *Thank you for my life as it is.* I send the thoughts off in a simple prayer. There's a lightness in it, a sense that I really am okay.

Reaching across the console, I take my sister's

hand, smile at her as we wind past the placid waters of Pamlico Sound. Her skin is ice cold, but still it warms me. "I'm so glad we came."

Her smile is radiant. "Me too."

She asks if we can drive up to Fairhope and visit the museum that e-mailed Evan about the research for his book—Benoit House, it's called. Lily wants to see if she can learn anything for her history report, and we both know that the museum has in its collection antique necklaces like the one that inspired Evan's novel. They think there might be some connection to the original settlers of Roanoke Island's Lost Colony.

During our long conversation on the dock, Lily asked RC about the necklace my mother left for us girls. As with so much of Mama's history, we've inherited only bits and pieces. My sisters and I each have a single, intricately carved bone bead. We don't understand the significance of them, except that they've been in my mother's family a very long time and are somehow connected to our ancestry among the Melungeons. RC could only tell us that she remembered Mama having the necklace and that perhaps she got it from her grandmother.

Sadly, when we reach the little community of Fairhope, we meet another dead end in Lily's quest to uncover our history. There's a locked gate barring the driveway of the Benoit House Museum. *Closed for private event,* the sign reads. A catering van and a florist's truck sit backed up to the towering Victorian house.

The wraparound porch has been laced with ribbon and white roses, and in the upstairs turret window, a bridal gown hangs waiting. Obviously someone is getting married this afternoon.

My mind runs quickly back to Paris, to Evan, to where he might be and what he might be doing right now. I try to remember the trip itinerary and to decide whether it would be all right to call him. I don't want to bust an event. He's notorious for forgetting to turn off the ringer on his cell phone when he's giving a speech.

I'm sitting there, tapping my fingers on the steering wheel and calculating the time difference, when I'm suddenly aware that Lily Clarette is looking at me. I have a feeling she's reading my mind again.

By now, it's nine o'clock in Paris—not a good time to call Evan. He'll be at one of the last tour events, I think. There's an evening cocktail reception. Unless I've lost track of the schedule, there's one tomorrow, too.

I picture him in his tux, tall and lean, dignified until he grins and makes a joke about the monkey suit. Suddenly the yearning is so powerful, I feel it stab. It's a little dagger to the heart.

Why hasn't he called today?

Insecurity takes another nibble.

Out of sight, out of mind?

Then again, I haven't called him since I flew into Greenville yesterday morning. I've been so focused on Lily. By the time I thought of it last evening, it was the middle of the night in Paris. Evan could be dealing with the same thing, hence the lack of phone calls. Busy days, short nights. With no helper there to handle details, schedules, clothes, communication, he'd have to take care of everything himself.

And he mentioned catching up with some friends in Paris. . . .

Female friends?

Stop. Stop that.

Again, I'm conscious of Lily studying me. I put the Jaguar in reverse. "I guess we should get out of the way before someone else needs to come in."

"This'd be a beautiful place for a wedding," my sister says wistfully. Like most girls her age, she has watched endless episodes of *Say Yes to the Dress*. Every once in a while, she worries that she should have married the hometown boy my father tried to betroth her to at seventeen.

"Yes, it would. Bummer that it's not open for us to talk to them about the necklace today, though."

"Maybe we can come back tomorrow." A more-than-casual glance slides my way. "Unless you're gonna get on a plane back to Paris, I mean."

"Lily . . ."

Both hands fly, palms out. "I'm just sayin' . . ."

"Let's go poke around that little bookstore we saw the sign for—Buxton Village Books. If they've got a copy of Evan's novel, we'll snap a photo to send to him. Then we'll drive back down to Hatteras and find Sandy's Seashell Shop."

"'Kay." She leans toward the window, still watching the graceful old house as we leave it behind. "Wonder who's gettin' married today." She goes on to talk about helping with an upcoming bridal shower in the dorm and what kind of a wedding she wants someday. Her roommate is an expert in all things upscale matrimonial.

"Really, you girls shouldn't be so focused on it. It's not healthy. Get your education first, then think about finding a guy. Or better yet, just wait until it happens. When the right man comes along, you'll know."

"I don't wanna be, like, over thirty and livin' by myself with a dog." Does she realize that she's just described my life—before the book tour whisked me away, that is? Now, I haven't seen my apartment mate, Friday the Antisocial Chihuahua, in over three months. He's temporarily residing with my best friend, Jamie, in her apartment, but time is running out. Jamie will be getting married and heading off on her honeymoon later this spring.

Weddings are a running theme lately.

Maybe that's God's way of hinting at me.

"Take time for yourself first, Lily. Decide who *you* want to be—that's all I'm saying. As beautiful as you are, guys will be standing in line when you're ready to start looking."

"*Pfff!* That's not what Marah Diane says. She says it was the dumbest thing I ever did, not marryin' Craig. She says if I thought I *had* to go to college, I coulda done it at Community . . . or online at the library."

I grind my teeth, thinking of the backward advice that's thrown at Lily every time she goes home to Lane's Hill. My sisters' lives are a far cry from idyllic. "Keep in mind that Marah Diane got married at sixteen and a half and started having kids. Does she really seem happy to you?" When I visit the family, what I see for the most part is my eldest sister yelling at her children, criticizing them, and complaining about how much trouble they are. If she's mad at her husband, the kids take the heat because it's forbidden for a woman of the Brethren Saints to talk back to a man.

"She's better now that the goat's-milk soap is bringin' in some money." Lily contorts her legs into the seat so that she's hugging her knees and resting her chin on them. "But you're right. It's not good, the way things are—not for her or Evie Christine. Coral Rebecca and Levi do all right."

We wind along Buxton Woods in silence, the ancient maritime forest, with its loblolly pines and live oaks, sheltering the road from the mist and wind.

Lily Clarette sighs. "But if it'd be wrong for me to get married *because* of the fam'ly, it'd be just as wrong for you to *not* get married because of them."

"You think *that's* what I'm doing?"

"Yeah . . . I kinda do." She pulls a face, and clearly it hurts her to say something that might upset me. The other side of that coin is that she loves me enough to do it anyway. "I know you're always real worried about bein' anything like our people, but a bat-blind fool can see you love Evan and he loves you. Y'all two are perfect for each other."

We pull into the parking lot of the bookstore, and the conversation ends naturally. Inside the little shop, the proprietor is knitting a hat behind the counter. She's delightful and gives us a tour of the historic building, even showing us the notches in the exposed rafters—evidence that the tiny house was constructed from old shipwreck timbers. Lily snaps photos and I make a mental note that this place needs to be on the next book tour. It's just too good to miss.

We leave with a brochure about Hatteras Island, postcards, and a stack of Lost Colony material for Lily's history report. The storeowner also fills us in on the research project at Benoit House Museum. "You won't have much luck getting to talk to them the next few days, though," she warns. "The museum director is out of town, so there won't be anybody around but volunteer docents. They don't know much about exhibits that are still in the works."

We thank her for her help and move on. It's time for us to make our way to Sandy's Seashell Shop.

As we drive back down the island, Lily homes in on the Paris conversation again. But in the Sandy's parking lot, she seems to regret having brought it up. "You're not mad at me, are you?"

"No, of course I'm not mad at you. I know you're only saying it out of love."

"'Kay."

We go inside and peruse the selection of seaside treasures offered up—everything from Christmas ornaments shaped like the Cape Hatteras lighthouse to stained-glass sun catchers to beach dresses for the coming summer. The wall across from the coffee bar is filled with signs bearing fun seaside phrases like *Sand, Sun, Surf* or *Home Is Where the Beach Is* or *Relax! You're On Island Time*. The place is being presided over by a Boston bulldog in brightly colored swim trunks. His matching bandanna has *Chum* embroidered on it. Lily quickly falls in love with Chum and carries him around the shop, lamenting the fact that pets aren't allowed in the dorm. She misses the ever-present plethora of dogs and puppies at my father's farm.

Before long, we have the chance to meet Chum's owner, Sandy of Sandy's Seashell Shop. Sixtysomething, with short, spiked-up blonde hair, she fashions many of the stained-glass and jewelry creations in the shop. I can't resist telling Lily to pick out one of Sandy's sea glass necklaces for herself. Lily debates forever, carefully examining one, then the next, and holding them to the light. So rarely in our childhoods were we ever allowed to select something that cost money in an actual store.

Finally, Lily chooses a moderately priced sea glass heart pendant. "This way we can get one for each of us." She holds out a cobalt-blue drop and smiles at me. "Sister hearts."

"That's really sweet." I take mine and slip it into place while Lily clips hers. We seal the deal with a hug.

Sandy is delighted. "My sister, Sharon, and I make those together. I love it when sisters buy them for each other. Made by sisters, for sisters."

Lily turns back to the case, her lips twisting to one side. She clutches a hand over her new pendant, studying the remaining sea glass creations. "Maybe we should get one for RC. To celebrate, kind of."

"RC doesn't quite seem like the jewelry type." As usual, Lily's thoughts are loving and sweet. But even though I feel a bond with RC that I hadn't expected to feel, a gift doesn't seem appropriate at this point.

Sandy looks at us with an expression of *Eureka!* as we walk to the checkout counter to pay. "Are you two related to RC? I thought you looked a little familiar. I was trying to figure out who you reminded me of."

"She's our half sister, but we only just found out. We haven't ever met before today." Lily spills the story so freely, I feel my checks heating up.

"It's complicated," I add.

Sandy doesn't seem at all concerned. Giggling, she swats a hand in the air, as if to wave away any notion of embarrassment. "Oh, honey, life usually is. You hear all kinds of stories, owning a coffee shop. Especially in a place like Hatteras." As she rings up my order, she goes on to tell us how she knows RC. They've been acquainted for quite a few years—ever since RC and Johnny bought the boat repair shop over in Elizabeth City. Part of the business was a mobile service on the Outer Banks. "They'll come over in the fall and winterize the boats, then come again in the spring, clean out the antifreeze, take the covers off and that sort of thing, wipe down the cabins, and make sure they're all ready to go." There's a flash of emotion then, and she picks up a few stray sugar packets on the coffee bar, shaking her head. "Of course, I don't know how they'll keep on, what with Johnny as bad as he's been with his Parkinson's disease lately. But they're trying, God bless them. They're good people."

The door chimes as it opens, and the phone rings almost simultaneously. "Well, speak of the devil, there's RC." Sandy moves toward the phone in a short-legged shuffle.

"I *thought* my ears were burning." RC grabs her ears and pulls them outward. She has ditched the bandanna. Without it, she looks younger and even more like us. "Don't listen to a word Sandy says." She sends a mock scowl toward the proprietor. "That's how she sells stuff in this place. Talks people's legs off until they give in and buy something just to shut her up."

"Now you know that's not true." Sandy scoffs and points at RC, but addresses us. "*I'm* not the one. It's that one *there*. That one there will talk your left leg off and then start on the right."

RC shakes her head and grins as she shrugs out of her coat and tosses it on the rack by the door. "That's the pot pointing at the kettle."

Sandy rolls a look at us just before picking up the phone. "Consider yourselves warned."

Seashell Sandy turns out to be absolutely right. This new sister of ours can talk just about anyone under the table. We spend hours making up for lost time, learning about one another and constantly being reminded that we've only scratched the surface. By the time we finally discuss leaving the shop, it's well past dark outside and Sandy has long since thrown RC a set of keys to the front door and gone home. It's like an episode of *Cheers*, where Sam Malone leaves Norm to close up shop. RC even serves us sandwiches and cookies from behind the coffee counter, then sticks a twenty in the cash register. She won't let me pay for the food, even after we argue about it.

I gather that this isn't the first time RC has made herself at home here. Apparently the women of Hatteras tend to hole up at Sandy's. They call themselves the Sisterhood of the Seashell Shop. RC is an honorary member, since she doesn't live on Hatteras full-time. The locals come here to pass the cold winter months, play board games, sip warm drinks, and keep one another company until the next season's tourists flock in. Sandy would've stayed, except she has guests at home.

When we do finally move stiffly out the door with RC, the night-cold of the nor'easter is a surprise. Clutching my sweater, I ask RC about the nearest hotel.

"No sense in that," she answers. "There's an extra bedroom at the place where we're staying. You two can have it. You can meet Johnny, too."

CHAPTER 7

By day three on the Outer Banks, it's official. I'm no longer the eldest of six siblings; I am the second in a line of seven. RC is our sister in every sense of the word. We're even kicking around plans to attempt a meeting between RC and our sisters back home, though we haven't told them about it yet. Delivering this news and arranging a gathering will require some careful handling. I've warned RC that the rest of the family lives within the confines of the Brethren Saints' lifestyle, and some of that might be a shock to her system. She's about as far from *confined* as can be.

This new sister of ours is a free spirit. She is, without doubt, the most peaceful soul I've ever come across, and that peace runs all the way to the core. She doesn't try to mold life into an imagined shape, but instead takes it as it comes.

"Expectation is the thing that'll kill you," she says as we walk along the shore near the place where she stays when she works here on Hatteras. It's not the fancy kind of beach house, towering three stories on stilts, but a little saltbox built in the fifties. Appropriately enough, the cottage is located on Providence Cove Drive.

"That's the mistake. See?" RC goes on, her olive skin reddened by the morning chill. "It's like, if you walked along the shore here and had it in your mind exactly what each wave was supposed to leave behind, instead of being surprised by what *does* turn up, you'd be upset that it wasn't like you planned. What's supposed to be a beautiful mystery would just be a constant disappointment. That's the way I look at it. Life is a beautiful mystery. Somebody *else* is in charge of the ocean. You don't get to make a list of what it should bring."

Her work-worn hands illustrate as we walk, our jackets bundled tight. I'm surprised that RC has turned philosophical. She doesn't seem like the type, at first, but these past two days, I've been wondering about that sense of peace she gives off.

"It's like with Johnny getting sick. Why'd that happen? He's a good man. I can't explain it, but it is what it is. I'm glad Johnny has good days when he can go out and work on the boats with me. Even on the days when his tremors are bad, I'm grateful he's there waiting when I come back in the evening. I'm happy we get to spend more time together. You *can* be happy where you are, *if* you stop writing the list. That's the truth. A long time ago, I tore up the list. Had to, otherwise life with Johnny would've made me crazy. The man's not a list maker."

I smile and nod and try to assimilate RC's views

on life into my own, but the two are polar opposites. *You, Jen Gibbs, are a list maker,* the still, small voice of wisdom whispers inside me. *You're trying to keep a death grip on the ocean.*

I gaze out at the sea, realize how completely pointless that is as the waves curl and break in random patterns, stretching toward our feet. They never quite reach us, just above the tide line. These early-morning journeys with RC, while Lily sleeps college-kid hours, have been so good. Not only have I come to know this new sister, but I've pondered my own life in view of what I've learned about hers. Despite the almost unspeakable things she endured growing up, she has chosen to be happy where she is, to live in the now.

My sister is proof that it's possible to leave the past in the past, to deny it any further power. I've been *stuck in reverse,* as RC would put it, still tripping over all the things I thought were behind me. I think about the hyperactive tennis game I've been playing with my heart—in one court one minute, in another the next. *Marry Evan? Yes. No. Maybe.*

Why the constant indecision? Why the lack of faith? Isn't the way RC loves Johnny and the way he loves her proof enough that we have the potential to heal from even the deepest wounds? Look what she has overcome.

Now she points toward a stretch of shore where, last night, we stood with Lily, admiring a sandcastle that some visitor must've spent hours building and perfecting when the nor'easter broke and left behind a sunny afternoon. This morning, the beach is as pure as a field of driven snow. Early sunlight casts diamond dust over the damp sand.

"Not a sign of it," RC observes. "See? It's ready for a new day. Clean slate." She brushes a hand toward the horizon. "Just another little miracle, isn't it?"

"I guess it is." I've never thought of the tides coming and going as miracles, but they are. They're proof of how very large God is and how very small I am.

I want to be like this stretch of freshly cleared shore. At times I think, *I'm ready. Let the waves wash over me.* But then I catch myself running from the tide just before it happens. Lily hasn't stopped nagging me about returning to Europe. I almost did it, but then my head filled with worries about trips to the airport and leaving Lily to drive Evan's Jaguar back to the mountains. She's too inexperienced to make that trip alone.

There are reasons not to go running to Paris, not the least of which being that Evan's book events are finished. He's been unexpectedly held over a few more days for a banquet sponsored by his French publisher. He'll see me when he gets home.

And once the tour is over, we're officially done doing business together, he reminded me on the phone last night, meaning that he wants an answer to the question he asked me in Bath.

Not if you write another book for me, I teased. *Then I'm your editor again.*

If that's the problem, I'll sell the next book to someone else, he joked.

I suspect that Lily really has filled RC in on all of this. I have a feeling RC's observations about the sandcastle and life lists are meant to show me that it's possible to let the ocean take care of itself.

"Guess we better get back to roust Lily and see how that man of mine's doing this morning." RC turns toward home, and I'm almost reluctant to make the change in direction. I enjoy this time alone with her. I've never had a big sister before.

I want to walk across that waiting stretch of new, sun-glittered sand.

I take one more look at it, and something shoots straight from my heart to my mouth without traveling through my brain. "Where's the closest airport?"

RC pauses midstride, turns and crooks a brow. The morning breeze snaps and pops her windbreaker. "Airport? Well, that'd be Norfolk."

My mind races toward that freshly laid sand. "I'm going to Paris. I am. I'm going to Paris to meet Evan. I can book a flight to Greenville for Lily and have someone come pick her up there and take her back to Cullowhee." No more excuses about where to leave the Jaguar or anything else. I'll find some sort of covered, secured parking for it and just . . . go.

"Well . . . well, that's a switch." RC blinks once, twice, three times, seeming strangely concerned. "You sure?"

I start to rethink it, then admonish myself. I am *not* backtracking this time. I'm not. I'm stepping out across that pristine sand, where all that existed yesterday has been washed away. I'm making new tracks. Watch me run. "Yes, I am. I'm sure."

RC pulls a cell phone from her pocket, and I think she's going to help me book a ticket. Instead, she says, "Let me text Johnny and make sure I'm right about the airport. It might be that, to go someplace international, you'd be better off to hop over to Raleigh. If you're gonna end up there anyway, you might as well just drive that direction and catch a plane there."

I stare out at the sea and take in huge drafts of cool salt air and watch the waves curl as RC hunts and pecks on the old-fashioned flip phone, apologizing all the while because she's a slow thumb typist. Messages go back and forth, but when it's said and done, she tells me, "Johnny's checking on it. He oughta have it figured out by the time we get back to the house. He's good with that kind of thing."

On the way home, it hits me that my decision to go means our time with RC will be ending. Lily will understand, but she'll miss being here with our new sister. "We really have to get together again soon, after I'm home."

"Oh, we will," RC promises confidently, but I notice that I keep having to slow my pace to match hers. Maybe she's sad about our visit ending too. "Soon." She pauses to pick up a tiny clamshell, its two halves still joined at the base. "Angel wings."

The iridescent interiors reflect the morning sun in miniature rainbow curls. "Amazing it made it here in one piece."

"I've never had sisters before." RC echoes my earlier thoughts and tips the shell into my palm. "I never had anything to do with my family, other than being in contact with Robby a little. My Johnny didn't have any family to speak of either. I did try to find Mama for a while after I was grown, but no luck. Johnny and me have made our tribe out of friends wherever we've lived. But it's nice to find some leaves on the family tree after all. Kinda fits with an old nut like me."

We laugh together, and RC shoulder-bumps me, her version of a hug. She's not the gushy type. The rest of the walk, we stroll in silence, zigzagging away from the chilly waves, each lost in our own thoughts of life and the sea.

When we get back to the cabin, Johnny is moving around the kitchen with his walker, making oatmeal. "Mornin', pretty lady," he greets RC cheerfully, his voice less affected by tremors than usual. His condition changes day by day. "That goes for the both of ya."

RC sidles into the tiny kitchen and kisses him tenderly on the cheek, cupping his face with one hand and holding it to hers. "I told you he was a charmer," she says to me. "If you can find one as good as my Johnny, you'd better grab him quick, while you can."

A private look passes between RC and Johnny. "You check on the airport for Jen?" she asks.

Johnny's mouth purses contemplatively. "Yup, I did. It'd be Norfolk. And lil' sister's already in there gettin' showered and packed and ready to go." He thumbs toward the bedroom where Lily was sleeping peacefully when I left. The door is open, but next to it, the bathroom door is closed.

I'm relieved that Johnny has already told Lily about my plans, and she's not protesting a plane ride back to Greenville. I was afraid she'd dig in her heels and insist that she should drive the Jaguar to Cullowhee while I flew to Paris.

But she comes out of the bathroom smiling, with her hair in a towel. "All I've gotta do is throw stuff in my duffel bag . . . well, and get my hair dry, of course." She's probably noticed that I've been keeping my things neatly stacked in my carry-on bag, as if part of me knew all along that I'd eventually muscle up my courage.

"Good. It won't take me long either. I'll get on the computer and book flights in a minute."

"I think Johnny was lookin' up some for you already." Lily glances toward the kitchen.

"You got a couple options late in the day," Johnny confirms. "Keep in mind, it's a far piece to the airport from here. You gotta go all the way up the Outer Banks to the north bridge, and then an hour and a half to Norfolk."

Lily nods along and I can see they've talked about this while RC and I made the trek home. "And, Jen, don't worry if you can't get us headed out at the same time. It's not a problem for me to hang around the airport and work on my research paper. I've still got a lot to do. I wish we could've stayed here 'til Benoit House Museum was open, though. Guess I can talk to them on the phone and stuff."

"Or come on over to Elizabeth City again," RC interjects. "Johnny and I'll bring you down here to Hatteras anytime you want."

Lily nods, beaming at the idea. Then she thumbs toward the front door. "Hey, ummm . . . can I have the keys? I thought it'd be easier to load our stuff if we backed the car up to the stairs."

"Let's just load it where it is. We don't have all that much to carry down." It's not that I don't trust Lily with the Jaguar . . . but I don't trust Lily with the Jaguar. That's Evan's baby, whether he admits it or not.

An eye roll indicates that Lily was hoping to get behind the wheel while she still could. "'Kay . . . I guess. Give me twenty minutes and I'll be ready."

CHAPTER 8

On the table, four steaming bowls of oatmeal and fresh fruit wait for a last breakfast together. "You got time for a little food," Johnny promises. "To catch one a them evenin' flights, you won't need to leave for hours yet." He insists that we sit down and eat, then sets the laptop computer by my spot so I can peruse the flights he has looked up.

I check the schedules, and we talk about timing while we're at the table. Finally I find one that leaves early this evening, makes a couple of connections, and ends in a red-eye to Paris. I'll be there in time to surprise Evan at his hotel. Lily can fly out at almost the same time and get into Greenville early enough to be picked up and driven back to Cullowhee.

Clicking Purchase, I'm both scared and satisfied. I cave in at the last minute and buy the trip insurance, just in case something goes wrong with this crazy plan of mine. After the fact, I'm irked with myself. *You are not backing out, Jen Gibbs. You're not.*

Across the table, Johnny tells RC that he thinks he

feels good enough to go help her with the boats today. A happy, contented look of love passes between them, and in it I see a deeper truth. The hardest thing about his illness is that it separates them. They've spent their entire adult lives together. They're two halves of one whole.

In them, I see what is really possible when love covers over past wounds and present struggles, when two people accept one another as they are, scars and all. *You and Evan could be this way,* a voice whispers inside me. *You just have to let go and let the tide come in.*

So that's my resolution. Let go. Take a leap of faith. Stop building higher and higher ramparts around the sandcastle.

Evan Hall was meant for me. We were meant for each other. I feel it in a way I've never felt anything before.

"You know . . ." Once again, I speak without thinking it through. "Since you two have work to do today, I think Lily and I will just head for the airport. I can ask for standby when we get there. With any luck, I'll make an earlier flight and that last connection won't be quite so iffy."

Shocked expressions come my way from all sides of the table. Lily gapes as if she fears I've been abducted by aliens and replaced with an impostor. *What have you done with my sister?* that look says.

"Sounds like you got your mind made up," Johnny assesses. "We'll miss ya." He and RC exchange another love-look, and he nods at her. "It'll be sorta lonely around here, our last few days on the Banks."

"We'll miss you, too." I speak for both Lily and me. Even though I'm excited about surprising Evan half a world away, saying good-bye stinks.

"Better get crackin'." Fortunately, RC is true to form—naturally unsentimental. Johnny volunteers to do the dishes, and RC helps us finish packing. Then we carry everything down to the Jaguar. I'm so worked up, I feel like I could fly from here to Norfolk . . . without an airplane.

The excitement lasts right up until I slide into the driver's seat to start the engine and let it warm while we go upstairs to make a last pass through the bedroom and say our final farewells to Johnny, who can't run up and down the steps like the rest of us.

I turn the key and nothing happens. The Jaguar is deader than a doornail.

Fifteen minutes of tinkering with switches, and it's still completely lifeless. Johnny makes his way down to look things over. Between the four of us, there's quite a bit of knowledge of engines and farm machinery, but the apparatus under the Jaguar's hood looks like it belongs in a fighter jet. We're afraid to mess with it beyond trying Johnny's jumper cables and battery tester.

"No tellin' who you can find to work on this thing around here," Johnny admits. "But don't worry, okay? If it's not fixed by lunchtime, we'll drive you to the airport and keep your car here. The folks who own this house are friends. They won't mind a bit."

I agree with the plan but hope that with enough

calling around I can find an insta-mechanic, and that the repair will be a quick fix . . . maybe a loose connection or something. I don't know what Evan will say if I have to tell him I abandoned his Jag at a beach house way down on Hatteras Island. Will my presence in Paris be enough to make up for an offense like that?

I go back upstairs and start working my way through the phone book while Johnny and RC gather their tools and cleaning rags for work. There's a boat they've promised to have ready today.

RC stops at the door, smiles. "You'll be here when we get back, right?"

"Yes. If I do get the car fixed, we'll hang around until after lunch and leave then." My standby-flight plan is toast now anyway. I'll just have to keep my fingers crossed for the connection to my overseas plane.

RC gives me a long, thoughtful look, and for a minute I wonder what she's thinking. "One way or another, we'll get you to the airport by the time that flight leaves this evening. Don't worry." She sends a patient smile. "Since you'll be here at lunch, we can do the hugging then."

"Rain check," I tease. RC not being much of a hugger, the promise of one lets me know how much she *feels* this new sister connection, how much it means to her.

"You got it." One of her now-familiar winks comes my way. "Hang in there, kiddo."

I watch her descend the stairs and disappear from

view. The little Hatteras house turns lonely and quiet, and despite a day that warms and becomes idyllic, this isn't where I want to be. After several futile attempts to find a mechanic who can work on a Jaguar *today*, I give up and call RC to let her know we'll need that ride to the airport, for sure. My repeated apologies for the imposition are met with a casual laugh.

"It's not every day you get to help out the course of true love," she jokes, then adds that they'll be home in a couple hours—plenty of time to offer taxi service. I tell her I want to at least pay for the gas, and she says we'll talk about it.

I call Evan just to hear his voice, but he doesn't answer. I text, but he doesn't respond. No doubt he has the phone on silent and has forgotten about it. He's as notorious for that as he is for forgetting to silence the phone before he steps up to a speaker's podium.

Finally, there's nothing left to do but distract myself by digging through some work projects. Sinking into an e-copy of a manuscript on my submissions pile is a surefire way to pass the time. Luckily, the story is compelling, and it does what all good books do: it takes me away from real life. My mind travels across miles and years and falls into a love story.

By the time I've skimmed through it, I'm aching for Evan. I want to talk to him, at least. I can feel myself losing my courage on this Paris thing. I need a little bolstering. I *can't* lose my courage. Not this time.

The past need not determine one moment of the

future. It's something my childhood mentor, Wilda Culp, told me. I guess it's taken me this long to finally absorb that lesson all the way to the core.

Another call to Evan produces no results. I phone the office instead and speak to George Vida's assistant, Hollis, who knows all. She tells me not to worry—Evan checked in with her earlier, and then he was turning the phone off for the day to sleep. He's been a little under the weather. Yes, he'll be in Paris a few days longer.

Long enough for me to get there.

CHAPTER 9

RC and Johnny come home at lunchtime, and we're on the road in less than an hour, rumbling up the Outer Banks in their old four-door shop truck, this time with the ocean on our right and the sound on our left. The water churns the world on one side, caresses it softly on the other. I'm more akin to the churning side right now. It's a time of change.

Rather than running away, I can feel myself stepping in. I'm ready.

It should be a long drive to Norfolk in the old truck, but the conversation on the way is filled with laughter and revelations, and the time rushes by. We talk about strange habits we have in common—certain foods we like to eat and clothing colors we prefer and subjects we were good at in school. When we arrive at the airport, Johnny insists on parking in the short-term lot and walking us in, even though I've promised that Lily and I can handle our luggage just fine.

"Nothing doing," Johnny says, thumping the

handicapped permit on the mirror. "Got my tag. I can make the walk."

I worry that we are wearing him out and he'll suffer for it later. He and RC have to make it all the way back to Hatteras yet tonight. I offered to pay for a hotel room here, but they refused.

We all proceed into the airport together, Johnny moving at a surprisingly rapid pace behind his walker. "Better hurry up. Don't wanna miss your flight." But we've arrived over three hours early. There's plenty of time for check-in and good-byes.

By silent, mutual agreement, we all wander to a stop some distance from the ticket counters, the four of us forming a little island as people pass by, preoccupied with their own business.

The farewells are sweet and sad. We all feel these new ties, still as fragile as spider thread. Stretch them too far and they'll break and float away on the wind. Lily keeps glancing toward the door, like she's thinking about running back to the Outer Banks instead of using her plane ticket. For half a second, I wonder if she's about to tell me she'll stay with the Jaguar and drive it back to Cullowhee once it's fixed. I don't want our time here to end with an argument about that.

Best to move along before plans go awry.

"Well, I guess we should get checked in," I say.

RC smiles at me tenderly, then sighs. My new sister's eyes are already so familiar—as if I've always known her, even though we've only just met. "Guess so. It was a good visit. Real good."

"Thanks . . . thanks for everything." Tears strain the words. I have to swallow hard to manage a few more. "I'll take that hug now."

Lily interrupts before I can reach for RC. A cell phone is shoved into my outstretched hand. "Here, take a picture of me and RC and Johnny, 'kay?" She's stalling, I can tell, but I oblige instead of reminding her that we already posed for dozens of pictures back at the beach house.

After I've snapped one, Lily grabs the phone. "Okay, now you three." She motions for Johnny and RC to relocate, and they move to stand beside me. Lily has us shift back and forth to get the picture just right. Suddenly she is Little Miss In Charge.

"Lily . . ." I'm getting antsy to be through security and on my way to Evan.

"I want to remember this," she protests. "Okay, now I want just you."

"*Lily* . . ."

"Smile. This is, like, the last time I'll see you single. When you come home, you won't be a Gibbs any-more." The pout lip is the one she deployed so skillfully as a child. It's still irresistible.

I strike the dorky selfie pose that Lily and her friends love on Facebook, hand on my hip, head tipped to one side.

She snaps several shots. "There, now that didn't

hurt so much, did it?" She tries to give me the phone. "Check the pictures and see if you like them."

"I'm sure they're okay."

"Check and see."

"No, it's fine, really. I hate pictures of myself anyway."

Lily rolls her eyes. "What*ever*." Glancing toward the ticket counter, she moves to grab her bags without even hugging RC and Johnny.

"Aren't you going to say good-bye?" I remind her.

"Oh, yeah . . . Good-bye." Lily isn't very emotional about this parting. I'm surprised. I thought she would be. Maybe it's just me. Maybe I'm making a big deal of it because I'm headed to another continent. It's not like we'll never see RC again.

But then, Lily ends up dragging out the good-byes anyway, chattering on about the museum on the Outer Banks and how, before we left the beach house, she read on the Internet that they have an internship program there. She'd like to come back and learn more about the Lost Colonists of Roanoke Island and whether those people really do have something to do with the story keeper necklaces and our heritage among the Melungeons of the mountains. "Besides, I like the beach a lot. It'd be fun to come back and . . ."

Someone taps me on the shoulder, and I jump at first. A sailor in uniform extends a hand my way. At first I think he's going to ask me to snap a picture for him. Instead he holds out what looks like a key chain and says, "I think you dropped this, ma'am." He releases it into my hand before I have time to argue. I catch it to keep it from falling.

It's fairly heavy, but there are no keys on the ring, just some sort of metal bauble clutched between my fingers. It rolls into my palm as I open my hand.

I do a double take, feel my mouth slowly dropping open. If I was looking for one final sign . . . if I *needed* one, here it is. A tiny silver replica of the Eiffel Tower catches the light against my skin. It's the sort of thing you might pick up in a tourist trap. But how did it get here? And why did that guy . . .

I glance up, and all eyes are on me. Mouths strain to withhold giddy grins. Faces beam with expectation.

"What's going . . . ?"

Snickering, Lily presses a hand over her mouth, extends the cell phone my way. "Look. Look at the picture."

"Huh?" I do as she asks, and as I focus on the tiny screen, everything is suddenly perfectly clear . . . Why there were problems with the Jaguar to prevent us from coming earlier for a standby flight. Why Johnny and RC were so happy to drive us all the way to the airport. Why Johnny insisted on walking us in. Why Lily was delaying just now. Why she took the pictures when and how she did. Why they're all smiling at me like three Cheshire cats in a tree.

They've been waiting for someone, and that's him

behind me in the picture. At six foot four, Evan Hall stands out in any crowd.

I whirl around, and he's only a short distance away. His grin stretches ear to ear. He nods at the tiny Eiffel Tower, forgotten in my hand. "It's not exactly Paris in the springtime." His eyes are the deep, fathomless blue of the ocean he has secretly crossed to come to me. The sort of ocean so powerful that it washes away the evidence of all things left behind by others. "But the Outer Banks in the springtime isn't bad either."

"No . . . no, it's not." I clutch the tiny souvenir of a trip that never was, run across the open space to Evan, and never look back.

About the Author

L isa Wingate is a former journalist, speaker, and the author of twenty novels, including the national bestseller *Tending Roses*, now in its eighteenth printing. She is a seven-time ACFW Carol Award nominee, a Christy Award nominee, and a two-time Carol Award winner. Her novel *Blue Moon Bay* was a Booklist Top Ten of 2012 pick. Recently the group Americans for More Civility, a kindness watchdog organization, selected Lisa along with Bill Ford, Camille Cosby, and six others as recipients of the National Civies Award, which celebrates public figures who work to promote greater kindness and civility in American life. When not dreaming up stories, Lisa spends time on the road as a motivational speaker. Via Internet, she shares with readers as far away as India, where *Tending Roses* has been used to promote women's literacy, and as close to home as Tulsa, Oklahoma, where the county library system has used *Tending Roses* to help volunteers teach adults to read.

Lisa lives on a ranch in Texas, where she spoils the livestock, raises boys, and teaches Sunday school to high school seniors. She was inspired to become a writer by a first-grade teacher who said she expected to see Lisa's name in a magazine one day. Lisa also entertained childhood dreams of being an Olympic gymnast and winning the National Finals Rodeo but was stalled by the inability to do a backflip on the balance beam and parents who wouldn't finance a rodeo career. She was lucky enough to marry into a big family of cowboys and Southern storytellers who would inspire any lover of tall tales and interesting yet profound characters. She is a full-time writer and pens inspirational fiction for both the general and Christian markets. Of all the things she loves about her job, she loves connecting with people, both real and imaginary, the most. More information about Lisa's novels can be found at www.lisawingate.com.